BENITO PÉREZ GALDÓS was born in Las Palmas (Canary Islands) in 1843. At the age of 19 he went to study law in Madrid, where he lived for the rest of his life. By 1865 he had abandoned his studies for journalism; he continued to write for the press throughout his life. His literary career was triggered by the discovery of Balzac in 1867; in 1868 he translated Dickens's *Pickwick Papers* from the French. His first two novels, *La Fontana de Oro* (1870) and *El audaz* (1871), were historical; in 1873 he embarked on the first of five series of historical novels, titled *National Episodes*, tracing the course of Spanish history from 1805 to the Restoration period inaugurated in 1875. In 1879, he abandoned the historical genre for his 'contemporary novels', the first of which, *Doña Perfecta*, had been written in 1876. In 1878 he discovered the work of Zola, which influenced his first major novel, *La desheredada* (1881). He never married but had affairs with women of all classes, including the novelist and feminist Emilia Pardo Bazán, and the peasant woman Lorenza Cobián, who in 1891 bore him a daughter, María. His best-known works were written between 1881 and 1897, including *La de Bringas* (1884), *Fortunata y Jacinta* (1886–7), *Miau* (1888), *Angel Guerra* (1890–1), *Nazarín* (1895), and *Misericordia* (1897). In 1892 he started to write for the stage, influenced by Ibsen. In 1897 he was elected to membership of the Spanish Royal Academy, and in 1898 he returned to the *National Episodes*, which he abandoned definitively in 1912 on going blind. At his death in 1920 he left behind him a total of 77 novels (including 46 *National Episodes*) and 21 plays.

JO LABANYI is Reader in Modern Spanish and Latin American Literature at Birkbeck College, University of London. As well as translating novels and short stories by Latin American writers, she is the author of *Myth and History in the Contemporary Spanish Novel* (CUP, 1989) and editor of *Galdós* (Longman, 1993). In 1985 she was awarded the Translators Association Twentieth Anniversary Short Story Translation prize for Spanish.

THE WORLD'S CLASSICS

BENITO PÉREZ GALDÓS

Nazarín

Translated, edited, and introduced by
JO LABANYI

Oxford   New York

OXFORD UNIVERSITY PRESS

1993

Oxford University Press, Walton Street, Oxford OX2 6DP

Oxford New York Toronto
Delhi Bombay Calcutta Madras Karachi
Kuala Lumpur Singapore Hong Kong Tokyo
Nairobi Dar es Salaam Cape Town
Melbourne Auckland Madrid
and associated companies in
Berlin Ibadan

Oxford is a trade mark of Oxford University Press

British Library Cataloguing in Publication Data
Data available

Library of Congress Cataloging in Publication Data
Pérez Galdós, Benito, 1843–1920.
[Nazarín, English]
Nazarín / Benito Pérez Galdós ; translated, edited, and introduced
by Jo Labanyi.
p. cm. — (The World's classics)
Includes bibliographical references.
I. Labanyi, Jo. II. Title. III. Series.
PQ6555.N413 1993 863'.5—dc20 92–41138
ISBN 0–19–282878–9

1 3 5 7 9 10 8 6 4 2

Typeset by Best-set Typesetter Ltd., Hong Kong
Printed in Great Britain by
BPCC Paperbacks Ltd
Aylesbury, Bucks

CONTENTS

INTRODUCTION

NAZARÍN, written and published in 1895, is best known outside Spain through Buñuel's film adaptation of the novel, made in Mexico in 1958. In 1970 Buñuel was to film another Galdós novel, *Tristana* (1892). Why should a director like Buñuel, known for his love of the surreal, be attracted to the work of Spain's major nineteenth-century realist novelist? Buñuel's 'readings' of Galdós highlight features of his work that do not fit easily with what is commonly understood by realism. For Galdós is in many ways a very modern writer, who plays with the craft of realism at the same time as he practises it.

Galdós's uneasy relationship to realism is partly explained by the fact that the realist novel in Spain did not get off the ground until after the Liberal Revolution of 1868, which opened the doors to the outside world. And it was not till the 1880s—when the political stability and economic growth of the Restoration period consolidated the power of the bourgeoisie—that the major works of realist fiction were produced: Leopoldo Alas's *La Regenta* (1884–5), Emilia Pardo Bazán's *House of Ulloa* (1886), and Galdós's *Fortunata and Jacinta* (1886–7), to mention only those readily available in English.[1] (In all, Galdós wrote 77 novels.) This late start meant that the Spanish realists were writing with a knowledge of earlier realist fiction that gives their work—in the case of Alas and Galdós at least—a self-conscious metafictional dimension rarely found (with the exception of Flaubert, himself a second-generation realist) elsewhere in Europe.[2] Fundamental here too is the Cervantine heritage, which of

---

[1] Published by Penguin in 1984, 1990, and 1985 respectively.

[2] Galdós had twenty novels by Dickens in his library, and in 1868, two years before publishing his first novel, translated *Pickwick Papers* (from French). In 1867 he bought Balzac's *Eugénie Grandet*, and in 1868 returned to Paris to buy the rest of his novels. In 1878 he acquired six novels of Zola, who considerably influenced his fiction of the 1880s.

course passed to England, France, and Russia in the course of the eighteenth and nineteenth centuries, generating the modern novel. Galdós's direct access to Cervantes allows him to exploit the ironic undermining of romance that gives birth to realism with a playful awareness that a sense of the real is created, not so much by referring to the real world, as through the dialogue with other literature. As in *Tristram Shandy*, with which Galdós's work has much in common, realism is a metafictional game. *Nazarín*—a direct reworking of *Don Quixote*—is Galdós's metafictional masterpiece.

Another consequence of the realist novel's late start in Spain is that the Spanish novelists begin to write at a time when the bourgeois values that make realism possible are already being called into question in England and, particularly, France (since the Enlightenment, Paris has been the central reference point for Spanish culture). In fact positivism had never really established itself in Spain, where even the most free-thinking intellectuals—Galdós among them—felt unable to adopt an entirely materialist position. The legacy of the past and the impact of new ideas combine to place Spain in a doubly ambivalent position with regard to bourgeois ideology. The result in the Spanish realist novel is an intense awareness of the coexistence of contradictory points of view, whose formal expression is irony. This ideological ambivalence was compounded in the late 1880s, at the high point of the Spanish realist novel, when the Russian novel became known in Spain. The year 1887 is the date of publication of the last part of Galdós's *Fortunata and Jacinta* (a watershed in his literary development), and the date of Emilia Pardo Bazán's lectures on contemporary Russian writers at the Madrid Ateneo. A copy of these lectures is listed in Galdós's library catalogue (in 1889–90 he had an affair with Pardo Bazán), together with the 1884 first French translation of Tolstoy's *War and Peace*, plus several other works by the same author and by Turgenev; Dostoevsky is mentioned by him in his journalism. The Russian writers were hailed in Spain, as in France, for their passionate interest in things of the spirit. Galdós's novels from the extraordinary

Angel Guerra[3] (1890–1) onwards will apply the realist techniques developed in the course of the 1880s to an analysis of paranormal phenomena and freakish characters that challenge the empiricist tenets and common-sense values on which realism is based.

Nazarín, like *Angel Guerra*, was strongly influenced by Galdós's reading of Tolstoy's *What I Believe* (his copy of the French translation *Ma religion* is heavily annotated), in which the Russian writer advocated a return to a primitive Christianity which has much in common with anarchist thought. In the nineteenth century, Spain—like Russia—was a country where religion had a strong hold even on those who, like Galdós, rejected the Church; and where the workers' movement was predominantly anarchist (the Spanish section of the First Workers' International was founded in 1868 by a delegate of the Russian anarchist Bakunin; only in the 1930s would the Socialist Party and its trade union, the UGT, start to attract large numbers). Galdós's novel dramatizes the clash between a capitalist work ethic that had belatedly and imperfectly established itself in Spain in the 1880s, based on the twin notions of private property and material progress, and illustrated by the reporter in Part I and the mayor in Part IV; and a doctrine of communal ownership in which labour is voluntary and material needs are reduced to a minimum, preached by Nazarín, a latter-day Christ (Nazarene) who is perceived by society as a dangerous anarchist. It is impossible to say whether this reaction against 'Victorian values' is a nostalgic return to pre-capitalist forms of social organization—still strong in the rural Spain for which Nazarín leaves the capital Madrid—or a radical anticipation of the anarchist Utopia, for it is both.

Nazarín is a register of the contradictions of late nineteenth-century Spain in its ambiguous relationship to modernity, but it also represents Galdós's attempt to mediate those contradictions. The economic boom of the 1880s had by

[3] Published in English by Edwin Mellen Press in 1991.

1892 come to a halt. The first May Day of 1890 had been celebrated by general strikes in Barcelona and Zaragoza: Galdós wrote a notable article on the occasion, opening with the words 'We are sitting on a volcano'.[4] And the 1890s were marked by an escalation of anarchist violence. In 1892 over 4,000 peasants took the town of Jérez de la Frontera with the cry '¡Viva la anarquía!'; in the ensuing repression, four anarchists were executed and hundreds imprisoned. In 1893 two bombs were thrown in Barcelona: one at General Martínez Campos, known for his repression of social unrest; the other in the Lyceum Theatre. In 1894, the year before *Nazarín* was published, an anti-anarchist law was passed to combat the threat of terrorism. (Further spectacular incidents would take place after the publication of *Nazarín*, with the bomb thrown at a Barcelona Corpus Christi procession in 1896, and the assassination in 1897 of Cánovas, the Conservative leader who had largely been responsible for the stability of the Restoration period.) Galdós's novel mentions Pope Leo XIII, who attempted to palliate the threat of social revolution with his 1891 encyclical *Rerum novarum*: a charter of workers' rights and employers' obligations. In 1894, just before *Nazarín* was written, a delegation of Spanish workers had visited Leo XIII, who urged Spanish bishops to set up Catholic workers' associations.[5] The Spanish press of the 1890s gave wide coverage to attempts abroad, in Belgium in particular, to set up Catholic trade unions. Nazarín's rejection of private property and material progress makes the authorities regard him as a dangerous anarchist, but his creed is, like that of Leo XIII, an attempt to defuse social tensions and prevent revolutionary violence: to 'save' the people from envy and hatred, as he puts it. Unlike Leo XIII, however, Nazarín does not talk of workers' rights, but preaches a doctrine of self-sacrifice and passive submission. Poverty and non-resistance to evil were central to Tolstoy's creed in *What I Believe*; but Tolstoy condemned

---

[4] See Benito Pérez Galdós, *Ensayos literarios*, ed. Laureano Bonet (Barcelona: Península, 1972), 183.
[5] See Peter Bly, *Pérez Galdós*: Nazarín (London: Grant and Cutler, 1991), 50.

the masochistic seeking out of suffering that Nazarín embraces and imposes on his followers. Nazarín, like Tolstoy, makes a political reading of Christ's teachings but (as also happens with Tolstoy) he simultaneously defuses the political implications of that reading.[6]

The 'evil' Nazarín combats in the novel is not, despite all his talk of injustice, social but 'natural': that of disease (the period 1885–90 had been marked by cholera outbreaks in Spain; the diseases encountered in the text are smallpox and typhus). The metaphor 'the Spanish disease'—taken from the agricultural reformer Lucas Mallada's book *The National Disease (Los males de la patria)* of 1890—would be used by the younger writers of the 1898 Generation (Unamuno, Ganivet, Baroja, 'Azorín', Maeztu) who from 1895 onwards undertook a 'diagnosis' of Spain's decline, aggravated by the loss of her last major colonies (Cuba, Puerto Rico, the Philippines) in 1898. In the work of the 1898 writers, the medical metaphor 'naturalizes' historical failure by presenting it as an organic, rather than political, malfunctioning;[7] the 'regeneration' they call for is not political but spiritual, as the religious term suggests. One suspects that Nazarín too is 'naturalizing', and thus depoliticizing, social ills by conflating injustice with disease; he too is seeking not political change but spiritual regeneration. Mallada had 'diagnosed' Spain's problem as rural underdevelopment; that is, the failure to modernize: the major outbreaks of social unrest in late nineteenth-century Spain did in fact occur in the rural areas. The 1898 writers will by and large reject the city (modernity) for a pre-capitalist rural order which is in effect the cause of Spain's social 'ills'. Nazarín, who also rejects the city for a return to nature, is equally blind in his failure to see that, by repudiating material progress, he is perpetuating the lack of

---

[6] See V. Colin, 'A Note on Tolstoy and Galdós', *Anales Galdosianos*, 2 (1967), 159, 161. Another possible source is Dostoevsky's political parable of the Grand Inquisitor in *The Brothers Karamazov*, in which Christ returns to sixteenth-century Spain; but Dostoevsky's Christ is very different from that of Galdós.

[7] See my article 'Nation, Narration, Naturalisation: A Barthesian Critique of the 1898 Generation', in P. J. Smith and M. Millington (eds.), *New Hispanisms: Literature, Culture, Theory* (Ottawa: Dovehouse, 1993).

sanitation that causes disease in the first place. The fact that he finally contracts typhus himself is perhaps Galdós's wry comment on his protagonist's ideological contradictions.

Or are they also Galdós's contradictions? In an 1885 article called 'The Social Problem', Galdós had seen unemployment and capitalist competition as the main contributing factors to social unrest; but in the 1890s, confronted with the spectre of social violence, his articles increasingly insist—in keeping with other Spanish intellectuals of the time—that what is needed are not political but moral and religious solutions (by which he did not mean a return to the established Church; Nazarín is arrested, among other things, as a priest who disobeys ecclesiastical orders).[8] By making Nazarín read a political message into Christ's teachings, only to deny the political implications of that message, Galdós is able to tackle the urgent contemporary issue of social injustice while avoiding conclusions that justify revolutionary violence against his own class.

We should however be wary of assuming that Nazarín's views are those of his author. Galdós allows the prostitute Ándara to voice with considerable eloquence the contrary view that money and food make life easier, and that the victims of injustice should fight to defend their rights. Nazarín's penultimate 'vision' in the novel appears to legitimize Ándara's 'revolutionary' stance by casting her in the role of shining warrior triumphant over the forces of oppression. This striking scene, which reads like a mixture of the biblical Armageddon and the anarchist apocalypse ushering in the new millennium, implicitly recognizes that the ultimate political consequence of Nazarín's doctrines is 'the destruction of the entire existing order', as the society priest Don Manuel Flórez will conclude in the sequel novel *Halma* (also 1895).[9]

[8] See in particular the 1893 article 'Confusions and Paradoxes' quoted in Peter B. Goldman, 'Galdós and the Nineteenth-Century Novel: The Need for an Interdisciplinary Approach', *Anales Galdosianos*, 10 (1975), 8; reproduced in English in Jo Labanyi (ed.), *Galdós* (London: Longman, 1993).

[9] See Benito Pérez Galdós, *Obras completas*, v, 7th edn. (Madrid: Aguilar, 1970), 1809.

The problem of interpretation is compounded by the fact that this apocalyptic vision is the product of a literally 'diseased' mind: by this stage in the novel, Nazarín is delirious with typhus. Right from the start of the book, his sanity is called into question: the parallels with the life of Christ are undercut ironically by a further set of parallels with Don Quixote (details of both sets of references are given in the Explanatory Notes).[10] The romances of chivalry that Nazarín sets out to enact are the Gospels; like Don Quixote, he will be brought home captive and defeated (if defiant). Several of Galdós's most notable characters are—like Don Quixote—simultaneously sane and mad. In the sequel novel *Halma*, Nazarín's trial concludes with the verdict that he is mad and therefore not criminally responsible; however the characters Don Manuel Flórez and Halma, after extensive dealings with him, conclude that he represents an inextricable confusion of sanity and madness, such that the boundary between the two categories—the socially acceptable and the socially unacceptable—becomes blurred. And if distinctions can no longer be made, the whole edifice of bourgeois rationalism—based on the ability to classify and analyse—collapses.

In Nazarín's case, the category confusion is compounded by reference to the theories of the Italian criminologist Cesare Lombroso, who first became known in Spain in 1888 and whose popularity reached a height precisely in 1895.[11]

---

[10] Bly (*Pérez Galdós: Nazarín*, 94) notes the possible influence here of Dostoevsky's *The Idiot* (1869), whose Prince Myshkin is also an amalgam of Don Quixote and Christ. Another possible model for Galdós's 'holy fool' is Wagner's *Parsifal*; Galdós, an accomplished musician, knew Wagner's operas, one of which features in *Fortunata and Jacinta*. Walter Pattison ('Verdaguer y Nazarín', *Cuadernos Hispanoamericanos*, 84 (1970–1), 537–45) and Matilde Boo ('Una nota acerca de Verdaguer y Nazarín', *Anales Galdosianos*, 13 (1978), 99–100) give information about a real-life prototype, the Catalan priest and poet Mosen Jacint Verdaguer, who worked with the poor and was confined to a lunatic asylum. Galdós first met Verdaguer in 1888, and sent him copies of *Nazarín* and the sequel novel *Halma*. For a summary in English of the information about Verdaguer, see Bly, *Pérez Galdós: Nazarín*, 96 and 100).

[11] For this and the following information on Lombroso, I am indebted to Luis Maristany's well-documented studies: *El gabinete del doctor Lombroso: Delincuencia y fin de siglo en España* (Barcelona: Anagrama, 1973); and 'Lombroso y

Lombroso's main works *Genio e follia* (*Genius and Madness*) (1864), *L'uomo delincuente* (*Criminal Man*) (1876), *L'uomo di genio* (*The Man of Genius*) (1888), and *Il delitto politico e le revoluzioni* (*Political Crime and Revolutions*) (1890) were translated into Spanish in the early 1890s; throughout the 1890s a flurry of Spanish publications on criminology and mental health appeared. Basing himself on Herbert Spencer, who had applied Darwin's theory of the evolution of species to the study of society, Lombroso argued that the various types of abnormality—criminality, anarchism, madness, and genius (the latter including the artist and the mystic)—were products of a related congenital malformation, manifested in physiognomical features such as shape of the skull and facial expression (Lombroso is clearly also indebted to the earlier nineteenth-century pseudo-science of phrenology).

From 1881 to 1883, the Madrid Ateneo had hosted a series of debates on the link between criminality and madness, in which Galdós's doctor friend Tolosa Latour—who provided the novelist with medical information for his novels, and let him examine interesting patients—had participated, arguing that mentally unsound criminals should not be held responsible for their acts. By 1888, when the Ateneo started to debate Lombroso's theories, the ground of discussion had shifted: it was increasingly argued that social deviants were irredeemable because their abnormality was congenital, literally 'monstrous'. As Spanish intellectuals found themselves confronted in the course of the 1890s with growing social violence, it became convenient to argue that the causes of terrorism were not social or political but physiological; in addition, the congenital nature of the abnormality justified the death penalty, for the problem could not be cured, only eradicated. The fact that, in *Halma*, the court verdict absolves Nazarín of criminal responsibility on grounds of insanity testifies to the influence on Galdós of Tolosa Latour, a champion of penal reform. As a journalist Galdós was an assiduous attender at the lawcourts, fre-

España: Nuevas consideraciones', *Anales de Literatura Española*, 2 (1983), 361–81.

quently interviewing the accused. It has been suggested that the birth in the nineteenth century of criminology, with its emphasis on techniques of police identification, played a key role in the development of the contemporaneous disciplines of psychology and the realist novel, equally concerned with defining individual identity.[12] Galdós defuses Nazarín's political threat, but the latter remains subversive because he eludes all definition: his individuality consists precisely in that which cannot be identified. Lombroso's theories, designed to label deviants, are used to create a deviant character who resists containment.

Galdós's medical interests are also evidenced in the novel's association of mysticism and hysteria. Nazarín's discussion of hysteria in Part III implies that Galdós was familiar with medical discourse on the subject; Tolosa Latour's psychiatric colleague Escuder discussed hysteria in his 1895 book *Locos y anómalos* (*Madness and Deviance*).[13] Late nineteenth-century medicine was obsessed with theorizing about hysteria, which was seen as an exclusively female disease, the term deriving from the Greek *hysteron* ('womb'). Since ancient times, hysteria had been seen as the symptom of a 'wandering womb', caused by frustrated maternity; pregnancy was the usual recommended 'cure'.[14] Charcot's famous experiments at the La Salpêtrière asylum in Paris in the 1880s, which showed that hysterical patients responded to hypnosis, demonstrated that hysteria was—as Nazarín will insist in Part III—a psychological and not a physiological disorder; as is well known, it was this which triggered the young Freud's 'discovery' of the unconscious. Freud's linkage of the unconscious to sexual repression is the direct consequence of his exploration of hysteria, still seen as the result of woman's failure to realize her sexual 'destiny'. If hysteria aroused such passions in the late nineteenth century,

[12] See Carlo Ginzburg's classic article 'Clues: Morelli, Freud, and Sherlock Holmes', in Umberto Eco and Thomas Sebeok (eds.), *The Sign of Three: Dupin, Holmes, Pierce* (Bloomington: Indiana University Press, 1988), 106–9.

[13] See Bly, *Pérez Galdós: Nazarín*, 58.

[14] For discussion of the discourse on hysteria, see Charles Bernheimer and Claire Kahane (eds.), *In Dora's Case: Freud, Hysteria, Feminism* (London: Virago, 1985).

it was because it raised fundamental issues about the relation of the mental to the physical. In Part V of the novel, Nazarín will ask whether reality is located in the external world of observable phenomena, or in the head which produces its own 'visions'. *Nazarín* is an exploration of the ways in which the mind can project reality on to the material world, transforming it in the process. It is in this sense above all that spiritual regeneration and madness are connected.

Nazarín's 'miracles' include his ability to cure the hysteria of his female disciple Beatriz, caused by a traumatic sexual relationship: with his quixotic ability to project his 'vision' on to the outside world, he is a kind of hypnotist. He does not cure Beatriz by removing her symptoms, but by channelling her negative projection of frustrated sexual desire into a positive projection of spiritual longings. Hysteria becomes mysticism, both of which consist in the ability to project mind on to matter in such a way that the latter is affected. In his film version, Buñuel—ever influenced by Freud—would interpret this as proof that mysticism is merely the sublimation of repressed sexual desire. Galdós does not imply that the link between hysteria and mysticism degrades the latter. *Nazarín* is an intriguing novel because it allows the materialist explanation typical of nineteenth-century realism (Nazarín *is* mad and by the end delirious with typhus; Beatriz *is* repressing her sexuality) to coexist with an exploration of the paranormal.

Both mysticism and hysteria, in their rejection of rational discourse, have been seen as specifically 'feminine' forms of self-expression.[15] In Galdós's novel, Nazarín and Beatriz share the same 'miraculous' power to project mind on to matter. Throughout the novel, Nazarín is described in feminine terms: when the narrator first sees him, he takes him for a woman; characters refer to him as an 'angel' (a term associated in nineteenth-century discourse with woman,

---

[15] See Bernheimer and Kahane (eds.), *In Dora's Case*; and Luce Irigaray, 'La Mystérique', in *Spéculum de l'autre femme* (Paris: Editions de Minuit, 1974), 238–52. Freud regarded hysteria as a feminine disorder that could however manifest itself in men.

the 'angel in the house'); when he falls ill, he fears his heroic adventures will end 'in an inglorious womanly swoon'. Nazarín causes such outrage, particularly to the other male characters, because his doctrine of passive submission is a refusal to 'act like a man'. (Nazarín's other female disciple, the prostitute Ándara who insists on the right to fight back, will occupy this masculine role.) As a latter-day Christ, Nazarín is the scandal of a 'feminine man' (Luce Irigaray has called Christ the 'most feminine of all men');[16] indeed he can be seen as a classic study in masochism, a supposedly female drive. In her brilliant book *Desire and Domestic Fiction: A Political History of the Novel*,[17] Nancy Armstrong argues that the realist novel sets out to 'feminize' its readership by prioritizing the private sphere of the emotions (associated with women) over the public sphere of political activity (associated with men). This she sees as a strategy of de-politicization, inasmuch as it creates a concept of the individual (whether male or female) that is defined by being in opposition to the political. Unlike most nineteenth-century novels, *Nazarín* is not a domestic drama (it takes place mostly outdoors), but its protagonist is an extreme example of the 'feminized man' who appears in so many realist works. Nazarín is shocking because he takes his 'feminine' values out of the home and into the public sphere (perhaps it takes a 'feminine man' to do this). His apolitical doctrine of non-resistance to evil joins hands with his 'feminine' insistence on the superiority of things of the spirit.

Nazarín is an aberration of nature in his combination of normally separate qualities: mad and sane, saint and anarchist/criminal, male and female. As such, he is a 'monster'. Monsters—from the Latin *monstrum* ('that which is shown or exhibited')—have been a perennial object of carnivalesque representation because they challenge norms of what is representable. Galdós's novel stretches the bounds of realism by attempting to represent the monstrous: that which, as an aberration of nature, defies the laws of form that make

---

[16] *Spéculum de l'autre femme*, 249.
[17] Oxford: Oxford University Press, 1989.

representation possible. This notion of the monstrous is personified by the dwarf Ujo who appears in Part IV: an amalgam of forms verging on the unimaginable. In this sense Buñuel's film dwarf, though a virtuoso exercise in the grotesque, is inevitably a disappointment, since he gives visual form to Ujo's formlessness. The whole novel betrays a fascination with the problem of representing the unrepresentable: from the opening description of the impossible perspectives of the boarding-house (an 'architectural joke') to the absurdity of Don Pedro Belmonte (another sane madman; Nazarín will vainly ask 'what kind of a man is this?') and of Beatriz's mystical vision (which leaves her unable to 'explain what it was she saw or even be sure she was seeing it'). Nazarín describes the printing press as a 'monster': for writing, in its attempt to represent the unrepresentable, has a monstrous quality.

We are constantly reminded of the inadequacy of words to represent their object. The novel starts by pointing to the discrepancy between the impressive street sign Calle de las Amazonas and the seedy alley designated by it; and warns us that Tía Chanfaina's boarding-house is no boarding-house in the normal sense of the word (neither is Tía Chanfaina her real name). The end of the novel gives us Galdós's version of the philosophical conundrum of the Cretan who says 'All Cretans are liars': a statement which if it is true must also, being spoken by a Cretan, be false. Here Nazarín, in hospital with typhus, has a vision in which Christ tells him He is a figment of his imagination: if the latter is a true statement, then the statement itself is unreliable. Christ will go on to deliver a final verdict on Nazarín's exploits: a verdict that, in addition to being inconclusive, defies interpretation given the doubts over the speaker's reality. Either way—voice of the supernatural or product of hallucination—language has a relationship to reality that defies empirical verification.

In the sequel novel *Halma*, Nazarín will be given the earlier novel *Nazarín* to read, in a direct analogy with Part II of *Don Quixote*, where Cervantes's hero reads and comments on Part I. Nazarín insists that the novel's representation is unfaithful because it depicts him as a saint. We are back to the Cretan philosopher: if Nazarín is a saint, by definition he will not see himself as such; his statement contradicts and confirms the novel's 'truth' simultaneously. In *Halma* Nazarín will also deny that his ideas are influenced by a reading of the Russian novel. By having his protagonist comment on works of fiction, Galdós makes him look real (outside books) at the same time as he turns the text into a metafictional discussion. Part I of *Nazarín* adopts a documentary stance by having Galdós as author interview Nazarín together with a journalist; but the supposed veracity of reportage is turned upside down when Galdós and the journalist come up with conflicting versions. To make matters more confusing, Galdós will end Part I by asking who wrote the rest of the novel, and refusing to tell us. As he nicely puts it: 'I myself would be hard pressed if I had to decide who had written what I write.' In Part III, the documentary claims of journalism are again exploded when Don Pedro Belmonte finds 'evidence' in the press for his ludicrous version of Nazarín's story. The fictional Nazarín looks real by comparison with the press cuttings; but this very scene is a reworking of Don Quixote's visit to the Duke and Duchess's palace in Part II of Cervantes's novel, as well as the result of Nazarín's literal ('realist') reading of the Gospels. In this proliferation of versions, the question of whether words are true is foregrounded and shown to be unanswerable. As with Don Quixote, there is even doubt about Nazarín's 'real' name. And the unrepresentable dwarf Ujo's name, we are told, is not a 'proper' name at all.

Throughout the novel, Nazarín is associated with the idea of carnival, incarnated in the 'monstrous' Ujo who, with his outsize head and tiny limbs, looks like the giant papier mâché heads that are an integral part of Spanish carnival festivities. This carnivalization underscores the subversiveness of Nazarín's doctrines which, with their repudiation of property and progress, literally turn the world upside down. Carnival is also the time when masks are worn: the problem becomes one of distinguishing the mask from reality. When the author first meets Ándara in Part I, he takes her face to be a mask because of the layers of make-up; when in Part III she takes the make-up off, we are left with a physiognomy so grotesque we can visualize it only as another mask: indeed, her ugliness conceals a brave and loyal spirit. When Nazarín abandons his priest's robes and dresses up as a beggar (in an absurdly heterogeneous collection of garments that rivals Ujo's 'monstrous' formlessness), he is donning a disguise that also reveals his true self. Carnival reduces everything to a play of appearances but, by turning the world upside down, it displays the truths that normally are repressed.

Above all, carnival is fun. *Nazarín* is a brilliant exercise in Cervantine wit, which achieves the seemingly impossible by giving us a comic version of the Gospels without in any way demeaning its latter-day Christ. Galdós's use of language is a carnivalesque celebration of the improprieties of popular speech, and of the incongruous mixing of disparate registers. The novel is an ironic study in the dissolution of forms, at the level of language as well as theme. In his 1897 speech on reception into the Spanish Royal Academy, Galdós suggested that contemporary society was threatened by loss of the distinctions that had previously given it structure. He went on to say that this crisis of forms offered the novelist new creative possibilities, for what was *Don Quixote* if not the swan song of a crumbling chivalric order.[18] *Nazarín* is in many ways the swansong of the nineteenth-century bourgeois order. The novel is an attempt to defuse the threat of revolutionary violence; but in preferring carnival to revolution Galdós is also opting for laughter as a weapon.

---

[18] See 'La sociedad presente como materia novelable', in Benito Pérez Galdós, *Ensayos de crítica literaria*, 173–82; reprinted in English in Labanyi (ed.), *Galdós*.

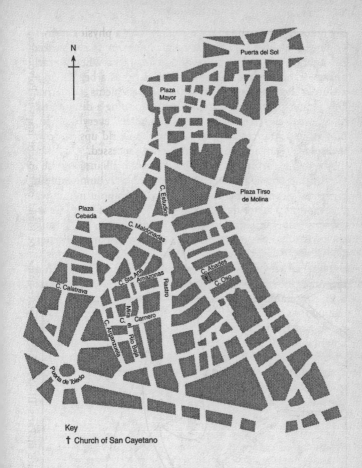

1. Map of Madrid, showing those streets mentioned in Parts I and II of *Nazarín* which still exist today.

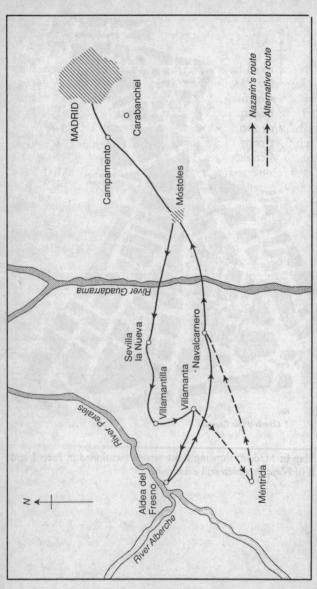

2. Map of Nazarín's route in Parts III–V. The only place-name not found on modern maps is Polvoranca, Ándara's birthplace.

NOTE ON THE TRANSLATION

I HAVE worked from the first edition of 1895, published by La Guirnalda, Madrid, in a print run of 1,000 copies. (Subsequent editions of the novel have only minor variants, mainly orthographical.) I should like to acknowledge my thanks to my former student Joyce Dowson for her wonderful gift of a copy of this first edition. I am also indebted to Professor Nicholas Round of the University of Glasgow for his meticulous and helpful criticisms of my translation; I have incorporated many of his suggestions.

Characters' nicknames have been left in the original Spanish, with a note on first mention explaining their meaning. Sums of money and measures of distance have been converted into rough English equivalents, since the Spanish often uses obsolete forms.

A major difficulty for the translator of Galdós is his virtuoso representation of colloquial speech. The number of low-life characters in this novel is particularly large, and the speech of each of them is sharply differentiated according to the proportion of popular idioms, improprieties, mispronunciations, and grammatical errors. I have done my best to adhere to this sliding scale of correctness/incorrectness, which situates the characters precisely in the social hierarchy (the rustic goatherd who appears briefly in Part III and the dwarf Ujo in Part IV being at the bottom end). In my rendering of the various forms of popular speech I have tried to avoid falling into pastiche, and for this reason have not used obvious literary models such as Dickens, but have gone to the source Dickens himself used for several of his novels: namely, Henry Mayhew's *London Labour and the London Poor* (1851, expanded edition 1861), which transcribes the speech of a vast range of working-class informants with a vivacity unparalleled in any fictional text (Dickens included). I have not used this model slavishly, but have tried to recreate something of its flavour and rhythms.

I have kept to Galdós's practice of italicizing his charac-

ters' most striking linguistic errors and colloquialisms, and
have also tried to maintain the distinction between straight-
forward mispronunciations and malapropisms. To convey
the latter, I have mostly had to change the joke but have
tried to do so in a way that seemed plausible. I have been
particularly aware of the difficulty of capturing the incongruous mixture of disparate registers that characterizes
the speech of Galdós's popular characters in such a way that
the linguistic inconsistency reads as that of the characters
and not as that of the translator.

Galdós also gives several of his low-life characters verbal
trade marks, mostly in the form of swear words, the repetition of which is a source of humour. On occasions this
device becomes a subtle form of characterization: for
example, the prostitute Ándara starts by alternating two
expletives (translated here as 'blimey' and 'holy smoke'),
drops them as she comes under Nazarín's influence, and
finally (in an endearing touch) picks up the blasphemous
'Christ Almighty' of the dwarf Ujo, who thus lives on in
her language after he has disappeared out of her life and
the novel. I have made a point of translating these verbal
trade marks by the same word or phrase on each occasion,
and hope the repetition is comic rather than tiresome.

A noticeable feature of the text is its use of what the
French call *style indirect libre*, which Galdós probably got
from Zola rather than Flaubert. I have indicated the trans-
ition from narration proper to free indirect style (that is,
verbatim reproduction of the characters' words but in
reported form) by the move to contracted forms (such as
'she'd', 'they've'), otherwise reserved for dialogue.

I am aware that my translation in no way does justice to
the range and inventiveness of Galdós's language, but I shall
be pleased if I have been able to convey something of its
humour, a feature of Galdós's writing which is not stressed
enough. *Nazarín* is an exploration of the fundamental principles of Christianity and their social implications, but its
brilliance and originality can be appreciated only if it is read
as a comic novel.

SELECT BIBLIOGRAPHY
IN ENGLISH

Biography

Berkowitz, H. C., *Pérez Galdós: Spanish Liberal Crusader* (Madison: University of Wisconsin Press, 1948).

General Studies of Galdós's Work

Bly, Peter, *Galdós's Novel of the Historical Imagination: A Study of the Contemporary Novels* (Liverpool: Francis Cairns, 1983).

Engler, Kay, *The Structure of Realism: The 'Novelas Contemporáneas' of Benito Pérez Galdós* (Chapel Hill: North Carolina Studies in the Romance Languages and Literatures, 1977) [does not discuss *Nazarín*, but gives an excellent account of Galdós's literary techniques].

Gilman, Stephen, *Galdós and the Art of the European Novel: 1867–87* (Princeton, NJ: Princeton University Press, 1981) [the best general book on Galdós, though it does not discuss the late novels].

Labanyi, Jo (ed.), *Galdós* (London: Longman, 1993).

Pattison, Walter T., *Benito Pérez Galdós* (Boston: Twayne, 1975).

Shoemaker, W. H., *The Novelistic Art of Galdós* (2 vols.; Valencia: Albatros/Hispanófila, 1980).

Urey, Diane F., *Galdós and the Irony of Language* (Cambridge: Cambridge University Press, 1982).

Studies of Nazarín

Bly, Peter, *Pérez Galdós: Nazarín* (London: Grant and Cutler, 1991).

Bowman, Frank P., 'On the Definition of Jesus in Modern Fiction', *Anales Galdosianos*, 2 (1987), 53–60.

Colin, Vera, 'A Note on Tolstoy and Galdós', *Anales Galdosianos*, 2 (1967), 155–68.

Dendle, Brian J., 'Point of View in *Nazarín*: An Appendix to Goldman', *Anales Galdosianos*, 9 (1974), 113–21.

Dolgin, Stacey L., '*Nazarín*: A Tribute to Galdós' Indebtedness to Cervantes', *Hispanófila*, 97 (1989), 17–22.

Goldman, Peter B., 'Galdós and the Aesthetic of Ambiguity: Notes on the Thematic Structure of *Nazarín*', *Anales Galdosianos*, 9 (1974), 99–112.

Parker, Alexander A., '*Nazarín*, or the Passion of Our Lord Jesus Christ according to Galdós', *Anales Galdosianos*, 2 (1967), 83–101.

Romero Pérez, Francisco, '*Nazarín*: Galdós' Enigmatic Apostle', *Revista de Estudios Hispánicos* (Alabama), 17 (1983), 189–98.

Sinnigen, John, 'The Search for a New Totality in *Nazarín, Halma, Misericordia*', *Modern Language Notes*, 93 (1978), 233–51.

Weiner, Hadassah R., 'A Note on *Nazarín*', *Anales Galdosianos*, 13 (1978), 101–3.

Ziolkowski, Theodore, *Fictional Transfigurations of Jesus* (Princeton, NJ: Princeton University Press, 1972), 68–78.

A CHRONOLOGY OF GALDÓS

1843   Born in Las Palmas, Canary Islands.

1862   Arrives in Madrid to study law.

1865   Starts to write for press.

1867   Visits Paris and discovers Balzac.

1868   Witnesses the September Revolution which overthrew the Bourbon Monarchy; translates Dickens, *Pickwick Papers*.

1870   First novel *La Fontana de Oro* published.

1873   Starts First Series of *National Episodes* (historical novels).

1876   *Doña Perfecta* published.

1878   Discovers Zola.

1879   Ends Second Series of *National Episodes*.

1881   *La desheredada* published in 2 vols.

1884   *La de Bringas* published.

1886   Made Liberal member of Parliament, representing a district of Puerto Rico.

1886–7   *Fortunata y Jacinta* published in 4 vols.

1887   Attends the writer Emilia Pardo Bazán's lectures on the Russian novel.

1889–90   Has affair with Emilia Pardo Bazán.

1890–1   *Angel Guerra* published in 3 vols.

1891   Illegitimate daughter María born.

1892   First play *Realidad* performed.

1895   *Nazarín* published.

1897   *Misericordia* published; becomes member of Spanish Royal Academy; sues his publisher and takes on publication of his own works.

1898   Starts Third Series of *National Episodes*.

1901   His anticlerical play *Electra* triggers left-wing riots.

1907   Elected Republican member of Parliament for Madrid; starts losing his sight and hires an amanuensis.

1910   Becomes Co-President of the Republican-Socialist Alliance with the founder of the Spanish Socialist Party, Pablo Iglesias; re-elected Republican member of Parliament for Madrid.

1912   Goes blind, operation for cataracts fails; abandons the Fifth and last series of *National Episodes*.

1915   Second operation for cataracts fails; last novel *La razón de la sinrazón* published.

1918   Last play *Santa Juana de Castilla* performed.

1919   Statue to Galdós, financed by public subscription, unveiled in Retiro Park, Madrid.

1920   Dies in Madrid, leaving his estate to his daughter María; huge crowds (but few official representatives) attend his funeral.

PART I

I

IT was a journalist, one of that new breed to whom we give the foreign name *reporter*—one of those who, like a hound on the scent of a hare, go hotfoot in pursuit of information, sniffing out arson, brawls, suicide, crimes comic and tragic, buildings flattened to the ground, and other such occurrences as commonly disturb the rule of Law and Order or in times of plague affect the nation's health—who was responsible for introducing me to the boarding-house of Tía Chanfaina* (registered in the parish records as Estefanía), situated in a street whose seediness and squalor could not provide a more ironic contrast with its ostentatious, highbrow name: Calle de las Amazonas. Those unaccustomed to the incorrigible facetiousness of the inhabitants of Madrid, that city or court of sarcasm and malicious equivocation, will not stop to wonder at the incongruous sight of that imposing street sign in that dingy alley, nor to enquire about the identity of the Amazons after whom the street was named, or where they came from, or how they ended up in the Fair Town of the Bear and Strawberry Tree.* Here we have a lacuna which my erudition will promptly fill, informing you, as befits a learned chronicler, that in the good old days there stood on that spot a playhouse from which a troupe of wenches, got up as mythological heroines, set out on horseback to take part in the festivities that greeted the entry into Madrid of Queen Elizabeth of Valois.* The ingenuous contemporary *informant* to whom I owe these pearls of wisdom* comments as follows: 'That *ad hoc* assembly of females caused a sensation in the streets and squares of the capital, with their daring acrobatics, somersaults and cavortings, the warriors making as if to seize them by the hair and dislodge them from the saddle, tumbling them to the ground.' Memorable entertainment it must have been, for from that day on the playhouse was called the Theatre of the Amazons; such is the glorious past of the street that in our times owes its reputation to Tía Chanfaina's liberal and hospitable establishment.

My guess is that the Amazons referred to by Philip II's chronicler, whose obedient servant I remain, were the sixteenth-century equivalent of a shameless bunch of trollops, or whatever the common word for such creatures may have been at the time. What I can affirm is that the awesome Estefanía la del Peñón,* Chanfaina, or whatever we are to call her, is one of their bastard progeny; the fruit, that is, of an unbroken line of fatherless viragos. For I swear that, when I try to apply it to her, the gentle name of woman eludes my pen, and it will be enough to acquaint my readers with her appearance, gait, raucous tone of voice, speech, and manners for them to recognize in her the most formidable harridan known to the city of Madrid in times past or future.

Despite which I truly thank God and my reporter friend for presenting me to that gorgon, for it was her barbarity that inspired the present story and led me to the singular character whose name provides my title. No one should take at face value the term *boarding-house* used earlier, for the only thing held in common by the various forms of lodging offered by Tía Chanfaina in that God-forsaken place, and those in the city centre known to all of us from our student days, if not beyond, is the name. The building had a spacious arched entrance like that of an inn, its plaster surface flaking in a thousand weird and wonderful shapes, with the bare masonry showing through in places and a wide dirt mark on both sides from the constant traffic, in this case of people rather than horse-drawn carriages. A drinks stall—jugs and bottles, a dusty glass container stacked with sugar sticks and swarming with flies, set on a wobbly, greasy trestle-table—reduced the gateway to near average proportions. The courtyard, like the entrance unevenly paved and more unevenly swept, littered with pot-holes, occasional clumps of straggly grass, puddles, mud, and broken pots or pitchers, was characterized by a lack of uniformity not so much picturesque as bordering on the fantastic. The southern wing must have been part of the original construction of the famous playhouse: the rest, dating from different periods, could well pass for an architectural joke: windows sinking to ground level, doors arching heavenwards, balustrades doubling as partitions, walls dripping with damp, bent rusty gutters, window-ledges lined with roof tiles, zinc sheets nailed over gaps in rotting timbers, edges battered out of shape, stucco daubed with swirls and diagonals of new white-wash, ridge tiles bristling with glass and broken bottles to deter burglars; here, rotting shafts holding up a gallery tilting like a beached ship; there, panelled doors with cat-holes so large a tiger could climb through, should any be around; cinnamon-coloured wrought iron; purple patches of brick-work like bruises; and finally the play of light and shadow on that profusion of cutting edges and menacing cavities.

One carnival time, as I well remember, my reporter friend decided to take me there for a lark. The first thing I saw was a ragged, one-eyed woman serving drinks behind the stall at the entrance, and on entering the courtyard we were confronted with the sight of a rowdy pack of gypsies camped there for the night, the men spread-eagled on the ground mending their pack-saddles, the women busy preening and picking lice out of their long matted hair, the half-naked children, with their black eyes and curly locks, playing with bits of rubble and broken glass. Their expressive terracotta faces turned towards us, and our ears were met by their sing-song tones offering to tell our fortune. Two donkeys, and an old gypsy with whiskers matching the docile creatures' soft furry coats, made up the scenario, complete with the appropriate background noise and musical accompaniment in the form of a gypsy girl's plaintive trills and the snip of the old man's scissors clipping one of the asses' rumps.

At this point there emerged from an aperture that might have been a gateway, doorway, or mouth of a cave, two scrawny honey-sellers, their legs encased in brown corduroy and black stockings, with leather sandals and thongs, tight-fitting waistcoats, kerchiefs round their heads, typical

products of the Castilian plateau, lean and dessicated like
meat cured in tinder. Tossing out the usual good-humoured
abuse at the gypsies, they made off with their pots and
weights to hawk their luscious wares through the streets of
Madrid. Then we saw two blind men grope their way along
the walls, one of them round and podgy, with a brown
leather cap, tasselled cloak, and guitar slung across his
back, the other clutching a violin with just two strings, and
wearing a scarf and a military officer's cap with no braid on
it. They were joined by a barefoot girl hugging a tambourine
and made their way out, stopping off at the entrance for the
obligatory drink.

There they got embroiled in a lively discussion with two
others likewise bent on sampling the liquor. These were in
fancy dress, one of them clad from top to toe in filthy floor
mats—if clad is the right word to use for something flung
over the shoulders—without a mask but his face blacked
with soot, holding a fishing-rod and a handkerchief knotted
at the corners, full of figs that looked more like turds. The
other had a mask in his hand, a horrid caricature of the
Prime Minister, and his body was swamped by a quilt
patched all over with different sorts of material in variegated
colours. Knocking back their drinks and proffering a string
of obscenities, they ran into the yard and up a staircase
composed of flaking bricks and rotting timbers in equal
proportions. A round of guffaws and the clatter of castanets
rang out from the corridor above; down came close on a
dozen masked figures, including two whose curvaceous
forms and short stature revealed them to be women mas-
querading as men, the others in hideous theatrical costumes
plus the odd one with his face daubed with red ochre, com-
pensating for the lack of a mask. At the same moment, two
men carried out an aged cripple wearing a placard round her
neck with her age—over a hundred—scrawled on it, an
effective publicity device for attracting alms; and took her off
to be deposited on the corner of Calle de la Arganzuela. The
old woman's face was a larger version of a horse-chestnut,
and she might have been taken for a mummy had her bright,
beady eyes not revealed a last spark of life in that bundle of
skin and bones, passed over by death.

After that we saw the body of a child of about two brought out in a coffin lined with pink calico and decked with artificial flowers. It was borne away with no show of tears or maternal grief, as if no one in this world lamented its departure. The man carrying it also stopped off for a swig at the gateway, and the gypsy women were the only ones to have a word of pity for that little creature whose stay on earth had been so brief. Boys in fancy dress, consisting simply of a cambric tunic or cardboard hat with strips of paper pinned on it, girls with shawls and flowers behind their ears in true Madrid lower-class fashion, made their way across the yard, pausing to hear the gypsies' ribald comments or to prod the donkeys, on whose backs they would gladly have mounted had their owners let them.

Before venturing indoors, the reporter filled me in with some choice information that, far from sating my curiosity, only served to whet it more. In earlier days Señora Chanfaina had taken in a better class of tenant, veterinary students, travelling salesmen with more money than manners, but as *business* shifted from that area to the Plaza de la Cebada the quality of her lodgers took a visible turn for the worse. Some of them simply rented what passed for accommodation, supplying their own food; others paid for board and lodging. The kitchen on the top floor was used by all and sundry, each providing his own pots and pans, except for the gypsies who cooked out in the courtyard on trivets improvised from bricks and stones. We finally went upstairs, eager to inspect every nook and cranny of that incredible mansion which harboured such a prolific and piteous share of humankind; and in a dingy room, the unevenness of whose cracked floor tiles emulated the waves of a stormy sea, we came across Estefanía, in bedroom slippers, washing her rough hands which she proceeded to dry on her hessian apron; with her voluminous bosom, averse to a corset's control, splayed out over her equally voluminous belly, her herculean arms, her thickset bull neck with its rolls of fat, her flushed face and the evident remains of a vulgar beauty, she was like a nymph on a painted ceiling, buxom, loud, baroque, designed to be viewed from a distance but seen close up.

Her hair was grey, done up in a mass of ringlets, waves, and curls. The rest of her person was in a state of disarray, suggesting total lack of any concern for neatness or desire to please. She greeted us with a broad smile and, in reply to my friend's questions, declared she'd had enough of always being on the go, and one of these days she'd drop it all and go into a convent or whatever charitable institution would have her; for it was like being chained to a grindstone, that business of hers, there was nothing worse than trying to get money out of the poor, particularly if, like herself, you were a compassionate soul by nature. For, she insisted, she never had the heart to demand the outstanding rent, and so that disreputable crowd had taken over her house like an occupying army; some of them paid the rent, others didn't, and every now and then someone would clear off with a plate and spoon or piece of clothing. As for her, she'd kick up a fuss and shout the house down, which put the fear of God in them, but she could never match her threatening words and looks with action, because if it came to a row, not that it often did, mind you, nobody could yell louder or swear worse, but in the end she'd let them get away with murder, any fool could wrap her round his little finger. This account of her character was made, it seems, in all sincerity, and her clinching argument was that after some twenty years in that nest of vipers, taking in lodgers from all walks of life, she hadn't managed to scrape so much as a shilling together to tide her over in case of ill health.

Just as she was explaining this, four masked women burst in, by which I mean not that they were wearing cloth or cardboard carnival masks, but that the wretches had coated their faces with rice-powder, circles of rouge, blood-red lipstick, not to mention other cosmetic horrors such as beauty spots, black pencilled eyebrows, and something like cats' paws painted round their eyes, to create a romantic effect. Their hands and clothes reeked of cheap perfume you could smell a mile off, and all of this, plus their language, made it abundantly clear we were in the presence of the most abject and degraded forms of human life. At first glance one might easily have thought they were in fancy dress and have taken their make-up for some bizarre kind of carnival mask. Such was my initial reaction, but I soon realized there was nothing uncommon about their faces, quite the contrary; or, to put it differently, for them every day was Mardi Gras or the start of Lent. Heaven knows what ungodly mischief they were up to, for the four of them and Chanfa were gabbling all at once, shrieking and gesticulating wildly, passing in a flash from anger to mirth, with the result that we were unable to make head or tail of it. But it was something to do with a pack of pins and a man. How did the pins come into it? And who was the man?

Tired of the hullabaloo, we slipped out into a corridor overlooking the courtyard, where I observed a window-box sprouting tufts of grass, rue, carnations, and other withered greenery, and sheepskin rugs and floor mats draped over the balustrade to dry. As we edged along it, afraid the creaking timbers would give way beneath our weight, we saw a narrow window on to the corridor swing open, and out of it peered a figure who at first sight we took to be a woman. It was a man. His voice rather than his face decided the matter. Oblivious to our presence as we stood watching him from some way off, he started to call out to Señá* Chanfaina, who took a while to respond, giving me and my companion time to study him at leisure.

He was a man in middle life, or to be precise young but prematurely aged, with a lean, almost emaciated face, aquiline nose and black eyes, olive-skinned, close-shaven, the most perfect Semitic type I ever saw outside North Africa, a classic beardless Arab. He was wearing a loose black robe I initially took to be a cape but then realized was a cassock. 'Is that really a priest?' I asked my friend, and his affirmative nod made me scrutinize him all the more carefully. Indeed my visit to what I shall call the *House of the Amazons* was turning out to be a rich source of material for an ethnographic study,* on account of the variety of species gathered under its roof: the gypsies, the honey-sellers, the women of ill repute, no doubt descended from some little-known branch of the ape family, and now this Arab in his black skirts, formed the biggest confusion of human types I had seen in all my days. And to complicate things still more the Arab was ... a Catholic priest.

My friend explained to me briefly that the Semitic priest lived in the part of the building overlooking the street, which provided superior accommodation to the rest, though it was not what you would call good either, and had its own access to the gateway via a private staircase, being entirely independent from Señora Estefanía's domains apart from the small window we saw him looking out of, and a door that provided no right of way because it was boarded up. So the priest did not form part of the formidable Amazon's family of lodgers. The latter finally heard her neighbour calling and came rushing out, and we overheard the following conversation which my excellent memory permits me to transcribe without omitting a syllable.

'Señá Chanfa, you'll never guess what's happened to me!'

'Heaven forbid! Don't tell me, not another disaster!'

'Why, I've been robbed. There's no doubt about it, I've been robbed. I thought as much this morning, when I heard Siona rummaging around in my chests. She went out to do some shopping, and when it got to ten and she hadn't come back, I got more suspicious, I mean my suspicions nearly stopped being suspicions. And now that it's got to eleven, or so I guess because she took my clock too, I know for a fact I've been robbed, I've checked my chests and my underwear is missing, every bit of it, and all my other clothes too, except for my priest's garments. As for the money that was in the sideboard drawer in this leather purse here, look, she's not left me a farthing. And to cap it all ... this is what hurts, Señá Chanfa ... the little I had in the larder has gone too, and so's the coal and tinder for the stove. And to cut a long story short, madam, I've tried to fix myself up with something to eat but can't lay my hands on a scrap of food, not even a crust of stale bread, or a plate or bowl either. All she's left me with is a pair of tongs, the bellows, the kettle, a strainer, and two or three broken pots. A regular clear out, Señá Chanfa, and I haven't had a bite all day, I'm feeling

faint and don't know where to turn ... So there you have it:
all I need is some food to keep me going. I won't miss the
other things, you can be sure of that.'

'God help you, Father Nazarín,* if your mother could see
you now! She'd wish she'd never had you! A man with such
bad luck, so *soft-witted* and *dim-headed*, it ain't natural* ...'

'But what do you expect? I ...'

'You, that's right, you ...! You've only got yourself to
blame, you're asking for it if people rob you and take advantage, you nincompoop, you ass, you cuckoo!'

The catalogue of obscenities that followed I shall suppress
out of respect for my readers. The gorgon waved her arms
about and ranted on, her torso bulging through the window,
while the Arab priest stood there demurely as if receiving a
string of compliments and endearments, looking just a trifle
subdued; he seemed barely touched by his misfortunes, or by
the torrent of abuse that was his neighbour's attempt at
consolation.

'If I weren't embarrassed to spank a grown man, and a
priest to boot, I'd be right in there now, and I'd lift up those
black skirts of yours and give you the hiding of your life ...
You ain't no better than a child, a babe in arms knows more
about the world than you do! And now you want me to stick
food down your gullet ...! It ain't the first time nor the
last ... Well, if you want to live like the birds in the air, you
can flit off into the countryside and hunt for berries; or sing
your head off on a branch till some flies drop into your
beak ... And if that head of yours needs examining, not that
I'm saying it does, mind you, then they can cart you off to
the *moony-bin*!'

'Señora Chanfa,' the priest replied with a composure that
was astonishing, coming over to the window, 'this paltry
body of mine doesn't need much to keep it going: a crust of
bread will do if you've nothing else to give. I'm asking you
because I consider you my neighbour. But if you say no
I'll take my request elsewhere, there are more charitable
souls around than you might think.'

'You can go to the Devil's Inn or the Papal *Nonce*'s
kitchen* for all I care, they're used to fattening up holy

jackasses, I mean, priests with nothing better to do . . . And anyway, Father, how come you're so sure it's Siona what's robbed you? You're trust and innocence itself, you let every Tom, Dick, and Harry have free run of the place; not to mention the trollops as come running to you with their sins and the like, or to pawn some valuable and then redeem it, or beg for money and generally drive you crazy. You never keep tabs on them what comes in the door, you just smile sweetly and say God bless. And then what happens? They lead you a merry dance, and by the time they've finished they've cleared out your bottom drawer.'

'It was definitely Siona. There's no need to malign anyone else. God be with her, and may she put it to good use, I'll not denounce her to the police.'

I was amazed by everything I had seen and heard, and even my friend, who had witnessed similar scenes before, was impressed on this occasion. I asked him to tell me everything he knew about this Nazarín who so intrigued and baffled me, and whose Islamic features seemed to grow more pronounced the more I looked at him. He replied: 'He's an Arab from La Mancha, born in the village of Miguelturra,* and his full name is Don Nazario Zaharín or Zajarín.* All I know about him are his name and place of birth, but we can always question him about his life and person, if you agree; I bet both are pretty remarkable, no less than his looks and what we've just heard him say. The locals generally regard him as a saint, but others think he's a fool. Which version is correct? If we talk to him, we ought to get a true picture.'

III

Worse was to come. The four hussies who had been chatting on intimate terms with Estefanía heard the accusation against La Siona, who was the aunt of one of them, and leapt to the accused's defence, hurling themselves at the window like panthers or lionesses. Their intentions may have been honourable but they went about it in such a shameless and bestial manner we had to intervene to shut their foul mouths.

There was no insult they did not hurl at the Arab priest from La Mancha, no obscenity they did not fire at him point-blank ...

'Look at him standing there like a stuffed dummy in those filthy rags of his, so skinny he looks like the oilcan at vespers. Fancy him trying to pin the blame on Siona, there's not a decenter *lady* in the whole of Christendom! A damned sight decenter than them blooming priests, all they do is cook up lies to swindle honest folks ... ! Just who does he think he is, and what's the use of wearing those big black skirts, so threadbare they look like a fly's wings, if he ends up living off charity and don't know how to make a living? Silly idiot, why can't he do like all them other priests up and down Madrid, and start up a trade in christenings and funerals ... ? They do very nicely out of it, thank you. They'll fix you up with a Mass any day of the week, but him, what does he get? Sod all: a life on the breadline, cheap chocolate for breakfast, a bit of liver and chard, goats wouldn't touch it ... And he has the cheek to say he's been robbed ... ! What's he got worth pinching, then, apart from his skin and bones, or his priest's tonsure and his Adam's apple ... No clothes, no sheets to his bed, no nothing ... unless you count the sprig of rosemary over his bedhead to keep the devils away ... ! They're what's robbed him, they're what's responsible for stealing his sermons and his holy oil, his masses and his *ora pro nobis* ... Robbed? Of what, I ask you? A couple of prints of the Holy Virgin, and a mouldy crucifix with cockroaches crawling up the stand ... ? Don't make me laugh ... So much for all that about our Mister *Domino Vobisco* here being robbed ... ! You'd take him for His Worship the *Pascual* Nuncio in person, or the *Heavenly Host* in the Corpus procession,* with all them holy relics in his house, not to mention the Holy Sepulchre of the eleven thousand virgins ... ! Why don't you get lost ... ? Why don't you take a running jump ... ? Why don't you ... ?'

'Off with you!' my friend intervened, shooing them out more by dint of force than persuasion, for the sight of a respectable, or seemingly respectable, citizen being abused by those vile creatures was altogether repugnant.

Getting rid of them was not easy: as they disappeared down the stairs, they left behind a trail of venom and perfume, and once down in the courtyard they proceeded to set to with the gypsies, and the asses into the bargain. Now that the coast was clear our only thought was to introduce ourselves to Nazarín; and, with his permission, we made our way to his lodgings, climbing the narrow staircase that led up from the gateway. Words cannot convey the desolation and penury of that house. In the sitting-room there was nothing to be seen but an antiquated wicker sofa, two chests, a sideboard, and a table with a prayer-book and two other volumes lying on top; leading off it was another room I shall call a bedroom because in it I could make out a bed made from wooden planks, with a straw mattress and limp pillow, and no trace of sheets or bedclothes. Three religious prints, plus a crucifix on a console, made up the sum total of the furnishings, together with a couple of pairs of worn boots set out in a row, and a few other objects of no importance.

Father Nazarín gave us a cool but polite reception, neither condescending nor over-unctuous, as if our visit were a matter of complete indifference to him or he felt obliged to pay us no more than the minimum formalities required by etiquette. My friend and I settled ourselves on the sofa, and he drew up a stool facing us. We could not take our curious eyes off him, and he returned our gaze as if he had seen us a thousand times before. Naturally enough the conversation centred on the robbery for want of any other topic and, when we urged him to report it to the police without delay, he replied in the most matter-of-fact manner:

'No, gentlemen; I'm not in the habit of informing on people...'

'What...! You mean to say you've been robbed so many times it's become a habit?'

'Yes, sir; several times, all the time in fact...'

'And you can say that without batting an eyelid?'

'You can see for yourselves I keep nothing in the house. I don't know what keys are. Besides, the little I own, or used to own, is hardly worth keeping under lock and key.'

'All the same, Father: property's property and, as the classical rules of proportion tell us,* what seems a little to someone else may represent a sizeable quantity for you. Why, this very day they've left you without your frugal breakfast or a shirt to your name.'

'Or soap to wash my hands ... Never mind, patience is a virtue. I'll find a shirt and breakfast and soap somewhere. And anyway, my good gentlemen, I've got my particular ideas on the subject, and I stick to them as strongly as my faith in Our Lord Jesus Christ. Property! For me it's just an empty word invented by egoists. Nothing belongs to anyone. Everything exists for the benefit of the first person who needs it.'

'Just imagine what would happen to society if everyone thought like that! And how are you going to tell who the first needy person is? We'd have to fight tooth and nail to be recognized as the first in need.'

With an affable but somewhat contemptuous smile, the priest replied with these or similar words:

'If you look at things from the point of view of present-day society, of course it sounds absurd; but you have to take a higher perspective, sir, so you can see things clearly. From down here on the ground, surrounded by so many super-fluous objects, we can't see the wood for the trees. But if other people see things differently that's none of my business, I'll say no more and please excuse me if . . .'

At that point we saw Señá Chanfa's shadow darken the room as her bosom blocked the whole window frame, through which she passed a plate with half a dozen sardines and a sizeable chunk of French bread, plus a pewter fork. The priest held out his hands to take it and, offering to share it with us, tucked in heartily. Poor man! It was the first bite he'd had to eat all day. Whether out of respect for us, or because her coarse manners had given way to pity, the fact is that Chanfaina's gift was not accompanied by verbal impro-prieties of any kind. Giving our good priest time to eat his fill, we proceeded to interview him as discreetly as possible. After plying him with questions and finding out his age, somewhere between thirty and forty, his origins, which were humble, being from a family of shepherds, his education, etcetera, I went on to explore more delicate matters.

'If I could be sure you wouldn't regard it as an impertinence on my part, Father Nazarín, there are a few things I'd very much like to ask you.'

'As you wish.'

'Feel free to answer or not, as you think fit. And if I touch on anything that's none of my business, just say so and we'll call it a day.'

'Go ahead.'

'Am I talking to a Catholic priest?'

'You are, sir.'

'And you're an orthodox priest, one hundred per cent orthodox? Isn't there something about your ideas or way of life that puts you at odds with established Church dogma?'

'No, sir,' he replied with a naturalness that guaranteed his sincerity, entirely unabashed by the question. 'I've never gone against the Church's teachings. I profess the true Christian faith and you can't fault me on that score.'

'Have you ever been cautioned by your superiors, by those whose job it is to interpret Church dogma and see its canons are observed?'

'Never. And it's never occurred to me I might stand in need of caution or correction.'

'One more question. Do you preach from the pulpit?'

'No, sir. The times I've given a sermon are few and far between. I speak to those who care to listen, quietly and in private, and talk to them about my ideas.'

'And your colleagues have never suggested your views smacked of heresy?'

'No, sir. I don't talk much to other priests because they don't talk much to me, and those that do can be sure there's not an ounce of heresy in me.'

'And do you have a licence to practise as a priest?'

'Yes, sir, and to the best of my knowledge no one has ever thought of revoking it.'

'Do you say Mass?'

'When I'm asked to. I don't go looking for services in parishes where no one knows me. I say Mass at St Cayetano's when I'm needed, and sometimes at the Olivar Oratory. But not every day or anything of the sort.'

'And is that your only source of income?'

'Yes, sir.'

'If you'll forgive my saying so, your existence sounds not a little precarious.'

'If you like, but it's my choice and I've no complaints. I don't care about making money. The days I have something to eat, I eat; and the days I don't, I do without.'

This was said with such frank simplicity, with such a total lack of affectation, that my friend and I were moved . . . truly moved. But more was in store for us.

IV

We could not ply him with enough questions, and he replied to them all, without betraying the slightest sign of irritation at our impertinence. Nor did he show any of the vanity you might expect in someone who finds himself the object of an interrogation, or *interview* as the fashionable term goes. After the sardines, Estefanía brought him a steak of some dubious species; but he refused it despite the Amazon's insistence, which made her fly off the handle again and call him a thousand names. But neither this nor our discreet attempts to encourage him to eat his fill were sufficient to change his mind, and he also refused the wine the harridan offered him. He rounded his meal off with a glass of water and a plain bun, giving thanks to the Lord for satisfying his daily needs.

'And what about tomorrow's needs?' we asked.

'Why, tomorrow I'll get my fill and if not I can wait till the day after, there are never two bad days in a row.'

The reporter wanted to treat him to a coffee; but he, admitting a partiality for it, would not accept. We both had to press him warmly before he eventually capitulated; we ordered it from the nearest bar, the one-eyed woman from the liquor stall at the entrance brought it up to us and, settling back to enjoy it as best we could, given the lack of table space and rough-and-ready service, we had a wide-ranging discussion and from several ideas he came out with deduced he was a man of no mean intelligence.

'I hope you won't mind', I ventured, 'if I say what was going through my head. It's clear you've had a good education. But I'm surprised there aren't more books in your house. Either they're not to your taste or you've had to sell them in some moment of need.'

'I used to have plenty of books, you're quite right, sir, and over the years I've given them away, till the only ones I've got left are the three you can see over there. I can say in all good faith that, prayer-books excepted, I've no interest in books of any kind, be they good or bad; there's little spiritual and mental profit to be had from them. My religious beliefs are firmly ingrained in my mind, and commentaries and paraphrases add nothing to the doctrine I know already. And what else do I need to know? Once you've supplemented your basic intuitions with a few ideas gleaned from your dealings with people and your observations of Society and Nature, what's the point of turning to books for further knowledge or new notions that only confuse and complicate what you know already? I've no time for books or newspapers. My ideas are quite clear in my mind and my convictions are unshakeable; they're emotional responses rooted in my conscience, and they blossom in the form of ideas and bear fruit in the form of acts. Does that sound pretentious? If it does, I'll say no more. Except to add that books mean no more to me than the cobblestones or earth I tread. And when I go into a bookshop and see all that paper printed, folded, and stitched together, and the streets inundated with newspapers day in day out, I feel sorry for all those people labouring through the night to churn out all that useless print, and sorrier still for the deluded souls who feel obliged to read it every day. There's so much written and published people will find themselves strangled by the monster that is the printing press, and they'll have to suppress the whole of past history. And one of the things that'll have to go is the fame and prestige attached to literary creation, one of these days the volume of material housed in libraries will reach such proportions there'll be no way of physically storing and preserving it. And when that happens you'll see how much notice people take of all those poems, all those novels full of lies, all those history books crammed with facts that get less and less interesting as time goes by till they run out of interest altogether. Human memory is too small a storehouse to contain the curiosity shop that is History. Gentlemen, the time is coming when life will be taken up solely with the present, and men will keep from the past only the revealed truths that last for ever. All the rest will be chaff, a trail of litter clogging up minds and buildings. When that time comes,' he added in a tone of voice I am bound to call prophetic, 'the Caesar of the day will issue a decree to this effect: "The entire contents of all public and private libraries are hereby declared null and void with no value beyond that of their constituent materials. Chemical analysis having shown that wood pulp, seasoned by time, provides a magnificent fertilizer for the land, we henceforth dispose that all books, old and new, be taken to large municipal dumps at the entrance to every village, so the farm labourers can help themselves to as much of the precious substance as they need, depending on the amount of land they have to till." It's coming, I promise you; and all that wood pulp will form a vast deposit like guano in the Chinchas Islands, and it'll be exploited by mixing it with other substances that accelerate the fermentation process, and transported by rail and steamer from Europe to the virgin territories that have never known literature or print or anything of the kind.'

His flight of fancy made us laugh heartily. My friend, judging by the wry looks he kept giving me as he listened, seemed to have formed a highly unfavourable opinion of the priest's mental state. I saw him more as an eccentric humorist. Our discussion showed no sign of losing momentum, and we darted from one subject to another. There were times when our good friend Nazarín struck me as a Buddhist,* and others when I saw him as an imitator of Diogenes.*

'That's as may be,' I said, 'but you could still live better than you do, Father. This is hardly what I'd call a home, and

I wouldn't exactly call this furniture either; apart from which you seem to have no clothes other than what's on your back. Why don't you apply for a Church post that allows you to live with a modicum of comfort? My friend here has plenty of influence in both the legislative chambers and whatever ministry you care to name; with a bit of help from my own contacts he can easily fix you up with a nice little living* somewhere.'

The priest gave us a slightly supercilious smile and assured us he didn't need a living, and the idea of singing in a choir didn't appeal to his independent spirit. We also suggested trying to get him a position as a coadjutor in some Madrid parish or as a village priest, to which he replied that, if offered such a post, he'd accept it out of a sense of duty and unconditional respect for the will of his superiors. 'But you can be sure they'll not offer me any such thing,' he added with conviction but not a trace of resentment. 'And with or without a fixed position you'd find me as I am, for poverty is the basic law of my existence; and my highest aspiration, if I may say so, is to possess nothing. If other people's idea of happiness consists of dreams of wealth, for me happiness is to dream of poverty, to delight in the very thought of it and, when things go wrong, to imagine something worse. An aspiration which is never sated because the more you have, the more you want; or rather the less you have, the less you want. I can see either you don't understand me or else you feel sorry for me. If the former is the case, there's no point trying to change your mind; if the latter, then I appreciate your pity and am glad my penury has served to inspire such a Christian sentiment.'

'And what then are your views', we asked him somewhat pedantically, keen to make the most of the interview, 'on the pressing problems of the day, on the current social crisis?'

'I know nothing about such matters,' he replied with a shrug of the shoulders. 'What I do know is that the more civilization—as you call it—advances, and the faster we supposedly progress, and the more machines and money we have, there are more poor people around than ever, and their poverty gets more grim and depressing and restive. And I'd like to do something to prevent the poor, my flock, from becoming infected with hatred for their fellow men. Of all the things we've lost, the saddest loss is that of patience, believe you me. Every now and then you come across it when you're least expecting it, but the day it runs out, God help this world of ours. If only we could tap a new seam of that precious gift, the supreme and most beautiful virtue taught by Our Lord Jesus Christ, mark my words, everything would sort itself out overnight.'

'You mean you're an apostle of patience?'

'I'm no apostle, my good sir, nor do I claim to be one.'

'You preach by your example.'

'I do what my conscience tells me, and if in so doing my actions serve as an example, and if someone chooses to follow that example, well and good.'

'And when it comes to social relations, your creed is passivity.'

'You've put the very word in my mouth.'

'And you let yourself be robbed without protesting.'

'Yes, sir, I let myself be robbed without protesting.'

'And you've no desire to better your lot, and you refuse to ask your Church superiors for a position.'

'That's right; I want nothing, I ask for nothing.'

'You eat when you've got food, and when you haven't you eat nothing.'

'Exactly. I eat nothing.'

'And if they threw you out of your home?'

'I'd go somewhere else.'

'And if you couldn't find anyone willing to take you in . . . ?'

'I'd sleep in the fields. It wouldn't be the first time.'

'And if no one gave you anything to eat?'

'As I said, there are always the fields.'

'And from what I've seen, it seems whores can insult you and you suffer in silence.'

'Yes, sir, I suffer in silence. I don't know what it is to show anger. Enemies are unknown to me.'

'And if someone abused you physically, if they hit you . . . ?'

'I'd take it lying down.'

'And if you were falsely accused ... ?'

'I'd not defend myself. I wouldn't mind what I was accused of if my conscience was clear.'

'But don't you realize there are laws and judges whose job it is to defend you against wrongdoers?'

'I find it hard to believe such things exist, and even harder to believe they'd defend the weak against the strong; but even if what you say is true, God's my judge and to win favour in his eyes I've no need of legal testimonies and lawyers and personal recommendations.'

'Passivity taken to such an extreme sounds positively heroic to me.'

'I don't know about that ... It's nothing special as far as I'm concerned.'

'What I mean is that you take on hunger, poverty, persecution, slander, every kind of ill, natural or social, that exists.'

'I don't take them on, I endure them.'

'And don't you ever think about tomorrow?'

'No.'

'Doesn't it worry you to think that tomorrow you may not have a bed to lie on or bread to eat?'

'No, sir, it doesn't worry me one bit.'

'And you rely on charitable souls like Señora Chanfaina here, who looks like a gorgon but isn't?'

'No indeed, sir, she isn't.'

'And don't you find the dignity of a priest's office incompatible with the humiliation of living off charity?'

'No, sir: there's nothing degrading or undignified about living off charity.'

'So your pride doesn't suffer when someone offers you food or clothing?'

'No, sir.'

'And presumably some of the things you get given find their way to others more in need, at least apparently, than you.'

'Sometimes.'

'And you accept charity for yourself, when you need it.'

'Of course.'

'And doesn't it make you blush?'

'Not at all. What is there to feel ashamed of?'

'So if, right now, we for example . . . out of pity for your plight . . . were to offer you, say . . . some of the money in our pockets . . . ?'

'I'd take it.'

He said this with such spontaneity and candour we had no reason to suppose he was moved to think and talk like that out of cynicism or a feigned humility masking an overweening pride. The time had come to bring our interrogation to a close for it was threatening to become intrusive, and we bade Don Nazario farewell with sincere protestations of pleasure at the happy coincidence that had allowed us to make his acquaintance. He thanked us warmly for our visit and kind attentions, and accompanied us to the door. My friend and I had left a handful of silver coins on the table without stopping to count them, for we had no idea what the needs of that aspirant to poverty might be: we simply threw them down in a little heap, whose sum total came to a little over five shillings but not more than six.

V

'That man's a charlatan,' the reporter said to me, 'a confidence trickster who's solved the age-old riddle of how to get something for nothing, an ingenious rascal who's developed scrounging to a fine art.'

'Hold on, my friend, let's not make hasty judgements that may prove wrong. If you've no objection, I suggest we come back and study his behaviour over a period of time. Personally, I don't feel I'm ready to give a clear verdict on that extraordinary individual we've just been talking to; he looks to me as much of an Arab as when I first set eyes on him, even if you tell me his birth certificate says he's a Moor from La Mancha.'

'Well, if he's not a confidence trickster, in my view he's mentally unsound. Passivity as extreme as that goes beyond

the call of Christian duty, especially in this day and age of
the self-made man.'

'But he's a self-made man of sorts.'

'And just what do you mean by that? I'd define his character as a total lack of character, a negation of everything that
makes a man human.'

'Well, my view or guess, subject to further information
and acquaintance without which I hesitate to pass judgement, is that this saint of ours has a highly developed
personality.'

'That depends what you mean by highly developed
personality. A loafer, a wastrel, or a scrounger can develop
certain talents to the point of genius, and can cultivate and
perfect certain faculties to the detriment of others, the net
result being . . . how can I put it? . . . a brilliance and artistry
surpassing our wildest imaginings. That man's a fanatical,
compulsive parasite, and it could be argued that he's got
no other vices because all his energies are concentrated on
cultivating and developing that single trait. You may say he's
an unusual case . . . No doubt; but I'm not persuaded he's
moved by motives that are purely spiritual. You can argue
that he's a mystic, an ascetic, a lover of wild herbs and spring
water, a Buddhist, a searcher after ecstasy, self-annihilation,
nirvana or whatever the word is. So he may be, but that
doesn't alter my view. Society, in its role as nursemaid or
tutor, ought to regard such types as corrupters of men, on
economic and political grounds, and lock them up in an
asylum. Let me put the following question to you: has this
man, with his obsessive altruism, brought any benefits to his
fellow men? My answer is: no. I can appreciate the magnificent contribution to social welfare made by religious institutions. The giving of alms is a private virtue that makes a
major contribution to the public good. But lone, individual-
istic, medieval practitioners of charity such as we have here,
do they tend the vineyard of the State? No. What they tend is
their own vineyard, reducing charity, so worthy when dis-
tributed systematically and rationally, to the level of plain
shirking. Society, and Christianity too for that matter,
requires everyone to work in his allotted place. Convicts

work, and so do orphans and old people in the workhouse. But this Moorish priest from La Mancha has found a way of getting out of any kind of work, even something as un-demanding as saying Mass. And here he is, without so much as lifting a finger, bringing back the Golden Age no less. I fear he'll have no difficulty finding disciples, teachings like that will spread like wildfire, attracting the idle masses. What can you expect from a man who suggests that books, im-mortal creations like books, and the press, a sacrosanct institution like the press, and all the modern products of print, that vehicle of change, that mother of invention... the whole store of ancient and modern knowledge, the Greek poets, the Vedas, all those stories that have come down to us through the ages, should be turned into mounds of agri-cultural manure? Homer, Shakespeare, Dante, Herodotus, Cicero, Cervantes, Voltaire, Victor Hugo, all converted into intellectual compost, so we can grow nice fat cabbages and cucumbers! He might as well have prophesied that the uni-versities would be turned into cowsheds, and the academies, atheneums, and conservatories into ale-houses or milking stables for asses.'

For all his admittedly witty comments, my friend was unable to persuade me or I him. The verdict on Nazarín, if such a thing were possible, would have to wait. In pursuit of further sources of information, we went into the kitchen where Chanfaina, sweating over an array of pots and pans, was in action frying and stoking, her tight white curls smudged with soot, her hands not still for a second, her right hand frantically stirring, her left hand wiping her runny nose. She immediately realized what we wanted to ask her, being a woman with her wits about her; and pre-empted our ques-tions with the following remarks:

'He's a saint... believe you me, gentlemen, a proper saint. But since saints get up my nose... why, the very sight of them makes me see red... I'd give that Father Nazarín a good wallop, I would, if it weren't for his being a priest, and pardon my saying so... For what use are saints, I ask you? No use at all. In ancient times it seems as they worked miracles, and with them miracles they gave people food, and turned stones to fishes, and brought the dead back to life or drove demons out of live men's bodies. But now, in these scientific times of ours, what with the *tellophore* or *tellophane* or whatnot, and the *realroads* and all those fancy inventions wandering the face of the earth, what good's a saint except to give the street urchins something to laugh at . . . ? The poor soul as you just seen, why he's got a heart of gold, a conscience pure and lily-white, and the meekness of a lamb; no one never heard a cross word leave his lips, you'd think he's a babe as was born yesterday, meaning he's got a saint's death coming to him . . . you can bet your boots on that . . . Rake around as you will, and there's not a single sin you can pin on him, big or small, unless it's the sin of giving away all he's got . . . I treat him like a child, I do, and scold him when I'm minded to. And does he get angry? Not a bit of it. If you raised a stick to him, not that I would, mind you, he'd turn and say thank you . . . That's the sort of man he is . . . And if you called him Jew dog, he'd smile like you'd offered him a bunch of roses . . . I've heard them clergy at St Cayetano's are none too keen on him, seeing as he don't bother with the formalities; and they only give him a Mass to say when there's one without a taker . . . The net result being that what he earns from the *ministry* is not worth writing home about. And me not being one to mince my words, I say to him: "Look here, Father Nazarín, why not get yourself another job, even if it's in a *funereal* parlour . . . ?" and he just laughs . . . And then I tell him he's cut out perfect to be a schoolmaster, what with that patience of his and being used to starving . . . and again he laughs . . . And that I will say . . . you could scour the world and not find an easier man to feed. He ain't particular if all he gets is a crust of bread or an ounce of lung. You can give him sheep guts and he'll down the lot, and not say no to a cabbage stump neither. Why, if he was a man and not the saint he is, the woman looking after him would be sitting pretty . . . !'

We had to cut Tía Chanfa short, for she looked set to go on six hours or more. And down we went to have a word with the old gypsy who, guessing what we wanted from him, lost no time in venturing his informed opinion:

'God be with you, gentlemen,' he addressed us, cap in hand. 'If it ain't too personal a question, might I ask if you just 'anded over some filthy lucre to that poor blighter Don Nazarín, God bless 'im? Cos you'd 'ave done better to 'and it straight to the likes of us; that way you'd 'ave saved us the bother of going upstairs to ask 'im for it, or you'd 'ave saved 'im from giving it away to the wrong sort of fellers . . . Between you and me the place is crawling with 'em, ready to scrounge money off 'im and rob 'im of everything down to the goodness of 'is 'eart, before he gets to give it to folks what deserves it . . . A better man you'll not find, I'll say that for 'im, present company excepted. Why, he's the prince of the 'eavenly angels, by the blessed crest of the cock that crowed at the Passion . . . ! And I'd rather confess with 'im any day than with God's 'ighness the Pope, I would . . . You can see 'is 'oliness coming out of 'is ears, and 'is eyes they shines with the *wondiferous* guiding star of the Blessed Virgin as art in 'eaven . . . So 'ere, gentlemen, you 'ave your 'umble servant, and the 'umble servant of all the family . . .'

By this time we had heard enough, nor at this particular point did we need to know more. At the entrance to the courtyard we had to force our way through a throng of horrible masked figures besieging the liquor stall. Picking our way through the combination of mud, scraps of material that had dropped from those vile bodies, and bits of orange peel and cardboard mask, we emerged into the street and made our way slowly back to the centre of Madrid, our Madrid, which seemed to our eyes a different and altogether superior city, in spite of the crass idiocy of modern-day carnival and the tiresome groups of revellers in fancy dress who kept plaguing us the whole length of our journey. I need hardly mention that we spent the rest of the day discussing that singular and still enigmatic character, thereby betraying the impact he had made on us. Time went by, and both the reporter and myself, forced to attend to other business, began to forget about the Arab priest, though every now and then he would crop up in the conversation. The patronizing diffidence with which my friend talked about him gave me to understand he had left little or no lasting impression on his

mind. Exactly the opposite was true in my case, and there
were days when I could think of nothing but Nazarín and
would take him to bits and reassemble him in my mind, piece
by piece, like a child dismantling a mechanical toy for the
pleasure of putting it together again. Did I end up manufac-
turing a new Nazarín out of the ideas in my head, or did I
manage to grasp hold of the genuine, real-life character? I
cannot say for sure. As for the pages that follow, are they a
true story, or one of those fabrications that, through a combination of the writer's skill and the reader's gullibility, form
something approximating to a semblance of reality? And I
can hear other questions being voiced: 'Who wrote the rest
of this book? Was it you, the reporter, Tía Chanfaina, the
old gypsy . . . ?' To such questions I have no answer, because
I myself would be hard pressed if I had to decide who had
written what I write. I accept no responsibility for the writing
process; but I can vouch for the accuracy of what is depicted.
The narrator remains anonymous. The narrative, imbued
with the spirit of things and with historical truth, speaks for
itself in all its transparency, detail, and authenticity.

PART II

I

ONE magnificent, calm, cool, moonlit night in the month of March, our good friend Nazarín was in his modest home plunged in rapt meditation, pacing up and down with his hands behind his back, or resting his body on the hard wooden stool so as to gaze through the murky glass at the sky and moon and fluffy white clouds, behind which the nocturnal orb kept darting in its game of hide-and-seek. It was already midnight; but he was unaware of the fact and still less concerned by it, being a man capable of contemplating without a stir the disappearance of as many clocks as exist in this world. When the strokes that rang out from those on the buildings nearby were few in number, he would register them; if they were many, his head was too occupied and restless to be bothered with counting them. The clock that guided him at night was his need for sleep, on the rare occasions when he truly felt such a need, and on that particular occasion his body had not yet advised him of its hankering after the makeshift bed on which for a few brief hours he was wont to rest.

All of a sudden, just as our good man was ecstatically pouring his thoughts out into the ravishing glow of the moon, the window went dark, eclipsed in its near entirety by a shadow moving towards it along the corridor. So much for the moonlight, and so much for Father Nazarín's blissful musings!

As the shadow neared the window, he heard a tapping from outside as if commanding or imploring him to open. 'Who can it be ... at this time of night ... ?' More raps, like a drum roll. 'If the shape's anything to go by,' Nazarín observed, 'it's a woman. Oh well, let's open up and find out who it is, and what on earth she wants from me.'

On opening the window the priest heard a muffled

whisper, like that of a masked figure putting on a false voice, which urgently pleaded: 'Let me in, please, Father, take me in and hide me ... They're after me; there's nowhere else I'll be as safe.'

'But my good woman ... ! Who do you think you are? Do I know you? What's the matter ... ?'

'Let me in, like I said ... I can climb in, don't be cross. A good man like you, you'll hide me, won't you ... ? Just until ... What the deuce, I'm coming in anyway.'

And true to her words she leapt in like a bolting cat, shutting the window behind her.

'But my good woman ... do you realize ... ?'

'Don't be cross, Father Nazarín ... You're so good, and I'm so wicked, and because I'm so wicked I says to myself: "There's one person in this world can get me out of this, and that's the blessed Nazarín." Don't you recognize me then, or are you acting daft ... ? Holy smoke ... ! It's Ándara, see ... ! Don't you know who Ándara is ... ?'

'Now I remember ... One of the four ... ladies ... who were here the day I was robbed, and who insulted me into the bargain.'

'It was me insulted you most and called you the rudest names ... Siona's an aunt of mine, see ... But what I says right now is, Siona's more of a thief than Old Nick, and you're a saint if ever there was one ... Holy smoke ... ! I don't mind saying so, honest ... !'

'Fine, so you're Ándara ... But what I'd like to know is ...'

'It's just that, bless you Father, so help me God, I just done someone in.'

'Mercy upon us!'

'When people starts casting *haspersions*, you lose your cool ... Any *feller* has his lapses ... I did her in ... or if I didn't, I near as did ... and I'm hurt, Father, look ... take pity on me ... she sank her teeth right into my arm and took a blooming great hunk out of me; then she went for this shoulder here with the carving knife and I'm bleeding.'

As she finished speaking she slumped to the ground like a sack of potatoes, in what appeared to be a faint. The priest pummelled her, calling her by her name. 'Ándara, Ándara, come round; and if you don't and you die of your terrible injuries, get ready to repent and recant your sins, so the Lord may receive you into His holy bosom!'

The whole of this scene was taking place in near total darkness, for the moon had gone behind a cloud as if in complicity with the wretched woman's search for sanctuary. Nazarín tried to haul her into a sitting position, which was not difficult for she was all skin and bones; but she flopped back on to the ground.

'If only we had a light,' the priest muttered frantically, 'then we could see . . .'

'You mean to say you ain't got a light?' the wounded harridan eventually murmured, coming round from her faint.

'I've got a candle; but what in God's name can I light it with, when there aren't any matches in the house?'

'I got some . . . here, take them out of my pocket, I can't move this right arm of mine.'

Nazarín patted the poor woman's body from the feet upwards like someone playing a tambourine, till something rattled inside the layers of clothing, permeated with a vile odour attempting to pass itself off as perfume. After a considerable amount of groping he found the grubby box, and was just about to strike a match to light the candle when the woman sat bolt upright, exclaiming:

'Close the shutters first. Blimey . . . ! Some neighbour poking around out there might see me and then we'd be done for . . .'

Having closed the shutters and lit the candle, Nazarín was able to inspect the poor woman's sorry state. Her right arm was scored all over with scratches and bite marks, and in the shoulder a stab wound was gushing with blood, staining her blouse and bodice. The first thing the priest did was extricate her from her shawl, after which he undid, or where necessary tore open, the bodice of her tartan smock. To make her more comfortable, he brought her the only pillow he had on his bed, and set about giving her the primary medical attention required, using the most rudimentary materials, washing the wound and staunching it with a bandage, which required him to tear into strips a shirt some friendly neighbours had given him just that day. Meanwhile a torrent of words came flooding from the harpy's mouth, as she recounted the tragic incident that was the cause of her plight.

'It was with Tiñosa,* it was.'

'What was, my good woman?'

'The fight I had, it was with Tiñosa, and it's Tiñosa I done in, supposing I did; right now I'm starting to have my doubts. Blimey, when I grabbed her by that topknot of hers and flung her to the ground, I rammed the darned knife into her with all my heart, hoping to get hers. Holy smoke . . . ! But as for now . . . I'd be glad if it turned out I hadn't killed her . . .'

'A right pair, the two of you. Tiñosa, you say . . . And just who is that good lady?'

'You know, one of them what was here with me that same morning, the ugliest of the four of us, she's got eyes like a half-dead sheep and a split lip, and her ear's torn from someone ripping off her earring and there's scars all over her neck . . . Holy smoke! She'd win first prize for ugliness any day, compared with her I'm like . . . the *Olympid* goddesses. So . . . it was all because Tripita* gave her a pack of black-headed pins . . . and it turned into a *bane* of contention . . . And we got into a proper *hargy-bargy* over whether Tripita is or ain't a gentleman . . . And when I said he was a toady and a pig, that set the feathers flying and she said I was this, that and the other and . . . a load of things you'd not say to nobody. And look here, Father, I may be a bitch, as big a bitch as they come, but I don't like folks saying so to my face, and specially not her, the biggest bitch in the business, why she's so hard-bitten even the cats turn tail when they see her coming . . .'

'That's quite enough, keep that foul tongue of yours to yourself or I'll wash my hands of you,' the priest reprimanded her sharply. 'Wretched woman, forget about all that anger, and remember you've just added murder to the list of your abominable sins, leaving your soul so sullied there's not the tiniest corner by which it can be plucked from the flames of Hell.'

'All the same ... Look, Father ... What I mean is, if they casts *haspersions* on me ... Holy smoke ...! I may be the lowest of the low but we all got our self-respect, and we likes folks to treat us proper ...'

'That's enough, I said ... and don't answer back. Give me a straight, sensible account of what happened, so I know whether to give you my protection or turn you in. And how did you manage to get away from the crowds that must have gathered to see what was going on, in your house or the street or wherever ... ? How come you didn't get arrested on the spot? And how did you manage to get here without being seen and slip into my house; and what made you decide to put me on the spot in the first place by asking me to take you in?'

'I'll tell you all about it, just like you ask; but first give me some water if you got any, and if not go and get me some, I'm dying of a thirst worse than all the flames in Hell ...'

'Water I do have, luckily. Drink that and tell me the whole story, if talking doesn't make you faint or feverish.'

'No, sir, I can go on talking till *tombsday* if you let me, and when I die I'll not stop talking till after my last breath. So I stabbed her here, see, and then here, begging your pardon ... and if they hadn't *unseparated* us I'd have skewered her good and proper ... Half her hair came away in my hands and I stuck these two fingers of mine in her eye ... To cut a long story short, they had to drag her away from me and they tried to *demobilize* me, but I clawed my way free like a tigress and dropped the knife and ran out into the street, and before they'd had a chance to come after me I was in Calle del Peñón. Then I worked my way back ... I could hear people shouting ... so I crouched down on all fours. Roma and Verginia was screaming and Tía Gerundia was saying: 'It was Ándara, it was Ándara ...' And the nightwatchman and a whole lot of other men ... all asking where I could have gone, this-a-way, that-a-way ... and they'd search me out and send me to jail* if not to the gallows ... When I heard that, blimey, I started to slink away, pressed to the wall for all I was worth, keeping to the shadows, till I slipped into Calle de las Amazonas here, without no one spotting me. There wasn't a soul in sight, they'd all gone to see what the deuce was up. I was trying to work out what saint in heaven to pray to and looking for some kind of hidey-hole, even if it meant the sewers. But the bleeding draincovers was too small, there was no way I could squeeze down them...! And my arm was throbbing like nobody's business and streaming with blood, holy smoke! I took refuge in the big gateway to this building here, it's always thick in shadow, and leant against the gatepost...I gave the gate a shove and it swung open before my eyes... Halleluyah, what a stroke of luck...! The gypsies often leave it unlocked, you see...I stole in on tiptoe like a ghost, thinking if the gypsies spotted me I was done for...But they didn't, the wretches. They was snoring their heads off, and the dog was out in the street somewhere...God bless the bitch that lured it out...! So I scuttled across the courtyard quick as a mouse, asking myself: "Now where can I go? Who can I ask to take me in? Chanfa, forget it. Jesusita and Pelada,* no hope. And if the Cumplidos find me here, that'll be my lot..." At this point it struck me there was one person might be willing to help me out, and that was Father Nazarín. And I bounded up the steps in a trice. Then I remembered at carnival time I'd given you the rough edge of my tongue, what with this red-hot temper of mine. I felt my conscience smart, holy smoke, just like my wound! But I said to myself: he's a good, simple saint of a man, and he'll have forgotten all about the blooming names I called him; and I ran to your window and knocked, and...oh God, it's really hurting now...! Oh God, oh God...! Father, for the love of Christ, you don't have some vinegar handy, do you?'

'No, my good woman, you know I have no luxuries in this house, no food or drugs in my cupboard. Vinegar! What do you think this is, the Promised Land?'

II

In the course of the night the unhappy woman's condition deteriorated so rapidly that Don Nazario (let us address him formally for once, instead of referring to him by the familiar Nazarín) was at a loss to know what to do with her, or how to resolve the tricky situation his widespread reputation for goodness had landed him in. Ándara (as she was known, her full name being Ana de Ara) fell into an alarming state of prostration, with intermittent bouts of unconsciousness and delirium. The worst of it was that, although the good priest knew she was suffering from weakness caused by excessive loss of blood, he had no immediate way of alleviating the problem, since the only items of food he had in the house were a bit of bread, a slice of fresh goat's cheese, and a dozen or so walnuts, none of them suitable for someone critically ill. But since there was nothing else at hand, she would have to make do with the bread and nuts till it was day and Nazarín could go out to buy something more nourishing. He would gladly have given her some wine, which is what she kept calling for; but such a thing never entered his frugal, modest dwelling. Since he could do nothing to help her regain her strength, he tried to find the wretched woman's body a more comfortable bed than the floor where she had been lying all this time; and discovering, after various vain attempts, that there was no way of getting her to move, for her muscles had gone limp like a rag doll and her bones were as heavy as lead, our good Nazarín had to brace himself and clumsily hoist that repulsive load on to his shoulder. Fortunately Ándara weighed next to nothing as there was practically no flesh on her (which made her present condition all the more dangerous), and for any moderately fit man lifting her would have been as easy as carrying a half-full wineskin. Even so the poor priest had a hard time of it and almost collapsed halfway across the room. But he finally managed to put his load down, and as her aching bones and lifeless limbs flopped on to the bed the wench murmured: 'God bless you, sir'.

Shortly before daybreak, in a moment of lucidity after babbling on about Tripita, Tiñosa, and other dubious individuals with whom she kept less than reputable company, the hussy said to her benefactor:

'Don Nazarín, sir, if you ain't got no food, I suppose at least you got some money.'

'Just what they gave me for today's Mass, but I haven't touched it yet and no one's asked me for it.'

'Thank God for that ... Well, as soon as it's light you can go and get me half a pound of meat to make me a stew. And while you're about it, you can bring me a quarter of a litre of wine ... But come over here so you can listen proper. You're an innocent what goes around like a saint, which means you always mess things up. Listen carefully to what I says, I know a shilling from sixpence, unlike some people ... Don't get the wine from Jesusa's brother's place, and not from José Cumplido's neither, they both knows you. "What's this?" they'll say, "Our saintly Nazarín buying wine when he never touches the stuff!" And they'll start gossiping and before we knows where we is, someone'll start snooping around and holy smoke ... they'll find me here ... ! And just think what they'd have to say about you ... ! You'd better get it from the tavern in Calle del Oso, or the one in Calle de los Abades, where nobody knows you, and anyway they're more honest there, I mean they don't water it down as much.'

'I don't need telling what to do,' the priest retorted. 'For one thing I don't care what people think about me, and for another it's not proper for me to take your advice nor for you to offer it in the first place. Nor, my wretched Ándara, have you any reason to be so sure my humble home is a harbour for criminals, and that I'll get you out of trouble by covering up for you. I won't inform on you; but I won't lie to anyone who comes looking for you either provided they do so with good cause, and if that's my position with regard to the law, I certainly won't help you wriggle out of the expiation the Lord has in store for you, because it wouldn't be right for me to do so, have you got that straight? I won't hand you over to the police: as long as you're here, I'll do everything I can to help you ... If nobody finds you, it's up to you to make your peace with God.'

'All right, all right,' the hussy sighed. 'But that don't stop you buying the wine where I says, for the simple reason they ain't so *adulterous* as they is round here. And if you ain't got enough cash on you, take some out of my skirt pocket, there ought to be a sixpenny piece and three or four coppers. Take the lot, it ain't no use to me right now, and while you're getting the wine, you can buy some cigarettes for yourself.'

'For me!' the priest exclaimed in horror. 'You know perfectly well I don't smoke . . . ! And even if I did . . . keep your money, you may need it before the day's out.'

'Well, it wouldn't hurt you to smoke since you ain't got no other vices, blimey! Not having no vices, none you could call a vice, why that's a vice of sorts too. Never mind, don't get cross with me . . .'

'I'm not. I'm trying to make you see you've got enough on your chest without indulging in idle talk and fancies. What you should be doing, wretched woman, is taking stock: pray to God and the Virgin Mary, search your conscience, reflect on all those sins of yours and remember that, if your faith and love are strong enough you can mend your ways and obtain forgiveness. I'm here at your side to help you, if you care to think about things more serious than dodging the law, money, wine, and cigarettes . . . Unless you want the cigarettes for yourself, in which case . . .'

'Oh no, sir . . . not me,' the wench protested. 'It's just that . . . What I mean is, if you want to take the sixpence, take it, it's not right you should fork out for everything . . .'

'I've no need of your sixpence. If I needed it, I'd ask you for it . . . Just get down to thinking about the state of your soul and what you have to do to repent. Remember you're injured, I can't give you proper medical care, and when you're least expecting it the Lord may strike you down with gangrene, typhus, or some other infection. None of which would be anything like as bad as what you deserve or as serious as the infection corrupting your soul. That's what you ought to be thinking about, my unhappy Ándara; we're all at the mercy of death but right now it's knocking at your door, and if it suddenly comes in, which well it might, and takes you by surprise, you know where you'll end up.'

All the time Nazarín was talking, and for some while after, Ándara said not a word, her silence showing that his exhortation had succeeded in instilling a vague fear in her soul. A considerable pause ensued, whereupon she started to heave one sigh after another, plaintively acknowledging that, if die she must, there was nothing for it but to resign herself. But she might well end up living if she had something to eat, and a bit of wine which would do to disinfect her wounds too. And if it came to the crunch she'd do her best to feel as contrite as she could, so the end found her well disposed and full of Christian sentiments. That apart, and hoping Nazarín wouldn't get cross with her, she'd venture to say she didn't believe in Hell. Tripita, who was ever so well read and bought *La Correspondencia* every evening, had told her all that stuff about Hell and Purgatory was a load of tommy-rot, and Bálsamo said the same.

'And who's Bálsamo, my good woman?'

'Why, he was a sacristan once and he studied to be a priest, and he knows the words of all the hymns, even the prayers for the dead. Then he went blind and took to singing in the streets with a guitar, and he got the nickname Bálsamo from a naughty ditty that always ended with the refrain *balsam of love*, and it stuck.'

'Well, you're free to choose between Mister Bálsamo's opinion and mine.'

'Oh no, father ... You know lots more than him ... How could you possibly think ... ! There ain't no comparison ... ! Why, he's a no-gooder, a real bad egg. He lives with a woman what goes by the name of Camella,* tall and lanky, all skin and bones. We call her that because in her time, before she lost her looks, they used to say she was the Lady of the Camelias.'

'I don't want to know about Camellas or Camelias, can we get that straight? Just forget about all those unsavoury acquaintances of yours, and think about cleansing your soul, which is going to take some doing. Right now, try and get some sleep; and I'll sit on this stool here against the wall till it starts to get light, which can't be long.'

Regardless of whether or not they slept, the fact is they both fell silent, and silent they were still when the first shafts of morning light stole through the cracks in the shutters. They took a while to light up the drab surroundings and outline the various objects, filling them in with their respective colours. At daybreak Ándara fell into a deep slumber, and when she awoke, well into morning, she found herself on her own. Hearing the sound of movement in the building, people coming in and out of the courtyard, the tenants going about their business, Chanfaina's booming voice in the kitchen, she panicked. Even though such noises were probably a normal part of the establishment's daily routine, the poor woman was on tenterhooks and in her state of nerves resolved to lie *doggo* on the thin mattress, doing her best not to make a sound, not to stir, not to cough, not to breathe more than was strictly necessary to avoid suffocating, so no false move would betray her presence in the priest's house.

But the power of fear to keep her awake proved less strong than the power of exhaustion to return her to oblivion, and she lapsed back into a profound lethargy, from which she was rudely awoken by Nazarín shaking her head from side to side, trying to get her to drink some wine. And how eagerly she gulped it down, how she licked her lips! Then she set about applying the same medicine designed for internal consumption to her wounds; and so great was her faith in the remedy, having no doubt seen it work on countless previous occasions, that it alone, in default of anything else to put her trust in, was enough to make the wretched woman perk up. Her apprehensiveness about the possibility of being discovered made her take a thousand ingenious precautions, such as speaking to Don Nazarín in sign language so the sound of her voice would not be detected by the neighbours' prying ears. They managed to say everything that needed saying by pulling faces and waving their hands in the air, though Ándara was hard put to it to communicate to him in that imperfect language certain rudimentary instructions about the stew on whose preparation the good priest was embarking. There was nothing for it but to resort to words, reduced to a barely audible whisper; in the end they managed to make themselves understood, Nazarín acquired some vital expertise in the culinary arts, and the patient sipped some stock which for all its lack of substance did her good; and what with that and the sops of bread she ate afterwards, she started to revive and return to her normal self. Having performed these charitable acts of hospitality Nazarín went out, leaving the house locked and the wounded woman to the company of her restless thoughts and that of the odd mouse sniffing around for crumbs under the bed.

III

The criminal spent the rest of the day alone, the good priest being in no hurry to come home. In the course of the afternoon the unhappy woman was beset by doubts and suspicions, as befits someone who has committed a crime. 'And what if he grasses on me?' she kept asking herself, obsessed with her chances of avoiding arrest. 'I don't know what to think, I really don't... Some folks says he's a saint, others says he's as big a rogue as they come... There's no telling... Blimey, holy smoke! I really don't think he'd grass on me though... What he would do, just suppose they tracks me down and asks him if I'm here, is say yes, he can't tell a lie for the life of him. Some kind of saint he is! If it's true there's a hell full of bonfires and pitchforks, it ought to be kept for folks what don't mind telling the truth if it sends some poor blighter to jail or the gallows.'

At one point in the afternoon, she had a dreadful scare when she heard Chanfa's voice right outside the window. She was talking to another woman who sounded, from her hoarse, throaty voice, like Camella. And Camella was such a bitch, so fond of sticking her nose into other people's business and broadcasting it to the winds! After they'd had a good natter, Estefanía tapped on the pane; but since the priest was not there to come to the window, the wretched women went away. Some other people, including several of the local street urchins, also knocked in the course of the day, which was perfectly normal and nothing to worry about, considering the needy from all the streets around were in the habit of visiting that friend and protector of the poor. By the time it got dark the hussy was in a state of total panic, desperate for the priest to come back so she would know whether or not she could count on his discretion in keeping her sanctuary a secret. The minutes seemed like hours; when at last she saw him come in the door, shortly after nightfall, she was on the point of scolding him for being so long, and would have done so had she not been so pleased to see him that she forgot to be angry.

'I'm not accountable to you for my movements and what I do with my time,' Nazarín replied to the impertinent barrage of questions which his protégée, if such she was, fired at him point-blank. 'How are you feeling? Any better? Is that stab wound of yours hurting any less? Are you getting back your strength?'

'Oh yes, sir, yes... But I've been scared stiff... Every other second I thought someone was coming after me to cart me off to jail. Tell me, am I safe here? I want an honest answer, not a pious one.'

'I've already told you,' answered the priest, taking off his mantle and biretta. 'I won't report you to the police... Just try not to do anything that gives your presence away... And ssh... there's someone out in the corridor!'

In effect, it was Estefanía who tapped on the window again and chatted to Nazarín for a few minutes.

'Well, well, our little saint's been out and about in the big city today all right,' said the Amazon. 'What's all this in aid of? Been to chat up the Bishop like I told you? If you don't bow and scrape you'll not get nothing. Did you get a Mass today, then? Good, that's what I like to hear. Keep on at it, do the rounds of the parishes shamelessly, chat them up... You'll soon see how the Masses fall into your lap. Good heavens, Father, I can smell... I declare there's a smell coming from your window... like that blessed *perfumery* those tarts puts on their persons... You mean to say you can't smell it? Why, it's enough to knock you over backwards!... It's not the first time, of course. Seeing as all sorts comes to visit you, and you make no distinctions and help them out not knowing them from Adam...'

'That must be it,' Nazarín answered unperturbed. 'All sorts come in here. Some of them smell and some of them don't.'

'And I can smell a good drop of wine, too... Don't say

your reverence is going off the straight and narrow . . . That's not communion wine, I know.'

'As for the first smell,' the priest said quite openly, 'I don't deny it. Whether you call it a perfume or a stench is open to question, but it's true there's a smell of it in my house. I can smell it myself and so can anyone with a nose. But wine I can't smell, I honestly can't, which doesn't mean there hasn't been any in my house today . . . There may well have been; but there's no smell of it, ma'am, no smell at all.'

'Well, I'd say there's a whiff of it . . . But there's no point having a row about it, your nose and mine must *whiff* different.'

Whereupon Señora Chanfa offered him some food which he refused, accepting only, on being pressed, a cinnamon bun and two chorizo sausages. With that the conversation drew to a close and the fugitive started to breathe freely again. 'I knew that darned *perfumation* on my clothes would give me away. I'd burn the lot of it if I could leave this place in my petticoats. I never dreamt when I put that scent on it'd get me into all this trouble. And it's a fine perfume, ain't it, father? Don't you think it smells real good?'

'No, I don't. The only scent I like is that of flowers.'

'Me too. But they costs a lot and you have to make do with looking at them in the park. Why, once I used to have a friend who kept bringing me loads of flowers, the very best; just that they was a bit dirty.'

'How come dirty?'

'From the rubbish. He was a dustman, my friend was, one of them what collects the rubbish each morning. And sometimes, at carnival time or when there was a ball on, he'd be cleaning the streets outside the theatres and rich people's houses, and he'd sweep up *camellas* by the dozen.'

'Camelias, you mean.'

'Camelias, and roses too. He used to wrap them all up carefully in a bit of paper and bring them to me.'

'Very gallant . . . ! Are you never going to stop babbling on and start thinking about important things like cleansing your soul?'

'If you say so, though I don't think I'm done for this time

round. I'm like a cat with seven lives. I been in 'ospital twice with a sheet pulled over my head, they all thought I was a gonner but I came out and was as right as rain.'

'I wouldn't be so confident if I were you, my good woman, just because you've had some near escapes in the past. Death is our constant bosom friend and companion. We carry it with us from the moment we're born, and the pains, tribulations, and frailties that constantly afflict us are simply signs of its caresses. I don't know why we should be so horrified by its sight when it exists within us all the time. I bet the sight of a skull scares the living daylights out of you, not to mention a skeleton . . .'

'Not half.'

'Well, that skull you're so scared of goes with you every-where you go: it's your head.'

'But not so hideous as them in the cemeteries.'

'Identical; except that it's clothed in flesh.'

'Do you mean to tell me, Father, that I'm my skull? And that my skeleton is these bones of mine, strung together like the ones I saw at the theatre once, in a puppet show? And that when I dance, it's my skeleton dancing? And when I sleep, that's my skeleton too? Holy smoke! And when I die, they'll pick up this fancy little skeleton of mine and tip it in a hole in the ground?'

'Exactly, like something that's no more use to anyone.'

'And when you die, do you go on knowing you're dead and remembering you were alive? And whereabouts in your body does your soul live? In your head or your heart? And why is it when you're scared you have your heart in your mouth?'

In reply Nazarín explained what the soul was in elemen-tary terms accessible to that untutored mind, and they went on conversing quietly well into the night after having some supper, forgetting about the neighbours who fortunately had forgotten them. Ándara, no doubt because of the enforced immobility which set her imagination racing, wanted to know everything, displaying an almost scientific curiosity which the good priest was sometimes able to satisfy and sometimes not. She was eager to know how you *get born*, and how it is that chicks come out of the egg looking like little cocks and hens ... why the number thirteen is unlucky, and why it brings good luck to pick up a horseshoe in the road ... She had no idea what makes the sun rise every day, why every hour is the same length, and why the days in a particular season are equally long or short each year ... Where did your guardian angel live when you were a *littl'un*, and why do the swallows leave in winter and come back in summer, and how do they always find their way back to the same nest ... ? And then it's odd how the number two always brings good luck, but having two candles lit in the bedroom brings you bad luck ... Then how come mice are so clever when they're so tiny, but you can dupe a big creature like a bull with a rag ... ? And what about fleas and other insects, do they have a soul of sorts? Why does the moon wax and wane, and how do you explain that when you're in the street and you meet someone who reminds you of someone else, you almost immediately bump into the other person ... ? And it's funny how you can have a hunch something's going to happen, and that when pregnant women start getting cravings, for aubergines say, the baby's born with an aubergine on its nose. Neither did she understand why souls get out of purgatory when you give the priest some money for a requiem mass, or why soap gets dirt off, and why Tuesday is such an awful day you can't put a foot right.

Nazarín was able to answer some of her queries easily but others were not so cut and dried, and when it came to the beliefs that could be classified as idle superstitions, he simply denied them outright, telling her to get such rubbish out of her head. So the evening went by, and a quiet uneventful night allowed the invalid to regain her energies. Three, four days elapsed, Ándara rapidly recovering from her injuries and getting stronger, the good Don Nazario going out every morning to say Mass and coming home late, with nothing disturbing the pattern or anyone discovering the criminal's whereabouts. Although she thought herself safe, she continued to go to inordinate lengths to ensure no sound or other sign of her presence reached the outside world. On the third day she got up from the mattress, no longer needed, but did not dare leave the bedroom; and whenever she heard voices she would hold her breath and quake. However, fickle fortune decided it had favoured her long enough, and on the fifth day all her precautions were to no avail and the wretched woman found herself faced with the imminent prospect of falling into the hands of the law.

At nightfall Estefanía came to the window and, calling out to the priest who had just got back, said: 'Come on now, you can't pull the wool over my eyes. Stop playing silly games, the cat's out of the bag and everyone knows the name of the minx you're hiding in that den of yours. Let me in the door round the other side, I want to come in and talk to you without the neighbours knowing.'

IV

Hearing this Ándara went as white as a sheet, not that there was one there to make the comparison, and had a vision of herself in jail, with chains round her ankles and handcuffs round her wrists. Her teeth were chattering as she heard Chanfaina come in; the latter made straight for the bedroom, declaiming:

'That's enough of this nonsense. Look here, you slut, I knew you was here all along. I sussed you out by that smell of yours. But I didn't like to say nothing, not for your sake but to save our Father here from trouble, God bless him: he's always landing himself in scrapes, what with that soft heart and silly angelic nature of his. And now listen to me, the two of you; if you don't do what I says, you're done for.'

'Is Tiñosa dead?' Ándara enquired, fear temporarily overcome by curiosity.

'No, she ain't. She's in the 'ospital with some kind of *interfection*, but they says she's not for pushing up daisies yet. If she'd kicked the bucket, you'd have swung for it.* So there . . . You can leave this place with that off your chest. Go where you like, just mind you make yourself scarce: they'll be here to arrest you before the night's out.'

'But who ... ?'

'Who do you think, you idiot? Camella's one for getting wind of things ... The other night she was at this window, with her nose pressed against the hinges like a ratcatcher's dog on the trail. She sniffed and she sniffed, you could hear her snorting from the gateway. Well, she's found you out and she's not the only one; there's no escaping now. Clear out while the going's good and find yourself some other hiding place.'

'I'll be off this second,' said Ándara, wrapping her shawl round her.

'Oh no, you won't,' Chanfa snapped, taking it off again. 'I'm going to give you one of mine, the oldest one I got, so folks won't recognize you. And I'll give you an old frock too. Leave those blood-stained togs of yours here and I'll hide them. ... I *hairby* declare I ain't doing this for a slut like you, but for our Father here, who's going to have questions asked about whether he is or ain't on the wrong side of the law, like yourself. The Magistrates is real sticklers, they won't leave no stone unturned. As for this little lambkin here, he's going to do what I says or else they'll have him up too, and he'll need all the help in heaven to get him out of a stretch inside.'

'So what am I to do then, if I'm allowed to know?' asked the priest, whose composure was starting to give way to mild concern.

'What you do is deny it, deny it and keep on denying it. This creature's leaving and finding somewhere else to hide. There ain't going to be no trace of her, *definately* no trace of her left behind: the likes of me is going to clear up and scrub the floor; and you, Mister Nazarín, God help me, when the police comes, you say no to everything, no she ain't been here, no it ain't true. And let them try and prove it, my foot ... ! Just let them try and prove it!'

The priest said nothing; but the fiendish Ándara nodded furiously, endorsing Estefanía's forceful arguments.

'The trouble is,' the latter went on, 'there's no way of getting rid of this darned smell ... What the deuce are we going to do about it ... ? You tart, you whore, you strumpet...! Why did you have to douse yourself with that blessed *patchouli* you can smell a mile off? You'd have done better to plaster yourself with the scent of all the rubbish tips in Madrid, you filthy slut!'

Having agreed on Ándara's *decamping*, that virago of a landlady, who was all go in moments of crisis, rushed back with the clothes Ándara was to put on instead of her blood-stained rags, to camouflage her escape to some safer place.

'How soon will they be here?' she asked Chanfa, keen to leave as soon as possible.

'We've got time to clean the place up,' the other woman replied, 'because first they've got to go to the Magistrate's Court to report you, and it'll be at least 10.00 or 10.30 before the cops* are here. That's what Blas Portela said and he's familiar with all the ins and outs of the law; if the gentlemen of the bar so much as scratch themselves he's the first to know. We've got time to give everything a good scrub and cover this vixen's tracks... And as for you, mister innocence itself, there's nothing for you to do right now except get in the way. Why don't you take a little walk?'

'I've got to go and see someone anyway,' said Don Nazario putting on his biretta. 'I've fixed an appointment with Señor Rubín,* the priest at St Cayetano's, after the evening service.'

'Off with you then... I'll go and get a bucket of water... And you in the mean time can take a good look round to make sure you ain't left behind no garter or button or haircomb, or no other filthy appurtenance of yours such as a ribbon or cigarette, for example... A right pickle you've landed this saint of ours in... Out you go, Don Nazarín, there's a good lad... We'll sort this mess out.'

The priest left and the two harpies got down to work. 'Go through the place with a toothcomb, shake the mattress, make sure you don't leave nothing behind,' Chanfa ordered.

And Ándara replied: 'Look, Estefa, it's all my fault, it's me what's caused the trouble... And since our good Father was kind enough to take me in, I don't want him to get hauled over the coals tomorrow or the next day because of me and my blinking perfume... So since I caused it all, I'll get down on my hands and knees till there's no whiff of that scent of mine . . . And as we got time . . . till 10.00 you say? . . . why not get on with what you got to do and leave me to it. I'll see it's all left ship-shape, don't you worry.'

'All right, I've got to cook supper for the honey-sellers and the four fellows from Villaviciosa . . . I'll fetch the water while you . . .'

'No need to bother. I can fetch the water from the drinking fountain on the corner. There's a pail here. I'll wrap the shawl round my head and no one'll recognize me.'

'That's true enough: you go then and I'll be off to the kitchen. I'll come back in half an hour. The key's in the lock.'

'I don't need it. It can stay where it is. I'll be here with the blessed water before you can count to ten . . . One more thing: before I forget . . . give me a sixpenny piece.'

'What do you want that for, you slut?'

'Have you got one on you or not? Let me have it, lend it me, you know I always keep my word. I want it to get a drink and a packet of cigarettes. When did I last tell a lie?'

'I wouldn't know, you do it all the time. There you are then, take the blinking sixpence and be done with it. You know what you've to do. Get cracking. I'm off. Wait for me here.'

The formidable Amazon went out, followed a couple of minutes later by the other harridan, after adding her own sixpence to the one her friend had lent her and picking up a bottle and medium-sized oilcan from the kitchen. The street was pitch black. She vanished into the darkness and came back shortly via Calle de Santa Ana, with the same objects tucked in the folds of her shawl. Nimble as a squirrel, she shot up the narrow staircase and into the house.

In the space of a few minutes, seven or eight at the outside, Ándara went into a broom cupboard off the kitchen, brought out a pile of straw she'd extracted from an old mattress, carted the lot into the bedroom wrapped in the mattress cover and spread it on the floor under the bed, pouring on top all the paraffin she'd brought in the bottle and oilcan.

Not satisfied with this, she ripped open with a knife the other mattress, also filled with straw, on which she had slept for the last few nights, and added one lot of stuffing to the other; and to clinch things she piled on top both mattress covers and every scrap of cloth she could lay her hands on, stacking on top of the bed the stool and even the wicker sofa. Having build her funeral pyre, she got out her box of matches and whoosh!... Just like gunpowder, blimey! Opening the window to get a good draught going, she stood contemplating the product of her labours for a while and only when the thick smoke from the combustible mound made it impossible to breathe did she make a run for it. Outside the door, at the top of the staircase, she paused for a moment to watch the flames spread and billow in the wind, and our friend Nazarín's house fill with black smoke, then she hurtled down the stairs and darted out of the gateway in a flash, muttering into her shawl: 'Just let them sniff me out now ... holy smoke!'

She went downhill past the Rastro and along Calle del Carnero, then down Mira el Río, where she stopped to glance up at the rooftops in the direction where she gauged Chanfaina's lodging-house ought to be. Until her eyes saw the column of smoke signalling the success of her efforts at fumigation, there was no way she could rest easy. If the smoke didn't start to rise into the sky soon, it must mean the neighbours had managed to put the fire out ... No way! Who could put out that regular inferno she'd sparked off in a few seconds flat! She scanned the horizon anxiously for ten or so minutes, thinking that if the fire didn't catch hold, rather than her definitive salvation it would be her perdition. She could cope with anything, even with being sentenced to rot in jail; but there was no way she could let the blessed Nazarín be falsely accused of having dealings with a whore ... Eventually, glory be to God! she saw a thick column of black smoke, blacker than Judas Iscariot's soul, spiral up into the heavens over the rooftops, and the cloud of smoke seemed to speak, voicing her thoughts: 'Let them smell me now ... ! Just let Camella come sniffing at the window like a bloodhound ... ! So you thought you could smell a rat, did you, gentlemen of the *bar-room* . . . ? Well, the only rats you're going to smell now are dead ones . . . blimey! And good luck to anyone who tries to sniff me out . . . Let them rake through the *ambers* . . . they'll see if they don't get their fingers burnt . . .'

She walked on and from the bottom of Calle de la Arganzuela she saw flames. All the surrounding rooftops were crowned with a reddish glow which the hussy observed with a fierce pride. 'I may be trash but I got my conscience, and my conscience won't let me stand idle while they call a good man bad and use a blinking smell to prove it, the *whiff* of my selfsame clothes . . . Not on your nelly . . . ! My conscience first every time. So bring on the fireworks! Don't worry, Nazarín; if you've lost the roof over your head that's no great shakes, you'll soon find some other garret . . .'

The fire was turning into a vast conflagration. Ándara saw people running in its direction, heard bells ringing. In her disturbed imagination she almost had the impression she was ringing them herself. Ding, dong, ding, dong . . .

'How could Chanfaina be so daft! Fancy thinking you can scrub bad air clean! Not on your life, holy smoke! It takes more than water, as the saying goes . . . What gets bad air clean is fire, for Christ's sake . . . ! Fire!'

V

Within a quarter of an hour of the fiendish woman's escape from Don Nazario's house, it had become a furnace and the flames were licking the walls of its cramped confines, devouring everything in sight. The neighbours came rushing out crazed with terror; but before they could fetch the first buckets of water, an elementary measure for quenching small-scale fires, a pillar of flames and smoke was billowing out of the window making it impossible for any human being to get near. The lodgers were running all over the place, rushing upstairs and down, at a loss to know what to do; the women were screaming, the men were cursing. There was a moment when the flames seemed to die down or abate inside the room, and a few people braved their way up the staircase from the gateway while others hurled pitchers of water through the window from the corridor. A good hosing down with a continuous supply of water would have stopped the fire spreading there and then; but by the time the fire brigade got there the whole building was liable to go up in smoke and all its inhabitants be burnt to death, if they didn't evacuate the place right away. Within half an hour they saw wisps of smoke curling up through the roof tiles (Nazarín's house was on the first and top floor), and it was clear the fire had spread sideways to the rafters. And where in God's name were the fire engines? By the time the first one finally got there the creaking roof timbers were burning like dry brushwood, and so was the corridor and the whole of the north wing. Anyone would have thought the building was made of tinder peppered with gunpowder; the flames latched on to it greedily and mercilessly, instantly consuming it; the worm-eaten timbers, the plaster, and even the brickwork caught fire, for the whole edifice was rotten and on the verge of collapse, coated with generations of layers of soot. It burned fast and furiously: the wind triumphantly fanned the flames, rewarding itself with a veritable firework display.

There is no need to describe the out-and-out panic of the building's destitute inhabitants. The fire was raging so fiercely and spreading so wildly it looked as though the whole block would soon be ablaze and burnt to a cinder. There was no way of putting that inferno out, even if all the hoses in Christendom were trained on it. By half past ten, the only thought in anyone's head was how to save their skin and the few possessions with which those miserable homes were furnished. And down from the upper corridors into the courtyard, and from there out into the street, flooded a stampede of men, women, and children, and with them the gypsies' donkeys, cats, and dogs, and even the rats that had made their nests in the rafters and assorted crannies throughout the building.

And all of a sudden the street was piled high with beds, chests, sideboards, and a thousand miscellaneous household items, and the air ringing with cries of woe and despair, which combined with the deafening roar of the flames in a frightful polyphony. The lodgers and those who had come to their assistance devoted all their energies to saving property and lives, including those of the maimed, crippled, and blind. Apart from one blind man who emerged with his beard singed, the rescue operation was carried out with no loss or damage to human life. What did disappear was a sizeable number of birds, which in most cases were not burnt to death but lost their owners in the panic, and one of the asses made off at full tilt, ending up in Calle de los Estudios. In the later stages of the operation, the fire brigade got down to work to stop the fire from spreading to the neighbouring buildings, and once this was achieved the worst was over.

Needless to say Chanfaina, from the minute her ample nostrils scented the first whiff of burning, single-mindedly set about saving her furniture which, though valueless except as junk, was the pride of the establishment. Aided by the honey-sellers and other obliging lodgers, she got *her chattels* out one by one and set up a regular bazaar in the street. Her arms and legs did not rest for a minute, nor her vigorous tongue which hurled the foulest, wildest insults at all and sundry, including the fire brigade and the fire itself. Her face was flushed as much from the glow of the flames as from the seething of her indomitable blood.

And just when she had got all her worldly goods out into the street, except for some pots and pans she was unable to salvage, and was settling down to the job of guarding them and fending off would-be marauders, who should turn up but Father Nazarín, as cool as a cucumber, would you believe it, as if nothing had happened, with the following angelic salutation: 'So we're homeless, are we, Señora Chanfa?'

'Too right, you simple simon of a saint, we bloody well is . . . ! And you just stand there all sweetness and light . . . ! It's all right for the likes of you what ain't got nothing to lose, and whom God rewards by taking the little you got; you never stop to think about respectable souls like us what has to lug all our things out into the street. Well, tonight you're sleeping under the stars like a proper gentleman. And what have you got to say about this terrible conflagration then? I hope you realize it started in your house, like a gunpowder keg blowing up ... They can say what they likes: it ain't natural. This was the work of human hands, mark my words; a fire as ... never mind ... enough said. At least the owner will be pleased, this lot wasn't worth a penny and the insurance will cough up; if they don't there'll be a heck of a fuss about this *hellocaust* in the papers, and somebody's going to be sorry, somebody whose name I won't mention to save their skin.'

The good Don Nazario shrugged his shoulders, not looking the slightest concerned or upset by the loss of his meagre estate, and flinging his mantle over his shoulder he offered his services to the neighbours to help them shift and sort their belongings. He did not stop till well into the night when, exhausted and unable to carry on, he finally accepted an offer of hospitality in the nearby Calle de las Maldonadas from a young priest with whom he was on friendly terms, and who happened to be passing the *scene of the incident* and saw him engaged in labours unworthy of a minister of the Church, as he made a point of saying.

The next five days he spent in his friend's home and company, living the tranquil, leisurely life of those who do not have to worry about the basics of existence; happy with the freedom afforded by his lack of possessions; gladly accepting what he was offered and asking for nothing; feeling fewer and fewer needs and appetites; with no physical desires and no regrets for the things that so preoccupy the majority; with nothing to his name but the clothes on his back and a prayer-book which his friend gave him. He was in his element with that carefree existence, plus the knowledge that his conscience was clear, and had forgotten all about his burnt-down home and Ándara and Estefanía and everything to do with the lodging-house and its inmates when one fine morning he received a summons from the lawcourt, requiring him to make a statement in connection with proceedings against a woman of ill repute by the name of Ana de Ara, etcetera, etcetera.

'Right, I'll be there,' he said picking up his mantle and

biretta, ready to comply with the summons without further ado. 'So, it's come up at last. I wonder what's become of Ándara... Perhaps she's been arrested... I'll go and declare the whole truth about my involvement, and say nothing about events I didn't witness or that aren't directly connected with my having taken the poor woman in.'

Admittedly his friend, whom he briefly put in the picture, did not look too pleased at what he heard and took a somewhat dim view of the whole ugly business and its likely consequences. Nazarín remained unperturbed for all that and set off to see the representative of the law, who greeted him courteously and took down his statement with all due respect, given the witness's ecclesiastical status. Incapable of telling less than the truth in any matter great or small, determined to stick to the truth not just out of a sense of duty as a Christian and as a priest but because of the boundless pleasure it gave him, he faithfully told the magistrate what had happened, gave a straight answer to every question he was asked, and signed his statement, to his complete and utter satisfaction. With regard to Ándara's crime, which he had not witnessed, he was generously non-committal, accusing and defending no one, and adding that he knew nothing of the erring woman's whereabouts but that she must have left her hiding-place the night of the fire.

He left the court feeling pleased with himself, so involved with the state of his conscience that he did not notice the magistrate had not treated him as courteously after his statement as he had before, but had looked at him pityingly, disdainfully, even reprovingly... Not that he would have cared much had he noticed. Back at his friend's house, the latter repeated his apprehensions about his having given that loose woman shelter, insisting public opinion and the law would not see Don Nazario as a man consumed by a passion for charity but as a harbourer of criminals, which meant he ought to start thinking about how to forestall the scandal, or at least work out a strategy for dealing with it when it broke. The well-intentioned little priest so went on about it he did not give him a minute's peace and quiet. He was an officious, interfering sort, with good connections all over Madrid, and once he took on an affair that was none of his business his energy was lamentable. He arranged to go and see the magistrate, and that night had the immense satisfacation of being able to address Don Nazario as follows:

'Now look here, my friend, the more honest we are with each other the better. You live with your head in the clouds and you don't see the dangers *looming*... looming, mark my words. Well, the first thing the magistrate asked me, and he's what I call a real gentleman, was whether you're mad. I told him I didn't know. I didn't dare deny it, because if you're in your right mind then your behaviour's even more incomprehensible. What on earth made you take in a vixen like that, a criminal, a...? For heaven's sake, Don Nazario, do you realize what you're accused of by the people who took the story to the police? Well, they allege you were maintaining notorious, dishonest, immoral relations with this and other *eiusdem furfuris*. My dear friend, can you imagine anything more shocking? I know it's a lie, of course. I know you well enough to be sure of that... You're quite incapable... And if you did allow yourself to be tempted by the demon of lust, you'd obviously do it with a better class of *femina*... I don't doubt you for a minute...! I concede it's all a big lie...! But do you realize what's about to hit you? It'll be easy enough for your slanderers to ruin your reputation; more difficult, much more difficult for you to undo the misunderstanding; slander sets all hearts racing and all tongues wagging, but no one gives credence to the defendant's statement or spreads it to the winds. This is a wicked world, men are mean and faithless, and they'll always cry for Barabbas' release and ask to see Christ crucified... And there's something else I have to tell you: they want to implicate you in the fire too.'

'In the fire!... me!' Don Nazario exclaimed, more in surprise than alarm.

'Yes, sir, they say it was that infernal basilisk who set fire to your house, which same fire, obeying the laws of physics, spread to the whole building. I know perfectly well you're innocent of this outrage, just like you are of the others; but be ready for them to come and drag you before Herod and

Pilate, interrogating you and implicating you in distasteful matters the mere mention of which makes the hair stand on end.'

And indeed the very mention of it seemed to make his own hair bristle in horror and shame, while Nazarín, faced by these forecasts of doom and gloom, remained unmoved.

'And to conclude, my dear Nazarín, you know I regard you as a friend, *ex tote corde*, and as a man of irreproachable, spotless conduct, *pulcherrimo viro*. But you live in cloud-cuckoo-land, to the detriment not only of yourself but of your closest associates, namely those whose home and hearth you share. I wouldn't dream of throwing you out, my friend; but I'm not the only one who lives here. My beloved mother, who holds you in high esteem, has been in a state of nervous agitation ever since she learnt about the legal imbroglio our guest is mixed up in. And she and I are not the only ones in the know, believe you me. Last night at Manolita's, the sister of the Vicar General at the Bishop's Palace, all her friends were going on about it. Some of them supported the accusations and some of them took your side. But as dear Mama says: "Now it's become a subject of gossip, however unfounded, we can't go on having that simple soul under our roof any more...".'

VI

'There's no need to say another word, my friend,' replied Don Nazario with his usual impassibility. 'I was thinking of leaving any day now. I don't like being a burden on people, and I've no wish to abuse the generous hospitality you and your good mother, Doña María de la Concordia, have lavished on me. I'll leave right away... You were about to say something else? You want to know how I'm going to counter these vile slanders? As you'd expect, my friend and colleague. I'll reply that Christ taught us to suffer, and that the best apprenticeship for those who aspire to be his disciples is to endure patiently, even gladly, the afflictions visited on us by human wickedness in its various forms. I've nothing else to add.'

Packing his bags being the easiest thing in the world, since he had no possessions other than those about his person, within five minutes of receiving this exhortation he was bidding his colleague and Doña María de la Concordia farewell, and left the house, setting off in the direction of Calle de Calatrava where he had some friends who would take him in for a few days. They were an elderly couple who since the year 1850 had had a shop there selling rope-soled sandals, twine, olive pulp, mule harnesses, corks, ash rods, and the odd earthenware pot. They greeted him as he had anticipated and accommodated him in a cramped backroom off the courtyard, fixing him up, amid the coils of rope and piles of pack-saddles and mule-collars, with a bed fit for a king. They were humble people and what they could not offer by way of material comfort they more than made up for with goodwill.

During the three long weeks Nazarín stayed at their house there occurred a succession of calamities and continual misfortune rained on his head, as if God were subjecting him to some decisive test. No parish had any Masses to offer him for the foreseeable future. In all of them he was given the cold shoulder and treated with a pitying disdain, and although he never once uttered an importune word he was rudely and harshly spoken to in one sacristy after another. Nobody explained the reasons for such behaviour, nor did he enquire. As a result life became impossible for the unfortunate priest since, having agreed with the Peludos* (as his friends in the Calle de Calatrava were known) to make a daily contribution to his upkeep, he found himself quite unable to keep his word. In the end he gave up doing the rounds of churches and oratories in search of Masses, which were clearly not forthcoming, and spent the days and nights shut in his dark room meditating and brooding.

One day he received a visit from an old priest who worked for the Vicar General and with whom he was on good terms, and that same evening he came back with a change of clothes. He told him not to stand for such humiliating treatment, but to go straight to see the Vicar General and be quite open with him about his difficulties and the reasons for them, so as to recover his former good reputation, which was being put in jeopardy by his inaction and the ill will of certain malevolent individuals who had it in for him. He went on to inform him that proceedings had already been set in motion to suspend him from office and to summon him to the Bishop's Palace to receive some form of sanction, if his statement showed him to be deserving of such. The combination of so many blows began to weaken the resolve of that man whose outward passivity belied an inner strength, founded on solid Christian virtues. He received no more visits from the elderly priest, and his lugubrious abode was given over to melancholy solitude and mournful contemplation. But this dismal isolation provided the climate for his valiant spirit to renew its vigour, implanting in him the decision to confront the situation imposed on him by human circumstance and to seek out a better life such as his soul had always yearned for.

The only time he now left his dismal refuge was at dawn, when he would set off for the Puerta de Toledo, keen to see and savour God's open fields and to gaze at the sky, listen to the delights of the dawn chorus, inhale the fresh air, and feast his eyes on the lush green of the trees and meadows, which in April and May, even in Madrid, are a visual treat and joy. He would walk on and on, in search of more open countryside and wider horizons, immersing himself in Nature, in whose bosom he could contemplate God undisturbed. How beautiful was the natural world, how ugly the world of Man...! His early morning outings, strolling along the highways and byways and every now and then stopping to rest, confirmed him in his belief that God, speaking to his innermost being, was commanding him to abandon all earthly pursuits, adopt a life of poverty, and break for good with the various forms of artifice that constitute what we take for civilization. His longing for such a life was so overpowering he could no longer resist its pull. To live in the midst of Nature, far from the wealth and corruption of the city, what more could he want! Only such a life seemed to allow him to follow the divine calling that spoke to his innermost soul; only such a life offered him the chance of purification on this earth and eternal reward in the next, and of practising charity in the way he so ardently desired.

When he got back home, well into morning, he would again become depressed and listless, and his conviction would begin to flag in the face of circumstance. There was nothing he would like more than to renounce the various material benefits of his ecclesiastical profession, so he could stop being a drain on the resources of the long-suffering, honest Peludos and earn his living by working or begging. But how could he get a job or ask for alms dressed as a priest...? He'd be denounced as a madman or a criminal. The logic of such thoughts led him to develop an aversion to his cassock, to those horrid, ungainly black robes he would gladly have exchanged for commoner garments. And one day, seeing his boots full of holes and having no money to get them mended, it occurred to him the best and most economical way of mending his shoes was to do without such things. He decided to give the idea a try and spent the whole day pacing barefoot round the courtyard with its cobbles and mud, for at one point there was a heavy downpour. He was happy with the results of the experiment; but reflecting that going barefoot is something you have to get used to, like everything else, he vowed to keep up the same training for a number of days till he had created a style of footwear that was immune to wear and tear, which was one of his more practical goals in life.

One morning, as he left home shortly after daybreak to take his walk out through the Puerta de Toledo, having sat down to rest about half a mile after the bridge, on the way to Los Carabancheles, he saw coming towards him a sinister-looking man, with an emaciated body and sallow face, sporting a variety of scars and dressed in rags, looking for all the world like a brigand or peddlar or something of the sort. And with the greatest reverence, quite literally, with a respect Nazarín was not used to receiving as man or priest, that repulsive individual came out with the following:

'Sir, don't you recognize me?'

'No, my good man . . . I've not had the pleasure . . .'

'I'm the one they calls Paco Pardo, La Canóniga's* son, don't you remember?'

'Pleased to meet you . . .'

'And we lives in that house over there you can see just this side of the cemetery . . . Well, Ándara's with us. We seen your worship sitting on this here stone several mornings, and Ándara, she says she's embarrassed to speak to you . . . Well, today she *exalted* me to come . . . with your leave, so here I am and . . . with your leave, I'm to tell you Ándara says she'll wash all your clothes . . . because if it wasn't for your worship here she'd be in the convent in Calle de Quiñones, otherwise known as the women's jail. And there's something else I'm to tell you . . . with your leave. And that's that seeing as my sister brings bits of rubbish and cast-offs and other such *goodies* back from Madrid, which we feeds to the pigs and chickens and between us lives off the proceeds, well the thing is, two days ago . . . I tell a lie, three days ago . . . she came back with one of them square priest's hats; she'd been given it at some house or other . . . Which, the hat I mean, is as good as new, despite its having belonged to a stiff, and Ándara says if you want it, not to have no *scrofules*, I'll take it to whatever address you care to give . . . with your leave . . .'

'You don't know what you're saying, the two of you. A hat? Why should I want a hat on my head when I don't even want a roof over it?' the priest replied vehemently. 'Keep it for someone who needs it, or use it to make a scarecrow if you've got a vegetable patch over there, as it seems, with peas or whatever you need to keep the birds off . . . and that'll be that. Thanks all the same. Good day to you . . . Oh, and as for washing my clothes, I appreciate it,' (this was spoken over his shoulder) 'but I've no clothes that need washing, thank God . . . the change of clothes I took off when I was given what I'm wearing now . . . well, I washed them myself in a puddle in the yard, and they came up a treat, believe you me. I hung them out to dry myself on a rope, that's one thing there's no shortage of where I live . . . So there you have it . . . Goodbye . . .'

Back home, he spent the whole day practising walking barefoot and by the fifth or sixth session he was getting quite adept at it and even enjoying it. In the evening, over his supper of fried chard and a bit of bread and cheese, he told his good friends and benefactors there was no way he could pay them what he owed them unless they offered him some trade or occupation, no matter how mean or lowly, that allowed him to earn his keep. Señor Peludo was scandalized by the idea. 'What, a priest like you! Heaven forbid! ... What would the *powers as be* say? And the ministers of the Chuch? ...' Señora Peluda reacted to her guest's suggestion less emotionally, and being a practical woman declared that work demeans no one because God himself *worked* to create the world, and she knew that down at the railway station they gave three farthings to anyone who offered to cart coal. If the humble priest wanted to quit the cloth to earn an honest living, she'd find him a *stablishment* where they paid handsomely for washing sheep tripe. Both of them, by now firmly convinced of the unhappy priest's total penury and seeing him as a simple soul incapable of earning his daily bread, told him not to worry about repaying what little he owed them since they, being good Christian folk and not incapable of the occasional saintly gesture, would *donate* him the meals accruing to date. It was as easy to feed three as two, and there were cats and dogs in the neighbourhood whose *consumption* was greater than Father Nazarín's ... *Seeing the which* he shouldn't worry about owing them that *outstanding* pittance, because all things could be forgiven, whether for the love of God or because you never know *where we is* and he who gives today takes tomorrow.

Don Nazario expressed his gratitude to them, adding that that night was the last he would burden them with his useless presence, at which they both tried to dissuade him from setting forth in search of adventures,* he with genuine protestations of warmth, she somewhat half-heartedly, no doubt because she was keen to have him off her hands.

'No, no: I've given it a lot of thought and your kind offer, for which I thank you, won't make me change my mind,' came the priest's reply. 'And now, my good Peludo, do you happen to have an old cape that's no use to you and that you could give me?'

'A cape . . . ?'

'One of those things like a blanket, with a hole in the middle to put your head through.'

'A hunting cape, you mean? Sure I've got one.'

'Well, if you've no need of it, I'd be grateful if you could let me have it. I can't think of any item of clothing that matches it for comfort, it keeps you warm and lets you move freely at the same time. And do you happen to have a fur cap?'

'There are plenty of new caps in the shop.'

'But I want an old one.'

'We've got old ones too,' Señora Peluda interjected. 'Remember the one you had on when you arrived from your village to marry me? A mere fifty-five years ago, that was.'

'An old cap like that is just what I want.'

'It's yours then . . . But you'd be better off with this other one I used to wear when I took the cart to Trujillo; it's made of rabbit fur . . .'

'That'll do nicely.'

'Do you want a sash to wind round your waist?'

'That'll come in handy too.'

'And how about this jerkin here? You could put it in a shop window if it weren't for the holes in the elbows.'

'I'll take it.'

They handed the pieces of clothing over one at a time, and he accepted them all eagerly. They all went to bed, and next morning the good Nazarín, barefoot, with the sash wound round the jerkin, the hunting cape over the top, the cap pulled down over his head and a stick in his hand, joyfully took his leave of his worthy benefactors and light of heart and foot, his mind fixed on God and his eyes on the heavens, set out for the Puerta de Toledo: as he passed through its archway he felt as if he were leaving behind a dark prison and entering that free, happy kingdom of which his soul aspired to be a citizen.

PART III

I

ONCE past the Puerta de Toledo he quickened his pace, keen
to get away from the metropolis and to leave behind the
sight of its narrow streets and the bustle of his noisy neighbourhood, which even at that early hour was beginning to
buzz with activity, like a swarm of bees leaving the hive. The
morning was crisp and clear. The beauties of sky and earth
were magnified a hundredfold in the fugitive's imagination
which saw in them, as if in a mirror, the image of his delight
at having finally gained his freedom, owing allegiance to
none but God. His rebellion, for rebellion it was, had not
been achieved without cost and he would never have done
such a thing, he who was so submissive and obedient, had
his conscience not told him it was his Lord and Master's
ineluctable command. Of that he had no doubt. But his
rebellion, conceding it merited such an unsavoury designation, was a technicality: a mere matter of shunning the
sanctions of his superiors, and eluding the petty intrigues and
harassments of a judiciary who did not represent justice or
anything of the kind ... Why should he have truck with a
magistrate who was prepared to listen to the vile slanders of
unscrupulous rogues? God, who could read his mind, knew
full well he was not running away from the Vicar General or
the magistrate out of fear, for his intrepid spirit did not
know what cowardice was and his steadfast will was imper-
vious to trials and tribulations of any kind, as befits a man
who had long savoured the mysterious pleasures of being a
victim of human injustice and wickedness.

He was not avoiding punishment but seeking it out, not
fleeing penury and adversity but courting poverty and
hardship. What he was escaping was a world and way of
life that cramped his spirit, intoxicated, as it were, with
dreams of a life of abstinence and penitence. And in order to

convince himself of the excusability, nay legitimacy of his revolt, he considered that, as far as Catholic dogma was concerned, his ideas were in entire concordance with the unchanging doctrines and teachings of the Church, which he had studied carefully and knew inside out. So he was not a heretic and could not be accused of the slightest deviance, not that such accusations worried him anyway for he was his own Grand Inquisitor. Clear in his conscience, he had no second thoughts about his decision and set off resolutely for the *wilderness*, as those open spaces seemed to his eyes.

As he crossed the bridge, a cluster of beggars plying the freest of trades on that spot eyed him in surprise and suspicion, as if to say: 'Who's this queer fish invading our territory without a licence? Blooming cheek ... !' Nazarín gave them a friendly nod and carried on his way without stopping to converse, eager to make good headway before the sun got high in the sky. On and on he walked, all the while pondering his new existence, subjecting it to a mental dialectic that tossed it this way and that, viewing it in every possible aspect and from every possible angle, favourable or unfavourable, so as to reach an objective verdict, as in a court case where both sides are given a hearing. 'Why don't you request permission to become a tertiary* in some monastic order?' And recognizing the validity of this argument, he came back with the reply: 'God knows if on my way I were to come across a monastery, I'd ask to be admitted and would enter it gladly, even if they imposed the strictest regime on me as a novice. But the freedom I seek can be found just as well wandering alone over hill and dale, as through submission to the harsh discipline of a religious institution. So I might as well opt for this life, since it's the one that suits me best and the one the Lord dictates to my conscience with a blinding clarity I can't ignore.'

Feeling a bit tired, half-way to Carabanchel Bajo he sat down to eat some bread, from the plentiful, fresh supply his friend Peludo's wife had put in his knapsack, and was accosted by a mournful, skinny mongrel who partook of his feast, and in return for those few crumbs befriended him and kept him company while he digested his frugal meal. He set out again followed by the dog and, still some way off from the village, felt thirsty and stopped at the first inn he passed to ask for water. As he was sipping it, three men chatting to each other on their way out of the inn stared at him with undisguised curiosity. There was obviously something about the way he looked that showed he was a bogus or makeshift beggar, and the thought made him uneasy. As he said 'God bless you' to the woman who had given him the water, one of the three men came over to him and said:

'Señor Nazarín, I knowed it was you from the sound of your voice. A right good disguise you got there. Might I ask ... with your leave, where you're going all dressed up like a tramp?'

'My friend, I'm going to find what I've always wanted.'

'And the very best of luck to you ... So don't you recognize me then? It was me what ...'

'I know it was you ... But I can't ...'

'What spoke to you a few days ago, down there ... and made you an offer ... with your leave, of one of them square priest's hats.'

'But of course ... ! A hat, which I refused.'

'Well, if there's anything I can do for you. Would your reverence like to see Ándara?'

'No, my good man ... Tell her from me to behave herself, or at least to do her best.'

'She's just over there ... See them three women on the far side of the road, *as it takes you*, picking thistles and purslane? Well, the one in the red petticoats, that's Ándara.'

'Give her my regards. And God be with you ... Ah, just one thing before I go: could you tell me where I can cut through from this road to the one ahead that goes from the Puente de Segovia to Trujillo? ...'

'Well, if you follow this here wall and carry straight on ... You go past Campamento, and follow the path all the way ... it's marked good and clear ... till you come out by the houses at Brugadas, *as it takes you*. You hit the Extremadura road right there.'

'Many thanks to you, and fare you well.'

He marched off followed by the dog, which seemed to

have thrown its lot in with him for the rest of the day, and he had barely walked a hundred yards when he heard a woman's voice desperately calling out to him from behind: 'Señor Nazarín, Don Nazario...!' He stopped and saw running full-tilt towards him a red skirt and lanky body with two arms sticking out on either side, flapping like windmill sails.

'I bet that's the wretched Ándara running after me,' he muttered, pausing for a few seconds.

So it was and the traveller would have been hard pressed to recognize her, had he not known she was in those rural parts. At first sight one would have been forgiven for thinking a scarecrow concocted of sticks and old clothes to keep the sparrows off the crops had miraculously come to life and acquired the gift of movement and speech, for the woman's resemblance to one of those country contraptions was complete. Time, which erodes the firmest constructions, had worn away and peeled off the cake of make-up on her face, leaving exposed the raw skin that in parts was cracked and in others swollen. One of her eyes was somehow bigger than the other and neither was a pretty sight, even less so her mouth whose lips were covered with sores, displaying her red gums and crooked teeth, many of which were decayed or missing. There was not a curve or suggestion of flesh on her body, which was all right angles, a bundle of bones... and her hands were black, and her toes stuck out of her filthy rope-soled sandals. But what most astonished Nazarín was that, as she approached him, the wench showed signs of bashfulness and an almost girlish shyness, betokening a transformation even more radical and extraordinary. If the errant priest* was taken aback by the sight of shame on that face, he was no less astounded to discover that Ándara was not the slightest bit disconcerted by his beggarly appearance. His transformation came as no surprise to her, as if she had foreseen it or found it perfectly natural.

'Sir,' the criminal said to him, 'I didn't want to let you go without saying hello to me... without me saying hello to you, I mean. The thing is, I been here since the day of the fire, and no one's seen me and I ain't scared of being caught no more.'

'All right, God be with you. What do you want with me this time?'

'I just wanted to tell you La Canóniga's my cousin, and that's why I came to hide here and they's treated me like a queen. I give them a helping hand with everything, and I'm through with that rotten Madrid as is honest folk's perdition. So . . .'

'God be with you . . . I'll be on my way.'

'Wait a minute now. What's the hurry? I say, have those cops from the lawcourts been after you? A right bunch of crooks they be! Something tells me they've been bothering you, and that sneak Camella's been telling tales to the law.'

'I've lost any interest I might once have had in Camellas, cops, or anything else. Forget it . . . And fare you well.'

'Wait . . .'

'I can't stop, I'm in a hurry. I've nothing to say to a degenerate like yourself, except to remind you of what I said when you were staying in my house; mend those ways of yours . . .'

'But that's just what I done . . . ! I swear even if I was pretty again, or just reasonable looking, I'd not tempt my luck or let Satan get his hands on me no more. Now the fiend's scared of me, I look such a fright he won't come near me. And talking of the Devil, if you'll not get cross there's something I'd like to tell you.'

'What's that?'

'That I want to come with you . . . wherever it is you're going.'

'Out of the question, my child. You'd have to endure all sorts of hardships, you'd have to suffer hunger and thirst . . .'

'That don't matter. Let me come with you.'

'You're a wicked woman. This reformation of yours is not to be trusted; it's a sour-grapes reaction to your lack of physical charms. Your heart is still diseased and prey to vice of one kind or another.'

'Want to bet?'

'I know you well enough...You set fire to the house where I gave you sanctuary.'

'So I did and I ain't sorry neither. Didn't they want to find me out and get you into trouble all because of my smell? Well, it takes fire to get bad air clean.'

'That's what I'm trying to tell you, to cleanse yourself with fire.'

'What fire?'

'The love of God.'

'Well, if I was *agoing* with you...those flames would touch me all right.'

'I don't trust you...You're rotten to the core. Stay behind on your own. Solitude is a great educator of the soul. That's what I'm looking for. Set your mind on God, offer him your heart, remember your sins and dwell on them till you repent and hold them in abhorrence.'

'Let me come with you then...'

'No. The day you succeed in becoming good, you'll find me.'

'Where?'

'I said you'll find me. Goodbye.'

And without waiting to hear more he made off at the double. Ándara was left sitting on the verge, picking up pebbles and tossing them down on the ground in front of her, her eyes fixed on the path down which the priest disappeared. The latter turned round two or three times and the last time he did so, at a fair distance by now, all he could see was a red dot in the middle of the green fields.

II

On that first day of his peregrinations, the fugitive had several encounters barely worthy of mention but included here for the simple reason that, being the first, they inaugurated his Christian adventures. Shortly after leaving Ándara he heard the sound of gunfire, which got nearer and nearer, blasting the air asunder and chilling the spine. In the direction from which the noise came, he saw detachments of soldiers running this way and that, as if fighting a battle. He realized he was near the army range where the nation's soldiers carry out their manœuvres. The dog looked him squarely in the eye, as if to say: 'Don't worry, my good master, it's all faked, the cadets keep at it all year round, firing at each other and chasing each other up and down. Besides, if we pay them a visit at meal time they're sure to give us a bite to eat, they're a generous lot and good to the poor.'

Nazarín stood watching that pretty sport for a while and, shortly after resuming his journey, still gazing at the wisps of smoke from the gun barrels curling their way up into the air, he met a goatherd driving some fifty goats. He was wizened and crafty-looking, and gave the wayfarer a wary look. This did not stop the pilgrim from greeting him courteously and asking if he had far to go to get to the road he was looking for.

'I can see *yer* be new to the trade,' replied the goatherd, 'and *ne'er* trod these parts *afore*. Where's *yer* hail from then? Arganda way? Well, hearken to me, them there Civil Guards* they got orders to *collar* every beggar they finds, and take 'em to the *confinements* in Madrid. 'Course they lets 'em out after, there ain't *sustainment* for all them vagrants . . . God speed, brother. I got naught to give *yer*.'

'I've got some bread,' said Nazarín, putting his hand in his knapsack, 'and if you'd like some . . .'

'Let's 'ave a look, me good man,' said the goatherd, scrutinizing the half loaf held out to him. 'This looks like French bread, French bread from Madrid, good stuff too.'

'Well, let's split this piece between us, I've got another bit left from the store Señora Peluda gave me when I left.'

'Much obliged. One good turn deserves another. Just carry on *forard*, *forard* all the way, and the Móstoles road's just twenty minutes' going. And come to think of it, got any good wine on *yer*?'

'No, sir, neither good nor bad.'

'Well I never . . . So long, friend.'

Next he came across two women and a boy carrying some chard, lettuces, and cabbage leaves, the ones from the bottom of the stalk that get fed to the pigs. Nazarín tried out his hand at his newly adopted mendicant's profession and the peasant women were so generous that, barely had he opened his mouth, they gave him two curly-leaved lettuces and half a dozen new potatoes, which one of them took out of a sack. The pilgrim put the gifts in his knapsack, thinking that if that evening he chanced on someone who'd let him bake them in the ashes of their fire, what with the lettuces he'd have a handsome feast. Having come out on to the road to Trujillo, he spotted a cart stuck in a pot-hole and three men struggling to lift the wheel free. Without waiting to be asked, he stopped to help and threw his admittedly meagre energies into the job; the operation being successfully concluded, they tossed a copper down on the ground for him. It was the first coin received by his beggar's palm. So far he'd had nothing but good luck, and the human beings he had encountered in those uncivilized parts seemed an altogether different breed from those he had left behind him in Madrid. On second thoughts, he recognized it was a mistake to jump to conclusions on the basis of one day's events; untold disasters were bound to come his way, and he was sure to have his fill of the trials, sufferings, hardships, and terrible mortifications he so ardently longed for.

He continued on the dusty road till dusk when he caught sight of some houses that might or might not be Móstoles, not that it mattered to him. The important thing was that they were places of human habitation and he made his way towards them to ask if he could spend the night there, in a woodshed, sheep-pen, or outhouse if need be. The first building was a big farmhouse, with a rudimentary roadhouse or refreshment stall built on to a side wall. Outside the entrance half a dozen pigs were rolling in the mud. In the background the traveller could see some irons for branding mules, a covered wagon with its shafts sticking up in the air and a row of chickens disappearing into it one after the other, a woman washing some dishes in a pond, a stack of pruned vine-shoots, and a withered tree. He meekly approached a pot-bellied old man, with a flushed face and respectable suit of clothes, who came out of the doorway, and courteously asked if he would give him permission to

sleep in a corner of the yard. Heavens above ... ! The mere
sound of his voice was enough to set the man off cursing and
swearing. The least offensive insult he came out with was
that he was sick to death of having thieves on his property.
Don Nazario did not wait to hear more and, saluting him
cap in hand, made off.

The woman washing up in the pond pointed to a bit of
open ground fenced off partly by a tumbledown wall and
partly by a hedge of brambles and nettles. The way in was
through a gap in the hedge and inside was an abandoned
building site, with brick buttresses about a yard high, overgrown with yellow weeds marking out the ground plan. The
area was covered with a carpet of wild barley a few inches
high, and on two walls jutting out from the main wall at the
far end rested a rickety roof improvised from sticks, furze,
straw, and mud, a highly precarious construction but not
without its uses for beneath it were sheltering three beggars:
a couple (married or otherwise) and another younger one
with a wooden leg. Comfortably installed in that rudimentary abode, they had made a fire and on it had a big pot,
whose lid the woman kept lifting in order to stir it, while the
man blew furiously on the flames to stop them from going
out. The one with one leg was busy cutting twigs with his
knife and stoking the fire with rhythmic precision.

Nazarín asked permission to shelter under that roof, and
they replied that it was common property and anyone was
free to come in or out without needing to wave a bit of
paper. In other words, they had no objection to the newcomer making himself at home in a corner but he shouldn't
expect a share of the hot dinner, for they were poorer than
poverty itself, and their business was not to give but be
given. The penitent hastened to reassure them, telling them
all he wanted was permission to put a few small potatoes in
the ashes, and offering them some bread which they had no
qualms about accepting.

'So how's things in Madrid?' the old beggar said to him.
'When we've *done* all the villages and hamlets round here,
we're thinking of giving it a try round about the feast of St
Isidore.* Been a good year then? Lot of poverty about?

Business as bad as ever . . . ? I've heard they're about to bring Sagasta* down . . . Who've we got for Mayor nowadays?'

Don Nazario answered affably that he knew nothing about business and commerce and couldn't care less whether Sagasta was in power or not, and that he was as close an associate of His Lordship the Mayor as he was of the Emperor of Humbug. With that, the fireside chat came to an end; the others ate their supper out of a big pan without inviting the new guest and he baked his potatoes, and the only thought in their heads was to find a cosy corner and settle down to sleep. The newcomer was left with the worst spot, barely under cover; but none of this dampened his steadfast spirit. He found himself a stone for a pillow and, wrapping himself in his cape as best he could, stretched himself out confident that his easy conscience and weary body would make him sleep soundly. The dog curled up in a ball at his feet.

In the middle of the night he was woken by the animal's growls, which turned into frantic yelps, and lifting his head from the rock-hard pillow Nazarín saw a figure, whether male or female he could not at first fathom, and heard a voice saying:

'Don't be alarmed, Father, it's me, Ándara; I been following you all afternoon and evening, like it or not.'

'What are you doing here, are you crazy? You'll disturb those *gentlemen* over there if you're not careful.'

'No I won't, let me finish. The wretched dog started yapping . . . but I crept in ever so quiet. I was following you and saw you come in here . . . Don't get cross . . . I wanted to obey you and not come after you; but my feet just brought me here. They did it *without thinking* . . . I don't know what's got into me. I got to go with your reverence to the end of the earth or it'll be the end of me . . . There, there . . . go back to sleep now; I'll lie down in the grass over here and rest, I don't blooming well feel like sleeping . . .'

'Get out of here, or at least keep your mouth shut,' the good priest said to her, placing his sore head back on the stone. 'What will those gentlemen have to say! See, they're complaining about the noise already.'

Indeed the one with the wooden leg, who was nearest, was making grunting sounds, and the dog once more called the importunate wench to order. Finally silence was restored, or would have been were it not for the awesome snoring of the older couple. At daybreak they all awoke, including Don Nazario, who was surprised not to see Ándara, which made him suspect her apparition in the middle of the night had been a dream. The three professional beggars chatted for a bit with the apprentice, and the old couple painted such a sorry picture of the bad luck they had had that year, that Nazarín felt moved to compassion and gave them all his capital earnings, that is, the copper the cart drivers had given him. Shortly after, Ándara appeared through the hedge, explaining to him why she had suddenly vanished before he awoke. The reason was that, not being able to sleep on that hard bed, she had got up before sunrise and, going out on to the road to see if she could make out where they were, she had discovered it was none other than the fair town of Móstoles, which she knew well having gone there several times from her village. She went on to say that, if Don Nazario gave his leave, she'd go and see if two sisters still lived there who were friends of hers; they were called Beatriz and Fabiana, and one of them got involved with a butcher in Madrid and they later married and he set up an inn in the village. The priest had no objection whatsoever to her going to look up her friends, or taking a one-way journey to the end of the world for that matter, because he had no desire to take the woman with him. And an hour later, while the pilgrim was conversing with a goatherd who generously gave him some milksops, he saw his self-styled protégée coming towards him in a state of acute distress, and *velis nolis* had to listen to a tale that initially was of no interest to him . . . The butcher-turned-innkeeper had died gored by a bull at the local *fiesta*, leaving his wife in penury with a 3-year-old daughter. The two sisters were living in a run-down tavern next to a stable, so hard up the poor women would have gone off to Madrid to earn a living walking the streets (which would have been easy for Beatriz, still young and pretty) if the little girl hadn't gone down with a *pernoxious* bout of typhus* which looked set, before the next twenty-four hours were out, to carry her off to Heaven.

'The little angel!' exclaimed the penitent, clasping his hands together, 'And the poor mother!'

'As for me,' the go-between went on, 'the minute I set eyes on that heart-rending scene, and the mother crying, and Beatriz snivelling, and the little girl with expiration writ all over her face . . . why, I felt such a stab of pain . . . and then I had this feeling all of a sudden, like my guts was crying out to me . . . A gut feeling like that can't be wrong . . . And with that I brightened up and said to myself: I'll go and tell Father Nazarín, to see if he'll come and look at the little girl and save her.'

'What are you saying, woman? Am I a doctor?'

'Not a doctor . . . something worth more than all the doctors ever invented. Only say the word, Don Nazario, and the little girl'll be healed.'*

III

'I'll come,' said the Arab from La Mancha, after hearing Ándara beg him for the third time. 'I'll come, but only to offer the poor women a few pious words of consolation . . . That's the limit of my powers. Compassion, my good woman, love of Christ and of one's fellow men are not medicine for the body. Off we go then, show me the way; but I can't heal the little girl, that's something only science can do, or in the direst cases God Almighty.'

'You don't expect me to fall for *excursions* like that, do you?' the wench retorted with the brazenness she had shown when hiding in the Calle de las Amazonas. 'Stop messing me around, your reverence, I know for a fact you're a saint. Well I never! Fancy trying to pull that one on me . . . ! And what would it cost you to work a miracle supposing you wanted to?'

'Stop blaspheming, you ignorant, ungodly woman. Me work miracles?'

'Well, if you can't, who can?'

'Me...? You must be crazy, me, the lowest of God's servants, work miracles? Whatever gave you the idea His Divine Majesty might have bestowed on me, a nobody, with no special merits, the wondrous gift enjoyed on this earth by a select few, a handful of chosen individuals, angels not mortal beings? Out of my way, wretched woman... Your foolish words, born not of faith but of facile superstition, are in danger of making me lose my temper despite myself.'

And so angry was he, he even raised his stick as if to strike her, something quite out of character that could only be the result of extreme provocation.

'Who do you take me for, you deluded, degenerate creature? Your mind's as diseased as your body...! Am I an impostor? Have I ever pretended to be more than I am...? Come to your senses and stop this talk of miracles or I'll think you're making fun of me, or that you're as ignorant and blind to God's laws as you were depraved in the past.'

Ándara was not to be convinced, attributing her protector's words to modesty; and taking care not to use the word 'miracle' again insisted on his coming to see her friends and the dying child.

'That's different. Of course I'll visit the poor souls to comfort them and beg the Lord to succour them in their hour of need. That I'd be glad to do. Let's go.'

It took them less than five minutes to get there, so fast did the harridan drag him through the muddy streets full of nettles and stones. In a seedy tavern, with a bare dirt floor, cracked walls that might have been shutters so much air and light did they let in, the ceiling almost completely hidden by cobwebs and the floor littered with empty barrels, broken pitchers, and unidentifiable bits and pieces, Nazarín set eyes on the sorry family, two women huddled in their shawls, their eyes inflamed from crying and lack of sleep, shaking and shivering. Fabiana had a headscarf tied tightly round her forehead, just above the eyebrows: she was dark, prematurely aged, wrinkled, and abjectly dressed. Beatriz, who looked a lot younger though in fact she was 27, wore her headscarf knotted jauntily under her chin, in Madrid working-class style, and her clothes, though basic, showed signs of a desire to please. Her face, while not beautiful, was attractive; she was tall and slender, with a well-proportioned, almost provocative figure, black hair, pale complexion, and blue eyes with deep red circles round them. She was wearing filigree ear-rings and the fingers of her hands, well groomed like those of a city woman rather than a peasant, were decked in rings of little or no value.

At the far end of the room, they had fixed up a length of string, with a curtain hanging from it like a theatre backcloth. Behind it was the bedroom and in it the bed, or rather cot, of the sick child. The two women welcomed the errant hermit with the greatest reverence, no doubt because of what Ándara had told them about him; ushering him to a bench they offered him a cup of goat's milk with some bread, which he accepted out of courtesy, sharing it with the wench from Madrid who downed it with relish. Two elderly women from next door poked their noses round the door to see what was going on, and settling themselves on the ground stared at the good Nazarín with more curiosity than surprise.

They all discussed the little girl's illness, which had been critical from the start. The day she fell ill, her mother had known something was afoot from the crack of dawn because when she'd opened the front door she'd seen two crows fly past and three magpies perched on a post outside. That on its own would have been enough to make her feel uneasy. Then, when she went out into the fields, she saw a nightjar hopping up and down in front of her. All those things one on top of the other bode very ill indeed. And when she got back home, lo and behold there was the little girl with a raging temperature.

Don Nazario enquired whether she had been seen by a doctor, and they replied in the affirmative. Don Sandalio, the local practitioner, had been to visit her three times and the last time he'd said only a divine miracle could save the child. They'd also sent for a healer famous for the cures she'd worked. She'd put a poultice of lizards' tails on the girl's forehead, the lizards having been caught on the dot of midnight ... This seemed to revive her a bit; but their hopes were soon dashed. The healer, distraught, had told them that if the lizards' tails hadn't produced the desired effect, it was because the moon was on the wane. Had the moon been waxing there'd have been no two ways about it.

Nazarín reproved them sternly, if not angrily, for believing all that silly nonsense, and exhorted them to trust only in science and after that in God above all else. The women fervently promised to do as the good priest said and, weeping and going down on their knees, implored him to take a look at the child and cure her.

'But my good women, how can you expect me to cure her? Don't be ridiculous. You're blinded by maternal love. I don't know how to heal the sick. If God has chosen to take the little girl from you, He has His reasons. Resign yourselves to your fate. And if He decides to spare her, it'll be because of your prayers, though there's no harm in my praying for her too.'

So strongly did they press him to see her that Nazarín went behind the curtain. He sat down next to the child's bed and contemplated her in silence for a while. Little Carmen's face was a deathly grey, her lips almost black, her eyes sunken, her skin hot and clammy, and the whole of her inert, prostrate body prefigured the stillness of the grave. The two women, mother and aunt, started to weep again like Magdalenes,* the neighbours who came in did the same, and against that chorus of female woe Fabiana said to the priest:

'Just suppose God wanted to work a miracle, can you think of a better chance? We know you're made of the stuff of angels, sir, going round in disguise without shoes on, asking for alms, just like Our Lord Jesus Christ, who had no shoes neither and ate only what folks gave him. Well, I say these times of ours ain't no different from those times of old; and what the Lord did then, why can't he do it now? By which I mean, if you choose to save the little girl she'll get better, sure as day. I know she will and I put my fate in your hands, holy Father.'

Extricating his hands from their kisses, Nazarín said to them firmly and gently:

'My good women, I'm a humble sinner like yourselves, I'm by no means perfect, far from it, and if you see me dressed so poorly it's because I've a liking for poverty, because I feel this is how I can best serve God; and I say that quite humbly, I wouldn't suggest that going barefoot makes me better than people who wear socks and shoes, or that being poor, destitute in fact, makes me superior to those who save and hoard. I can't heal the sick, I can't work miracles, and the idea that the Lord might choose to work them through me has never entered my head; for only He, when he chooses, can bend the laws of Nature He's created.'

'Yes, you can! Yes, you can! Yes, you can!' came the chorus from all the women in the room, young and old.

'No, I can't, I keep telling you ... and you'll make me lose my temper, for heaven's sake! Don't ever expect me to lay claim to powers I haven't got, or to pretend to a higher status than the obscure, lowly position I deserve. I'm just like everyone else, I'm not a saint, I'm not even a good man ...'

'Yes, you are! Yes, you are!'

'Come on now, stop contradicting me or I'll be straight out of the front door ... You're gravely offending Our Lord Jesus Christ if you imagine this humble servant of His to be capable of imitating, not Him, it'd be madness to suggest such a thing, but even the select company of saints to whom he gave miraculous powers, to set an example to the gentiles. Forget it, my good women. I appreciate your good intentions; but I don't want to encourage you to have unrealistic hopes. If God has disposed that the little girl should die, it's because death is best for her and the corresponding grief good for you. Resign yourselves calmly to His heavenly will, which doesn't mean you shouldn't pray to the Lord and His Holy Mother, entreating them ardently and devoutly, beseeching them with all your heart and soul to save the child's life. As for me, there's only one thing I can do and you know what that is.'

'What, Father, what ...? Do it right now.'

'The same as you; ask God to restore this innocent child to her natural health and beauty, and offer him my health and my life, in whatever form he may choose to take them. In return for answering our prayers, may he bestow on me all the calamities, adversities, sufferings, and ills that can afflict man on this earth... May he strike me down with the most horrible, abject, repulsive forms of disease, blindness, leprosy... anything, everything, let it fall on my head, in exchange for restoring the life of this little lamb and relieving you of your suffering.'

There was such heartfelt passion and unshakeable conviction in his words that the women started to fall about shouting in a sudden delirious frenzy. The priest's ardour fired them like a spark igniting a powder-keg; tears poured out, hands pressed frantically together, entreaties and lamentations joined in a single howl. Meanwhile, the pilgrim solemnly and silently placed his hand on the little girl's forehead, as if to gauge the fever consuming her, and remained in that posture for quite some time, oblivious to the distraught women's imprecations. Shortly after he took his leave, promising to return later, and when he asked where the village church was, Ándara volunteered to show him the way; off they went and there he stayed for the whole of the rest of the day. The hussy did not venture past the church door.

IV

At dusk, when he emerged from the church, Nazarín immediately bumped into Ándara and Beatriz who had come to fetch him. 'The little girl's not got any worse,' they informed him. 'She even seems to have a perked up a little... She opened her eyes for a bit and kept staring at us... We'll have to see if she pulls through the night.'

They added that they'd prepared him a modest supper, which he accepted not wanting to appear unsociable and ungrateful. When they got to the inn Fabiana seemed to have brightened up a bit, having spotted signs of improvement in the child at noon; but in the afternoon her temperature had shot up again. Nazarín gave instructions to go on giving her the medicine prescribed by the doctor.

In the sepulchral light of an oil lamp hanging from the ceiling they ate their meal, the priest declining to indulge in more than half a boiled egg and a bowl of vegetable soup with a thin slice of bread. As for wine, he would not touch a drop. Despite the fact that they had made him up a cosy bed with some blankets and straw, he refused to stay overnight and resisting their well-meant solicitude, which came from the bottom of their hearts, insisted on sleeping with his dog on the building site where he had spent the previous night and where he had all the room in the world. Before going to bed, they sat up talking for a while, the conversation ceaselessly coming back to the subject of the sick child and how, when someone is ill, we must always be prepared for the worst.

'And she's sick too, you know,' said Fabiana pointing in Beatriz's direction.

'She looks healthy enough to me,' observed Nazarín, paying her more attention than he had up to now.

'It's those blinking nerves of hers,' said Ándara. 'She's been like that since she came back from Madrid; but you'd not think so to look at her, would you? She gets prettier by the day. It's all because of a nasty turn she had, or a host of nasty turns that *feller* gave her . . .'

'Shut up, you idiot.'

'All right, I'll not say another word.'

'What she's got,' Fabiana added, 'is heart sickness, meaning she's bewitched, because believe you me, Father Nazarín, villages like this are full of ill winds and people as cast the evil eye.'

'I've already told you not to be superstitious; I'll say it again.'

'What's wrong with me,' Beatriz ventured somewhat bashfully, 'is that three months ago I lost my appetite, but so much so that even a grain of wheat was more than I could swallow. Whether it's because someone's cast a spell on me, I've no idea. And the not being able to eat led to not being able to sleep; and I'd wander round the house all night with a lump here in the pit of my stomach, like I had a slab of granite lodged in it.'

'And then,' Fabiana continued, 'she started having these terrible fits, so terrible, Señor Nazarín, all of us put together wasn't strong enough to hold her down. She'd scream and foam at the mouth, and then she'd shout the place down, *proclaiming* things as made you blush to hear them.'

'Don't be daft,' said Ándara, in all good faith; 'that's what's called having the devils in you. I had them in me too when I was growing up, and what cured me was a dose of . . . what's it called? . . . *broom ride* . . . or something.'

'Devils* or not,' Beatriz asserted, 'I went through *regular* agonies, Father, and when the fits came over me I could have killed my mother, if I'd had one, and I'd as soon have grabbed a baby or someone's leg to gnaw at it or bite it off . . . And when the attacks were over, I'd feel so terrible I wanted to die. There were times when all I could think of was death and how to do myself in. And the worst of it was the sudden terrors. I couldn't walk past the church without feeling my hair stand on end. I'd sooner have died than go inside . . . As for seeing a priest in his long robes, a blackbird in a cage, a hunchback, a sow with piglets, things like that paralysed me with terror. And the sound of bells . . . that drove me beserk.'

'Why, that's not witchcraft,' said Nazarín, 'nor the work of the Devil. It's an illness that's very common and well documented, called hysteria.'*

'*Isterics*, that's it; that's what the doctor said. There was no knowing when the fits would start and they'd stop just as sudden. Have I taken anything for it? God knows the things I've taken! Elder twigs soaked in water on a Friday, whey from a black cow, ants mashed with onion . . . And that's not counting all the crosses and medals and dead men's teeth I've worn round my neck!'

'And are you recovered now?' Nazarín enquired, studying her again.

'Not completely. Just three days ago I had another of my hating spells, wanting to hurt someone, I mean; but not so bad as before. I'm getting better.'

'I sympathize with you. It must be terrible to have an illness like that. What's the cure? It's got a lot to do with the imagination, and the way to a cure is through the imagination too.'

'What do you mean, Father?'

'You have to get it into your head that these attacks of yours are imaginary. Didn't you say God's holy temple filled you with terror? Well, get over that terror by going inside and fervently begging the Lord to cure you. I promise you there are no devils in your body right now, if devils is the proper word for the strange emotional disorders produced by the nervous system. Just convince yourself these symptoms of yours aren't a sign of internal damage or physical mal-functioning, and the symptoms will go away. Stop brooding, go for walks, keep yourself occupied, eat as well as you can, don't spend so much time thinking, try to sleep, and you'll get over it. Right, ladies, it's late and I'm off to bed.'

Ándara and Beatriz accompanied him to his outdoor abode, and left him there after making him up as good a bed as they could from grass and stones. 'You can't imagine, Father,' Beatriz said to him before she left, 'how much better I feel after what you said about this sickness of mine. Whether it's devils meaning devils, or devils meaning nerves . . . the truth of the matter is I've more faith in you than in all the doctors in Christendom . . . Goodnight then.'

Nazarín prayed for some while and slept like a log till daybreak. He was woken by the merry warbling of the assorted birds that had their lodgings in the surrounding hedges and, not long after, Ándara and her friend arrived to tell him the good news. The little girl was better: she'd had a relatively peaceful night, and had woken up bright-eyed and responsive to the world around, suggesting she was over the worst. 'If this ain't a miracle, let God come and see for Himself!'

'It's not a miracle,' he reproved them sternly. 'God has taken pity on her grieving mother. For all we know he'd have done so without our prayers.'

They set off together and found Fabiana delirious with joy. She flung her arms round the priest and even tried to kiss him, at which he put his foot down firmly. There was reason to be optimistic; but it was too soon to be sure of the little girl's recovery. She might well suffer a relapse and then the poor mother would be even more distraught. Anyway, whatever the outcome they'd know in due course; if they'd excuse him, he'd be on his way as soon as he'd snatched some breakfast. The three women's heartfelt insistence that he stay was to no avail. There was nothing else he could do for them; he was whiling away his time on matters of no substance when he ought to be embarking on his singular, holy mission.

It was an emotional farewell, and despite his strict instructions to the harpy from Madrid that she was not to come with him, she insisted in her blunt fashion that she'd gladly follow him to the world's end; her heart demanded it so strongly, her will could not resist its pull. So they set off together, followed by such a crowd of urchins and village crones that, to escape that unwelcome escort, Nazarín had to leave the road and, striking out across country to the left of the highway, set off in the direction of a clump of trees on the horizon.

'Know something?' said Ándara when the last straggler had dropped behind. 'Beatriz said to me last night that, if the little girl gets better, she'll do the same as me.'

'And what's that?'

'Why, follow you wherever you decide to go.'

'Then she can forget all about it. I don't want any followers. I'd rather be on my own.'

'Well, that's what she wants to do. She says it'd be a way of doing penance.'

'If she feels called to do penance, well and good; but that doesn't mean she has to follow me. She can abandon all her worldly goods, which by the look of it wouldn't be much of a sacrifice, and take to the roads to live off charity . . . but by herself. We all have to live with our conscience, and that means we're all on our own.'

'But I said it was all right for her to come with us . . .'

'And what made you think you could take the liberty . . . ?'

'I took the liberty, sir, as you say, because I care about Beatriz and I know this life would do her good. Meaning the exercise and penance will help her get over what's eating her soul, and that something's a bad man who goes by the name of Pinto* or Pintón, I forget which. But I've met him, he's a

good-looking fellow, a widower, with a mole just here with
hairs sticking out of it. Well, he's what's driven her out of
her mind and put the devils in her body. He leads her a
merry dance; one minute he sends her packing, the next he's
all over her, it ain't no wonder she's so *istericated*. It'd do
her the world of good, it would, sir, to set up as a pilgrim
and clear all that mischief out of her head, for if there ain't
no devils in her heart or guts and *vitals*, there's plenty of
them in that brain of hers. It all started with a miscarriage;
and if you really want to know there were two of them...'

'Why are you telling me all this? You're a hopeless
chatterbox, it's none of your business,' Nazarín scolded her.
'What have I got to do with Beatriz and Pinto and...?'

'Because you ought to take her under your wing; if she
don't join us on our pilgrim's way and look to her soul a
little, it won't be long before she plumps for a less honest
calling that's more to do with looking to her body. Blimey,
she's been on the verge once already! At the time the little
girl fell ill her trunk was packed ready to leave for Madrid.
She showed me the letter she got from Seve summoning
her and...'

'That's enough gossip, I said.'

'I've nearly finished... Seve said she was to come right
away and when she got there... Well...'

'Stop it! Beatriz can do what she likes... No, anything but
that... She mustn't be enticed by that schemer's call... She
mustn't rise to the Devil's bait, with its false glitter... Tell
her she's not to go, that what she'll find in Madrid is vice
and corruption and sin, and a dishonourable death when
she's past repenting.'

'But bless you Father, how can I tell her all that without
going back to Móstoles?'

V

'You go, and I'll wait for you here.'

'She won't listen to anything that comes from me. Now if
you was to go in person and put it nicely, she'd be saved

from perdition for sure. She's got faith in you and ever since you explained her illness a bit, she's convinced she's cured and ain't had no more fits. So we'll go together, if you've no objection.'

'Give me time to think it over first.'

'And that way we'll find out if the little girl's dead or better.'

'In my heart of hearts I know she's better.'

'Then let's go back, sir . . . so we can see for ourselves.'

'No; you go and tell your friend . . . Forget it, I'll decide tomorrow.'

They found shelter in a sheepfold after dining off the meagre takings from that day's begging, and when next morning Nazarín headed off in the direction he'd been taking since leaving Móstoles, Ándara said to him:

'I suppose you know where this path's taking us?'

'Where?'

'To my village, holy smoke!'

'I told you to stop swearing in my presence. If I hear one more swear word from you, I won't let you come with me. All right then; where did you say we're going?'

'To Polvoranca, which is where I come from, sir; and to be honest I'd rather not go near the place, I got relatives there, some of them quite well-to-do, and my sister's married to the inspector of taxes. Polvoranca's not just any old village, you know, some of the folks there are filthy rich and own up to six yokes . . . of mules, I mean.'

'I quite see why you're embarrassed to go back to your home village,' the pilgrim replied. 'That ought to show you! If you'd behaved yourself, you'd be able to go anywhere with your head held high. All right, we won't go there; let's take this path instead, we can find what we're looking for either way.'

They carried on walking all day, the only event worth mentioning being the desertion of the dog that had been following Nazarín since Carabanchel. Whether because the animal also had respectable relatives in Polvoranca or because he wasn't keen to leave his hunting grounds, namely the immediate environs of Madrid, the fact is that at dusk he *handed in his notice* like a disgruntled servant and made off for the capital in search of a more profitable position. After spending the night in the open fields, under an ash tree, the travellers found themselves once again approaching Móstoles, where Ándara had been leading them without Don Nazario realizing.

'Don't tell me we're back at your friends' village again! Now listen to me, my good woman, I'm not going into the village with you. You can go and see how the little girl is, and while you're about it you can tell poor Beatriz from me that she's not to be tempted by the lure of sin, and if she wants to become a pilgrim and live a life of poverty, she can do it perfectly well without me . . . Go on then, off with you. I'll wait for you by that old mill wheel you can see between those two half-dead trees over there, a mile or so outside the village. Don't be long.'

He made his way over to the mill at a leisurely pace, had a drink of water, took a rest, and the wayfarer* had been gone for less than two hours when Nazarín saw her reappear, not alone but with a fellow-traveller who, as they drew close, he recognized to be Beatriz. Tagging along behind were some of the local urchins. Before they reached the spot where the mendicant was waiting for them, the two wenches and the boys started to shout out in excitement: 'Have you heard . . . ? The little girl's better! Alleluyah! God bless Saint Nazarín! The little girl's better . . . completely better! She's talking and eating as if she'd been raised from the dead.'*

'Calm down, my good women. You can give me the good news without broadcasting it to the winds.'

'But we feel like broadcasting it to the winds!' Ándara cried, jumping up and down.

'We want every living creature to know, the birds in the sky, the fish in the river, the lizards under the stones as well,' cried Beatriz, radiant with joy, her eyes aglow.

'It's a miracle, holy smoke!'

'That's enough.'

'It may not be a miracle, Father Nazarín; but you're a good man and the Lord grants everything you ask.'

'Stop talking about miracles and calling me a saint, or I'll hide myself away in shame and embarrassment, and that'll be the last you'll see of me.'

The urchins were making as much of a racket as the women with their gleeful squeals and cheers.

'If you come into the village, Father, you'll be carried shoulder high. Everyone thinks the little girl was dead and that just by laying your hand on her forehead you've brought her back to life.'

'Good Lord, what nonsense! Thank heavens I didn't go with you. But that apart, praise be to God for his infinite mercy . . . And Fabiana must be relieved.'

'Overjoyed, Father, beside herself with happiness. She says if it wasn't for your coming to the house, the little girl'd be dead and buried. And that's what I think too. And do you know what the village women are doing? They're queuing up to come into our hovel and asking if they can sit on the stool the holy man sat on.'

'What on earth's got into them? How can they be so simple-minded and ignorant!'

At that point Don Nazario noticed that Beatriz was barefoot and wearing a black skirt, with a shawl wrapped round her shoulders and crossed over her chest, a knapsack on her back, and a scarf knotted firmly under her chin.

'Are you going somewhere, my dear?' he asked; and no one should be surprised at that intimate form of address,* which he used quite spontaneously with people from the lower classes.

'She's coming with us,' Ándara declared point-blank. 'I told you so, Father. There's only two ways she can go: thataway to Seve, like I said; and thisaway.'

'Well, she can complete her pious mission alone. The two of you can go off together and leave me in peace.'

'Never,' replied the young woman from Móstoles. 'You shouldn't be going around on your own like this. The world's full of wicked people. If you take us with you, you needn't worry about things; we'll look after you.'

'I said no, I'm not the slightest bit worried and I'm not afraid of anything.'

'But what's wrong with having us around? Hard to please,

ain't he now...!' said the one from Polvoranca in a cajoling
tone. 'And what if we gets the devils in our bodies, who's
going to drive them out? And who's going to teach us about
things of the spirit, things like the soul, God's glory, charity,
poverty? Leave me and her on our own! A right pickle we'd
be in. Who'd have thought it...! And that's what we get
for loving you, with all our hearts and not an ounce of
malice...! Wicked we *been*; but if you leave us behind,
what'll become of us?'

Beatriz said nothing but dabbed at her eyes with her
shawl. The good Nazarín lapsed into silent meditation for a
while, drawing lines in the earth with his stick, and finally
announced:

'If you promise to be good and do whatever I say, you can
come.'

After saying goodbye to the street urchins of Móstoles,
which meant giving away the few farthings they'd gleaned
that day, the three penitents set off, taking a little path to the
right of the main road as you go towards Navalcarnero.
The evening was muggy; at nightfall a gale blew up, against
the full force of which they had to battle for they were
going westwards; the sky was riven by terrifying flashes of
lightning followed by fearsome thunderclaps, and rain
started to bucket down soaking them to the skin. Fortunately
they chanced on a ruined hut and there took refuge from the
raging storm. Ándara scraped together some firewood and
tinder. Beatriz, being a woman of foresight, had some
matches on her and got a magnificent fire going, and the
three of them huddled round it to dry themselves off. Having
decided to spend the night there, for they were unlikely to
find a safer or more comfortable shelter, Nazarín gave
them his first lesson in religious instruction, something the
wretched women had forgotten or never had. For over half
an hour they sat listening to his eloquent words, free from
unnecessary embellishment, as he spoke to them about the
beginning of the world and original sin, with all the sorry
consequences it had brought, till God in his infinite mercy
chose to free mankind from the grip of evil through the act
of redemption. The errant hermit explained these rudimen-

tary notions in simple language, illustrating his arguments with examples to make them clearer, and they listened with rapt attention, especially Beatriz who hung on every syllable and was quick to grasp everything, engraving it indelibly on her mind. Then they recited the rosary and the litany, and repeated various prayers which their teacher wanted them to learn by heart.

Next day, after kneeling to say their prayers, they set out on their way with excellent results: the two women, who went on ahead to ask for alms in the villages or hamlets through which they passed, collected a fair amount of coppers, vegetables, stale bread, and other miscellanea. Nazarín was starting to think his penance was going too well to qualify as such, for ever since he'd left Madrid good fortune had rained on him. No one had treated him badly; he'd met with no obstacles; he'd been offered charity almost every time he'd asked for it, and he'd not known hunger and thirst. And what's more he'd been able to enjoy the priceless gift of freedom, his heart was overflowing with happiness, and he was getting fitter all the time. He'd not even had a bout of toothache since he took to the roads, and besides how wonderful it was not to have to bother about shoes or clothes, nor worry whether his hat was new or shabby, or whether he was got up respectably or not. As he hadn't shaved, and indeed had stopped shaving some time before leaving Madrid, he now had a nearly full-length beard; it was black streaked with silver, finishing in a neat point. And with the sun and country air his skin was starting to take on a beautiful, deep tan. His clergyman's physiognomy had vanished without trace and his Arab features, freed from that mask, stood out in all their pristine splendour.

Their progress was halted by the River Guadarrama, whose waters were swollen from the recent storm; but without too much ado they found a ford further upstream where they could wade across, and carried on through countryside less bleak and arid than that on the left bank, at regular intervals glimpsing houses, villages, ploughed fields, not to mention trees and shady groves. In the middle of the afternoon they caught sight of a cluster of large white buildings, set in green woodland, with an elegant red-brick tower that looked like that of a monastery. As they got nearer they saw to their left a drab, dingy mud-coloured settlement, with another little tower like that of a village church. Beatriz, who was good on the geography of the area, informed them: 'That's Sevilla la Nueva, it's almost deserted, and those big white buildings with trees and a tower are La Coreja, a large estate. The owner's living there at present, a man called Don Pedro de Belmonte; a rich aristocrat, well preserved, a good hunter, a great horseman, and the most quarrelsome individual in the whole of New Castile. They say he's a terrible man, with the foulest temper, and I've also heard it said he gets drunk to drown his sorrows and, when he's had a drop too many, he beats the living daylights out of everyone and goes on the rampage... He's so strong that one day, out hunting, just because a man riding past on his donkey refused to *remove* himself, he grabbed donkey and man, lifted them clear of the ground and hurled them into a gully... And a boy who scared off some hares he was hunting was beaten up by him so badly he had to be carried out of La Coreja on four men's shoulders, more dead than alive. In Sevilla la Nueva they're so scared of him that, when they see him coming, they all cross themselves and make a run for it, because once, I'm not joking, as a result of some quarrel or other over water rights, the infamous Don Pedro stormed into the village just as everyone was coming out of Mass, and started raining blows right, left, and centre till over half the population was left flat on the ground... So, Father, I think we'd be well advised to keep our distance; he's often out hunting in these parts, and he's sure to spot us and want to know what we're up to.'

'Well, what you say has excited my curiosity,' Nazarín observed, 'and the portrait you've painted of this monster makes me feel more like going on than turning back.'

VI

'Don't go looking for trouble, sir,' cried Ándara, 'if that brute of a man decides to go for us, there'll be no escaping.'

At that point they were approaching a narrow path lined on both sides with black poplars, which appeared to be the driveway to the estate, and no sooner had the three pilgrims set foot on it than three huge dogs the size of lions sprang out on them, barking furiously, and started to savage them before they could beat a retreat. What jaws, what fangs! They mauled Nazarín's leg and Beatriz's hand, and ripped the other woman's skirt to shreds, and even though the three of them bravely tried to beat them off with sticks, the ferocious hounds would have made a meal of them if they had not been brought to heel by a gamekeeper who emerged from a clump of bushes.

Ándara, arms akimbo, let out a torrent and a half of abuse at the house and its confounded dogs. Nazarín and Beatriz did not utter a murmur. And the wretched gamekeeper, instead of apologizing for the damage the vicious beasts had done, hurled the following churlish warning in the pilgrims' face: 'Out of here, ruffians, vagabonds, thieves! And thank your lucky stars the master didn't catch you; if he had, by Christ, you'd not be in a hurry to stray into La Coreja again.'

The two women edged away timidly, dragging Nazarín with them almost by force for he seemed not to know the meaning of fear. By a brook in a shady elm grove, they sat down to recover from the fright and wash the good priest's wounds, bandaging them with some cloths the ever-provident Beatriz had brought with her. For the whole of the rest of the afternoon and evening, till prayer time, they went on talking about their near escape and Beatriz proceeded to relate further outrages attributed to Señor de Belmonte. Rumour had it he was a widower and had murdered his wife. His family, who were from the Madrid aristocracy, had broken off relations with him and banished him to that country residence as if under house arrest, with a large staff of well-trained servants, partly to cater for his domestic and hunting requirements, partly to keep an eye on him and warn his relatives of any escape attempt. This information made Nazarín even keener to meet the monster face to face. Deciding to spend the night in the shelter of the elm grove, they said their prayers and had supper, and by way of *table-*

talk Nazarín declared nothing in the world would stop him paying a visit to La Coreja, where he sensed he would be subjected to some major ordeal, or would at least know punishment, humiliation, and adversity, which is what his soul desired above all else.

'For after all, my daughters, we can't have good fortune all the way! If we weren't sent opportunities for suffering, and terrible misfortunes, starvation, cruelty from man and beast, this life we've chosen would be a piece of cake, and any man or woman in their right mind would volunteer for it. So what were you expecting? A bed of roses? All that insisting you wanted to follow me, and as soon as a chance for suffering arises you talk of backing out! Well, if that's what you wanted you needn't have bothered; and I say to you quite seriously that, if you can't face the uphill paths overgrown with briars and you want it to be easy going and flowers all the way, you'd be better off turning back and letting me get on with it.'

They tried to dissuade him with every argument in the book, including some that were not devoid of good sense, for example: if they came across evil they should tackle it and fight it but it was surely foolhardy to go searching it out. They argued their case as best they could, given their rudimentary rhetorical skills, failing to persuade him that night and again next morning.

'Precisely because the owner of La Coreja is said to be stony-hearted,' he said to them, 'precisely because he maltreats his inferiors and abuses the weak, that's why I want to knock at his door and talk to him. That way I'll see for myself whether or not his reputation is deserved, for sometimes, my good women, public opinion gets things wrong. And if there's evidence that the gentleman ... what did you say his name was?'

'Don Pedro de Belmonte.'

'Well, if this Don Pedro of yours does turn out to be a monster, I want to ask him for charity in the name of the Lord, to see if the monster softens and gives me something. And if he doesn't, that's too bad for him and his soul.'

He refused to listen to further arguments and, seeing the

two women quake and blanch with fear, he ordered them to stay behind while he went on his own, intrepid and ready for whatever might befall him, for better (which meant being savaged by the dogs) or worse (which meant death). He set off, and they shouted after him: 'Don't go, don't go, that brute'll kill you ... Father Nazarín, for the love of God, we'll never see you again ...! Come back, come back; the dogs are on the loose and there's a crowd of men coming, and one of them with a gun looks like the owner ... Holy Jesus, Blessed Virgin, protect us in our hour of need!'

Don Nazario headed straight for the gateway to the estate and advanced boldly up the driveway without meeting a soul. As he neared the house he saw two men coming towards him and heard dogs barking; but they were hunting dogs, not the ferocious mastiffs of the previous day. He walked on resolutely, and when he got close to the men he saw them both halt as if waiting for him. He returned their gaze and, commending himself to God, carried on walking unhurriedly and determinedly. When he reached them, before he had a chance to get a good look at them, an irate, stentorian voice boomed: 'And where do you think you're going, you wretch? This isn't a public footpath, devil take you! It's the driveway to my house.'

Nazarín stood to attention in front of Don Pedro de Belmonte, for the man addressing him was none other than he, and in a steady, humble voice, for all its humility without a trace of cowardliness, said to him: 'Sir, I come to ask for alms, in the name of the Lord. I know perfectly well this is the driveway to your house and, since I assume every household in this god-fearing land is inhabited by good Christian souls, I took the liberty of entering. If in so doing I've caused offence, I beg your pardon.'

Having concluded his speech, Nazarín was able to take a long look at the imposing figure of La Coreja's elderly owner, Don Pedro de Belmonte. He was so tall the word giant would not be out of place, well-built and elegant, about 62 years old; but a more handsome example of old age would be hard to find. His tanned face, the pronounced curve of his slightly thickset nose, his bright eyes set beneath bushy eyebrows, his pointed, curly white beard, his broad, unfurrowed brow betrayed a haughty, aristocratic tempera- ment, more used to giving orders than receiving them. Nazarín had only to hear him speak a few words to ap- preciate his lively temper and despotic mien. The strange thing was that after unceremoniously throwing him out, as the penitent was meekly bidding him farewell, cap in hand, Don Pedro began to stare at him with an intense curiosity.

'Come here,' he ordered him. 'What I normally give the tramps and vagabonds who come anywhere near my house is a good thrashing. Come here, I said.'

For a second Nazarín baulked, for with all the valour in the world it was impossible not to be intimidated by that arrogant gentleman's flashing eyes and thundering voice. He was dressed in a lightweight, well-cut suit, which he wore with the refined ease of a person accustomed to moving in sophisticated circles, riding boots, and on his head a brown trilby tilted over his left ear. His shotgun was slung behind his back and a stylish cartridge belt was strapped round his waist.

'And now,' Nazarín thought, 'this good sir is going to get out his gun and stick the butt into my stomach, or split my head open with the barrel. May the Lord protect me.'

But Señor de Belmonte went on and on staring at him, without so much as a word, while the man who was with him, also armed with a shotgun, stared at the two of them.

'Pascual,' the gentleman said to his servant, 'what do you make of this fellow?'

Since Pascual did not reply, no doubt out of respect, Don Pedro came out with a cavernous guffaw and, looking Nazarín squarely in the eye, added:

'You're a Moor... Wouldn't you say he's a Moor, Pascual?'

'I'm a Christian, sir,' the pilgrim replied.

'A Christian by religion... That's as may be... But that doesn't stop you being a thoroughbred Arab. Aha! I've a good eye for people. You're an Arab and you're from the East, from the sublime, poetic Orient. There's no fooling me...! The minute I set eyes on you...! Come with me.'

And he started to make off for the house, insisting the beggar walk at his side while the servant brought up the rear.

'Sir,' Nazarín repeated, 'I'm a Christian.'

'We'll see about that . . . You can't fool me! You might as well know I've been in the Diplomatic Service, as consul first in Beirut and then in Jerusalem. Altogether I spent fifteen years in the Orient,* the best years of my life. Now there's a culture for you!'

Nazarín thought it best not to contradict him and followed him meekly, waiting to see what all this would lead to. They went into a large courtyard where he heard the same dogs as the day before . . . He recognized them by their bark. Then they went through a second archway, coming out into a bigger yard than the first, where some rams and two Friesian cows were grazing on the thick grass. After that yard was another smaller one, with a waterwheel in the middle. That extraordinary series of walled enclosures made Nazarín think of a fortress or citadel. He also saw the tower they had spotted in the distance, which was a huge dovecote, with thousands of pairs of those beautiful birds fluttering round it.

The gentleman removed his gun and handed it to his servant, ordering him to retire, and sat down on a stone ledge.

The first exchanges of conversation between the beggar and Belmonte could not have been stranger.

'Tell me: if right now I were to throw you into this well, what would you do?'

'What do you expect, sir? Drown, if it's got water in it; and if it hasn't, crack my skull open.'

'And what do you think? That I'm capable of throwing you in? . . . What have you heard people say about me? In the village they must have told you I'm a monster.'

'Since I always tell the truth, sir, I have to say the reports I've had of you are not flattering. But I'd like to think your fiery temper is not incompatible with a noble heart and an upright, Christian spirit that stands in love and awe of God.'

The gentleman stared at him again with such intensity and curiosity that Nazarín did not know what to make of things and felt slightly at a loss.

VII

All of a sudden Belmonte started to lash out at the servants for supposedly letting out a goat that had eaten a rosebush. He called them loafers, renegades, Bedouins, Zulus, and threatened to flay them alive, cut their ears off, or slit their gullets. Nazarín was indignant but managed not to let his feelings show. 'If that's how he treats his servants, who are almost part of the family,' he mused, 'what will he not do to me, a poor vagrant? It's a wonder none of my bones are broken yet.' The gentleman came back to his side having run out of steam, and carried on fuming for a bit like a volcano throwing up debris and gases after the eruption is over.

'Those scoundrels are enough to try anyone's patience. They do things wrong just to vex and annoy me. It's a pity we don't still live in feudal times, when you could have the satisfaction of stringing up on a tree anyone who got out of hand!'

'Sir,' said Nazarín, resolved to give the noble gentleman a lesson in good Christian behaviour, no matter how dire the consequences of provoking his wrath might be, 'you can think of me what you will and you may find me impertinent; but I'll explode if I don't point out that your way of treating your servants is un-Christian, anti-social, barbarous, and uncouth. How you react to that is up to you; I entered this house poor and naked and that's how I'll depart. Servants are people, not animals, they're as much God's children as you are; and they've got their dignity and self-esteem, like any feudal baron, real or would-be, in times past or present. And having said that, which I regard as my bounden duty, I beg to take my leave.'

Again the gentleman surveyed him from top to toe, face, clothes, hands, his bare feet, the remarkable shape of his skull,* and what he saw, together with the beggar's urbane way of speaking, so incompatible with his apparent status, evidently astounded and threw him.

'All right, thoroughbred Arab or bogus beggar or whatever you may be,' he said to him, 'how come you know such things, and how and when did you learn to express them so articulately?'

And without stopping to wait for an answer he got up and imperiously ordered the pilgrim to follow him.

'Come with me ... I want to cross-examine you before I respond to what you've said.'

He led him off to a large room furnished with antique walnut armchairs, tables to match, chests and bookshelves, and pointing to a chair he sat down too; but almost immediately he got up and paced to and fro in an obvious state of nervous agitation that would have thrown men of less mettle than our valiant Nazarín.

'There's an idea going round my head ... what an idea! Just supposing ... ! No, impossible. But it has to be possible ... The Devil take me if it's impossible. Stranger things have been known to happen ... Damn it, I thought as much from the very start ... ! I'm not a man to be taken in by appearances ... Oh, the Orient! What magnificence ... ! Only there do people know the life of the spirit ...'

And he kept on repeating the same phrases, striding up and down without looking at the priest or else stopping to stare at him head on, incredulous and somewhat abashed. Don Nazario didn't know what to make of things and whether to regard the owner of La Coreja as the greatest eccentric God had let loose on this earth, or to see him as a sophisticated tyrant preparing his guest for some terrible torture and first playing cat-and-mouse with him.

'If I show any sign of weakness,' he thought, 'I'll be sacrificed unceremoniously and stupidly. Let's make the most of things, and if this raging giant is going to do something dreadful to me, we'll at least see to it he hears some good Christian truths first.'

'My good sir, my dear brother,' he said to him, getting up and adopting the calm, courteous tone he habitually used to reprove sinners, 'pardon me for daring to address your eminence as an equal, speaking as I do from a position of inferiority. Christ commands me; I must and I shall speak. I see Goliath before me, and ignoring his strength I take aim with my sling. My ministry requires me to counsel those in error; I am not intimidated by the arrogance of my interlocutor; my humble appearance does not suppose ignorance of the Faith I profess, nor of the Catholic creed which I can impart to anyone in need of such instruction. I am afraid of nothing, and if someone were to sentence me to martyrdom as my reward for preaching the gospel, I would embrace that martyrdom gladly. But first I have to tell you that you stand in mortal sin, that your pride is a grave offence to God, and that if you fail to mend your ways your noble birth, your riches, and distinctions will be to no avail; such things are idle vanities and useless ballast that will pull you down the more you try to climb. Anger is one of the greatest evils, it leads to other vices and deprives the soul of the peace of mind it needs to conquer sin in other spheres. The wrathful man is in the pay of Satan, who knows well how little resistance he meets from ill-tempered souls. Control your outbursts, treat your inferiors with courtesy and humanity! I don't know whether your heart is touched by the love of God; but without love for your fellow men that highest form of love is unattainable, for the plant of love has its roots on this earth, roots that are the kindness you show your neighbour, and if that plant's roots are withered, how can its upper reaches bear flowers and fruit? Your look of amazement as you listen to what I say shows you're not used to hearing such home truths, especially not from someone barefoot and in rags. Which is why Christ's voice spoke to my heart, insisting I enter your estate fearing nothing and no one, and why I entered, and why you have me here in the lion's den. Bare your teeth, sharpen your claws, devour me if you will; but I'll die urging you to mend your ways, because Christ sent me here to show you the light and tell you you're damned if you don't soon heed the call.'

Much to Nazarín's surprise, not only did the owner of La Coreja not fly into a rage at his words but on the contrary he was listening to him keenly, with respect even, though not exactly with deference, staggered by such reasoned arguments coming from one so humble.

'We can discuss that later,' he said, quite unruffled. 'There's an idea going round my head . . . an idea that keeps nagging at me . . . You'd better know that for some time now I've been plagued by loss of memory, it's what makes me keep losing my temper . . .'

All of a sudden he slapped his forehead and with the words: 'I've got it. *Eureka, eureka!*' he almost literally bounded into the next room, leaving the good pilgrim alone, even more bewildered. The door having been left open, the latter could see him in the adjoining room, which was a kind of library or study, rummaging through the sheaves of paper piled on a big desk. First he skimmed through a series of newspapers, of outsize dimensions, seemingly foreign, then he flicked through some magazines till finally he got out a drawerful of folders through which he rifled frantically. All of this took a good hour. Nazarín looked on as servants came into the study and took orders from their master, who it must be said addressed them more politely than before, and eventually servants and master disappeared through yet another door that led into the innermost recesses of that vast building. Finding himself on his own, the good priest took a calmer look at the room where he was sitting; the walls were covered with old religious paintings, of considerable quality: St John the Baptist admonishing Herod in the presence of Herodias; Salome dancing; Salome with John the Baptist's head;* on another wall saints of the Dominican Order; and over the mantelpiece a fine portrait of Pius IX.* The more he saw, the more the house and its owner remained a mystery to him. He was just beginning to fear he'd been abandoned in that solitary chamber when a servant came to fetch him and told him to follow in his footsteps.

'What do they want with me now?' he wondered as he trailed after the retainer through a sequence of drawing-rooms and corridors. 'Lord have mercy on me; and if I'm being taken off to be imprisoned, drowned, or beheaded, may death find me ready to face it as I've always wished.'

But the dungeon or tank to which he was taken was a well-proportioned, bright, spotlessly clean dining-room, where he saw the table magnificently laid with china and crystal as fine as any in Madrid, with just two places set, facing one another. Señor de Belmonte, who was waiting for him in a black suit and a shirt with a dazzling white pleated front and collar, his hair and beard carefully groomed, indicated one of the chairs to Nazarín.*

'Sir,' the penitent stammered in confusion and embarrassment, 'how can I be seated at such an elegant table dressed in these rags of mine?'

'Sit down, I said, and don't oblige me to repeat the invitation,' the gentleman insisted in a tone of voice that belied the harshness of his words.

Realizing it ill became his genuine modesty to protest too much, Don Nazario sat down. To go on refusing would have been a sign not so much of a vocation for poverty as of overweening pride.

'Sit down I will, sir, and I accept the undeserved honour you do a poor vagabond by inviting him to share your table, when yesterday he was savagely mauled by the dogs of this house. This act of charity cancels out part of what God commanded me to say a little while ago. Anyone capable of such an act is not, and cannot be, an enemy of Christ.'

'Enemy of Christ! What on earth made you say that?' the giant exclaimed genially. 'But the two of us get on famously!'

'I'm delighted to hear it ... But if I accept your generous invitation, my good sir, I beg you to allow me not to depart from my custom of eating only the necessary to satisfy my hunger. No, don't pour me any wine; I never touch it or any other kind of alcohol.'

'You may eat what you like. I'm not in the habit of pressing my guests to eat more than their fill. You'll be served everything and it's up to you what you do with it; you can eat too much, too little, or nothing, as you please ... And in return for that concession, sir, may I ask your leave ...'

'There's no need for that. You can do what you like with me, with my leave or without it.'

'Your leave to interview you.'

'On what subject?'

'On the pressing problems of the day, social and religious.'

'I'm not sure if my limited knowledge will allow me to give you the informed replies you're obviously expecting ...'

'Oh! If you start by denying your knowledge, just as you conceal your status, we'd better call it a day.'

'I'm not concealing anything; I'm exactly what I appear to be; and as for my knowledge, I'm bound to declare it's greater than you'd expect from the life I lead and the clothes I'm wearing, but I don't think it great enough to be worth displaying to someone as well educated as yourself.'

'We'll see about that. I'm not very learned; but my travels in the East and West have taught me something, as have my dealings with people, the richest and best source of education in the world; and what with my accumulated observations and a few books here and there, specializing in religious matters, I've built up a modest stock of ideas that are my most prized possession. But to get to the point . . . I'm dying to ask you . . . What's your view of the present spiritual state of humankind?'

VIII

'Now there's a question . . .' Nazarín muttered, looking down at his feet. 'The subject's so complex I don't know where to start.'

'I mean, the present state of religious belief in Europe and the Americas.'

'I believe, sir, that the advances of Catholicism are such that the coming century will see the breakaway churches reduced to a position of insignificance. And for that we've largely to thank the wisdom, the exemplary goodness, the exquisite tact of the incomparable leader of our Church . . .'

'His Holiness Leo XIII,'* Señor de Belmonte added with a convivial gesture, 'to whose health we drink this toast.'

'No, I'm sorry. I don't drink, not even to the Pope's health, because neither the Pope nor Christ our Saviour would want me to change my way of life . . . As I was saying, Man is beginning to show signs of weariness and disenchantment with scientific speculation, and of a welcome return to the spiritual.* It had to happen. Science has failed to resolve any of the big questions raised by the enigma of our origins and destiny, and its extraordinary practical applications have also failed to live up to their promise. With all the advances in technology people are less happy, there's more poverty and hunger, and the distribution of wealth is increasingly unjust.* Everything is crying out for a return to the forgotten paths that lead to the sole fount of truth; that is, religious faith, the ideals of the Catholic Church, whose ability to survive and endure are amply proved.'

'Quite so,' affirmed the aristocratic giant, who incidentally was tucking in heartily while his guest merely picked at the succession of succulent dishes. 'I'm delighted to see your ideas coincide with mine.'

'The current state of the world is such,' Nazarín continued, becoming more expansive, 'you'd have to be blind not to see the signs of a new religious dawning. Winds of change are blowing, announcing that we're nearly out of the desert and that the Promised Land is near, with its pleasant valleys and fertile hills.'*

'True, true. I couldn't agree more ... But you'll have to admit society is growing tired of wandering in the desert, and if it doesn't get what it wants pretty soon, it'll lose patience and go overboard. Where's the Moses to keep it in check, whether by force or persuasion?'

'The Moses ... ? Why, I've no idea.'

'To find that Moses should we look to philosophy?'

'Certainly not; philosophy's just a play of hollow words and conceits, and philosophers are the hot air stifling and tiring mankind on its arduous journey.'

'Will we find that Moses in politics?'

'No, politics has burnt itself out. It's fulfilled its function and what used to be called political problems, that is, issues of freedom, human rights, etcetera, have been resolved without mankind finding a new heaven on this earth.* After winning all those rights the peoples of the world are as hungry as ever. So many political gains and so little bread to go round. So much material progress and every day fewer jobs and more unemployment. It's no good looking to politics now, it's given all it had to give. For long enough it's turned our heads, whether liberal or conservative, with its public and private wranglings. The best thing the politicians can do is pack their bags, they've nothing of substance to offer mankind; we're tired of empty speeches and trite slogans, and of seeing non-entities promoted to mediocrities, mediocrities promoted to celebrities, and celebrities promoted to the status of national hero.'*

'Bravo, bravo. I'm amazed at your clarity of exposition. So will our Moses come from the warrior caste? Will he be a dictator, a general, a Caesar . . . ?'

'I wouldn't like to say. There's no way we, or I, can know. All I can affirm is this: that we've only a few more miles to go before getting out of the desert, and by miles I mean relatively long distances.'

'Well, as far as I'm concerned the Moses who'll lead us to our destined goal is certain to come from the religious fold. Don't you think that one of these days, when we're least expecting it, we'll see the appearance of one of those towering giants of the Christian faith, no less great than St Francis of Assisi, or as great if not greater, who'll lead mankind to the end of its travails before despair hurls it into the abyss?'*

'That seems the most logical supposition,' said Nazarín, 'and if I'm not mistaken that superhuman saviour will be a Pope.'

'You think so?'

'Yes, I do, sir . . . It's just a hunch of mine, one particular view of the philosophy of history, God knows I wouldn't want to give it the status of dogma.'

'No, of course not . . . All the same that's what I think too. It'll be a Pope. Which Pope? Who knows!'

'Our intellect has too much confidence in its ability to penetrate the mysteries of the great beyond. There's enough for us to busy our heads with in the present. The world is at sixes and sevens.'

'It couldn't be worse.'

'The society of men is diseased. It's looking for a cure.'*

'Which has to be that of Faith.'

'And those blessed with the gift of Faith must take responsibility for guiding those less fortunate. On this road, as on all roads, the sighted must give a helping hand to the blind. What's needed are examples, not empty clichés. It's not enough to preach the teachings of Christ; we must put them into practice by living as he did, in so far as the human can imitate the divine. To spread the gospel in this society of ours, the faithful must renounce the superficial advances of History, like streams flowing down to the foot of the mountain, and espouse and practise the basic truths. Don't you think so? If you want to demonstrate the power of humility, you've got yourself to be humble; if you want to exalt poverty as the highest state, you've got yourself to be poor, and at the same time be seen to be poor. That's my creed . . . I mean, my personal interpretation of Holy Roman dogma. What's the remedy for social unrest and the increasingly violent struggle between rich and poor? Poverty, renunciation of all worldly goods. What's the remedy for the injustice that sours the world, despite the political advances we're so proud of? Why, passive acceptance, surrender to evil, just as Christ surrendered to his enemies without a fight. Such non-resistance to evil can lead only to good, just as strength is born of meekness and the espousal of poverty will by definition provide consolation for all and an equal share of Nature's resources. That's what I believe,* that's my vision of the world, based on total faith in the spiritual and material efficacy of the Christian ideal. It's not enough for me to achieve personal salvation; I want everyone to be saved and the world to be rid of hatred, tyranny, hunger, injustice; no more masters and slaves, no more divisions or wars or politics. That's my view, and even if it sounds absurd to someone as educated as yourself I'll stick to it come what may, wrong if I'm wrong, or right if, as I believe, my mind and conscience are illumined by God's truth.'

Don Pedro listened to the whole of the last part of this meaty discourse in a state of profound reverie, his eyelids lowered, his hand caressing an outsize wine glass, still half full. Then he murmured faintly: 'True, true, so true . . . ! To be in possession of the truth . . . what bliss . . . ! To put it into practice, more blissful still . . . !'

Nazarín said grace at the end of the meal, and Don Pedro went on gently moaning with his eyes closed: 'Poverty . . . such a lovely idea . . . ! But I can't, I can't . . . The thought's exquisite...! To go hungry, naked, and live off charity... It's sublime... I can't, I can't.'

When they got up from the table, the giant's tone of voice and manners were quite different from what they had been that morning. His fiery temper was silenced, what spoke was the geniality that comes with breeding. He was another man; his lips were fixed in a beaming smile; the sparkle in his eyes made him look years younger.

'Now, Father, I'm sure you'd like a rest. You must be used to taking a siesta...'

'No, sir, I only sleep at night. I spend the whole day on my feet.'

'Not me. I get up very early and by this time of day I need a little nap. You should have a rest too. Come with me now.'

Like it or not Nazarín was taken off to a richly furnished bedchamber not far from the dining-room.

'Yes, sir... Yes indeed,' Belmonte pressed him warmly. 'Take a rest now, you could do with it. With that itinerant life of poverty, self-denial and abstinence, toil and hardship, you deserve a little reward. One mustn't abuse one's physical energies, my friend. Oh, I admire you, I respect and revere you, precisely because I lack the strength to imitate you! The thought of abandoning my high position, concealing my illustrious name, renouncing comfort, wealth and...!'

'I never had to renounce such things because I never had them in the first place.'

'What! Come now, sir, you've kept the pretence up long enough, indeed I'd call it a farce if I weren't afraid of offending you.'

'What on earth do you mean?'

'That with that Christian disguise, that long tunic like one of Christ's disciples, you may take other people in but not me, I've recognized you, I've the privilege of knowing who I'm addressing.'

'And who am I, Señor de Belmonte? Tell me if you know.'

'But why go on pretending? You...'

The owner of La Coreja took a deep breath and, in a tone of courteous familiarity, putting his hand on his guest's shoulder, spoke as follows:

'Forgive me for finding you out. I'm speaking to the Reverend Bishop of Armenia who for the last two years has been touring Europe on a holy pilgrimage ...'

'Me ... ! Bishop of Armenia!'

'To be more precise ... you see, I know everything about you ... to be more precise, the Patriarch of the Armenian rite who bowed to the authority of the Holy Roman Church, swearing allegiance to our great Pope Leo XIII.'

'In the name of the Blessed Virgin, I pray you, sir!'

'Your worship is travelling round the nations of Europe as a pilgrim, barefoot and poorly clad, living off public charity, to fulfil a promise made to the Lord if He permitted your flock's entry into the mainstream of the Christian fold ... Why, it's no use denying it and keeping up the pretence, much as I respect it! Your Most Holy Worship was given authorization to comply with your vow in this manner, temporarily renouncing all your honours and privileges. I'm not the first to find you out! You've already been sighted in Hungary, where it was rumoured you'd performed miracles! And you were also spotted in the Alps, in Valence, capital of the Dauphiné ... Look, I've got the press reports here that talk about the distinguished Patriarch and describe that physiognomy, that outfit of yours with an accuracy little short of astonishing! ... Which is why, as soon as I saw you nearing my house, bells started ringing in my head. Then I checked the story out in the newspapers. The spitting image, the spitting image! What an incredible honour you do me!'

'My good sir, please, I beg you to listen to me ...'

But the deluded giant would not let him get a word in edgeways, overriding Nazarín and drowning his words with his own verbal outpourings.

'But we've met before, I lived in the Orient for years; Your Reverence can't keep your pious act up with me! I'll talk to you straight, if you keep insisting ... You're an Arab by birth.'

'By the Passion and Death of Our Lord Jesus Christ!'

'A genuine Arab. I know your history inside out. You were born in the beautiful land where they say the earthly paradise was located, between the Tigris and the Euphrates, in the region of Aldjezira,* otherwise known as Mesopotamia.'

'May God have mercy on me!'

'You see, I know, I know all about you! And your Arabic name is Esrrou-Esdras.'

'Holy Mary!'

'And the Franciscans on Mount Carmel baptized you and educated you, and taught you the Spanish you speak so beautifully. After that you went to Armenia, where Mount Arafat is, I've visited it ... the place where Noah's ark came to rest ...'

'Mother of God!'

'And there you became a priest of the Armenian rite, so distinguishing yourself by your wisdom and virtue that finally you were appointed to the Patriarcate, where you successfully undertook the glorious enterprise of restoring your orphaned church to the bosom of the great Catholic family. So I won't tire you any more, Your Reverence. Take a rest in this bed here, you can't have abstinence, hardship, and mortification all the time. Every now and then you have to put up with a bit of comfort; and above all, Your Grace, you're in my house and in the name of the sovereign law of hospitality I order you to go to bed and sleep.'

And without allowing him to protest or waiting for a reply, he went out of the room laughing and the good Nazarín was left on his own, his head ringing as if he'd been subjected to the noise of a prolonged artillery bombardment, unsure whether he was asleep or awake, whether what he had seen and heard was real or dreamt.

IX

'Heavens above!' exclaimed the blessed priest, 'what kind of a man is this? I've never come across such a raving lunatic in all the days of my life! He wouldn't even listen to my replies and explanations ...! Can he really believe that story he came out with ...? That I'm Patriarch of Armenia and my name's Esdras and ... Sweet Jesus, Holy Mary, get me out

of here before it's too late, that man's head is like a huge
birdcage packed with larks, canaries, thrushes, cockatoos,
and parakeets all singing at once...I only hope it isn't
catching! Christ have mercy upon us...! Who'd have
thought God could create such things, so many different
types and species! You think you've seen it all, and you find
there are still more wonders and curiosities waiting to be
discovered...And he's expecting me to get into a handsome
bed like that, with a damask quilt...! Lord above! To think
I came here expecting to be persecuted, humiliated, even
martyred...and what do I find but a jocular giant who seats
me at his table, calls me Bishop, and ushers me into this
elegant bedroom here to take an afternoon nap! Now would
you say a man like that is bad or good...?'

The poor semitic priest was plunged into a quandary from
which there seemed to be no exit, so tricky and vexed was
the question his brain had chosen to probe. Before he could
decide how to classify Pedro de Belmonte's moral character,
the latter came back having slept his fill. As soon as he saw
him come in the door, Nazarín went up to him and, before
he could so much as open his mouth, grabbed him by the
lapels and said to him with unaccustomed vehemence:

'Now listen to me, my good sir, you didn't give me a
chance to tell you I'm not an Arab nor a Bishop nor a
Patriarch, and I'm not called Esdras and I'm not from
Mesopotamia; I'm from Miguelturra and my name is
Nazario Zaharín. Can we get it established that none of
what you see in me is an act, unless that's what you call the
vow of poverty I've taken on myself, which doesn't mean I've
renounced...'

'Monsignor, Monsignor...I quite understand why you
want to keep up the pretence...'

'Which doesn't mean I've renounced, if you'll let me finish,
honours or revenue because I never had such things nor do I
aspire to them nor...'

'But I'm not going to give away your secret, damn it! I
wholly approve of your keeping up this charade of yours
and...'

'And nothing of the sort...You're dreaming, you're out

of your mind, this whole business is nonsense. I've taken to the roads as a penitent to satisfy a burning desire I've felt ever since I was a child. I'm a priest and, although I've not asked permission to give up the cloth and live off charity, I consider my actions to be entirely orthodox, and I profess obedience and respect for everything the Church commands. If I've opted for freedom rather than an enclosed order, it's because individual penance seems to me to offer more hardships, more indignities, and a more obvious renunciation of worldly goods. I defy public opinion, I brave hunger and exposure to the elements; I seek humiliation and martyrdom. And on that note I'll take my leave, Señor de Belmonte, and please let me thank you for all the kindness you've shown me, and assure you I'll always remember you in my prayers.'

'My thanks to you, not just for the honour Your Reverence has done me . . .'

'Here we go again!'

'The extraordinary honour of gracing my house with your presence, but also for offering to pray for me and commend me to God, which is something I could do with, believe you me.'

'I do indeed . . . But will you please stop calling me Your Reverence . . .'

'All right; I'll drop the formalities, so as to go along with your profession of humility,' replied the gentleman, who would let himself be flayed alive rather than admit that anything he'd said or claimed was wrong. 'You're quite right to insist on travelling incognito, to avoid gossip . . .'

'For heaven's sake, sir . . . ! Never mind, just give me leave to depart. May God correct your obduracy, which is a form of pride, and if the bitter fruit of pride is anger, the fruit of obduracy is falsehood. So you see how many evils pride brings in its wake. My final words as I leave this noble house are to beg you to mend your ways in this and other respects, and to think of the life everlasting, at whose door you should not go knocking with your soul weighed down by so much luxury and material comfort. Because the life you're leading, my dear sir, may help you live to a ripe old age; but it won't give you eternal salvation.'

'I know, I know,' the good Don Pedro repeated with a rueful smile, ushering Nazarín out through the first courtyard. 'But what can I do, Your Excellency? We don't all have your incredible stamina... When you get to a certain age, I fear, you're too set in your ways to give things up and change your lifestyle. Take my word for it: when your body isn't going to be around much longer, it seems a shame to deny it its little treats. I'm weak, I admit it, and there are times I think I ought to give my body a good talking to. But then I feel sorry for it and say: "Poor little body, to think you've got so few years to go...!" That's a form of charity too, don't you think? After all, if the poor devil's partial to wining and dining, what can I do except indulge it...? And if it likes to pick a quarrel, then let it have its way... It's just a bit of good, clean fun. Old age needs its playthings just like childhood. Now when it was a few years younger, it used to go for other things... a good wench, for example... That's something I've cut out altogether... Absolutely out of the question. Totally forbidden. And it can just put up with it... The only sins I allow it are trifles such as eating, drinking, smoking, and scolding the servants... Enough said, sir, I don't want to keep you. Pray to God for me. It's lucky for those of us who have our faults that perfect beings like yourself exist to intercede for us, and through their extraordinary merits obtain salvation for others as well as themselves.'

'But that won't do at all.'

'Oh yes it will, if we do our little bit too. I ought to know... May your life of penance, most Holy Father, lead you to the perfection you desire and may God grant you the strength to continue your noble, saintly labours... Farewell, farewell...'

'Farewell, my good sir: please don't come any further,' Nazarín said to him when they got to the last courtyard. 'That reminds me, I left my knapsack over there by the waterwheel.'

'Don't worry, they'll be here with it in a minute,' replied Belmonte. 'I ordered them to stock it up with provisions, they always come in handy, believe you me, and even if you prefer a diet of wild grass and stale bread, it's not a bad idea to have something a bit more nutritious on you in case of illness . . .'

He made as if to kiss his hand but Don Nazario managed by a supreme effort to extricate himself, and at the outermost bounds of the estate they said goodbye with mutual demonstrations of affection. Seeing that the mastiffs were roaming around loose, Don Pedro commanded them to be chained up and ordered Nazarín to pause for a minute. 'I heard', he said, 'that yesterday, much to my chagrin, owing to the negligence of these rogues here, my dogs bit you and the two holy women who are your travelling companions.'

'They're not holy women, anything but.'

'You can pretend all you like . . . But their stories are in the European press as well! One of them is a lady of noble rank, a canoness from Thuringia, the other's from a discalced order in the Sudan . . .'

'Heaven help us, what madness is this . . . !'

'But it's in the papers! All the same, I respect your pious disguise . . . God speed. The animals are under control.'

'May God be with you. And may He show you the light,' said Nazarín, not wanting to go on arguing any more and keen to be on his way without further ado.

The knapsack, stuffed with food parcels, was heavy and, what with this and his hasty retreat, he was quite out of breath by the time he got to the elm grove where Ándara and Beatriz had stayed waiting for him. The two women, made restless and anxious by his long absence, rushed to greet him rapturously as soon as they caught sight of him, having fully expected never to set eyes on him again or at least that he would emerge from La Coreja with a broken skull. Great was their surprise and joy to see him in one piece and good spirits. The holy pilgrim's opening words gave them to understand he had quite some tale to tell, and the knapsack's weight and bulk had them bursting with curiosity. Back in the elm grove Nazarín found an old woman he had not met before, Señá Polonia, who was from Beatriz's village but had moved to Sevilla la Nueva. She had been passing by on her way back from a piece of land she owned, where she had

gone to sow some turnips, and spotting a familiar face had
stopped off for a chat.

'Heavens above, you can't begin to imagine how strange
that Don Pedro is!' said the good priest, dropping to the
ground after Ándara took the knapsack off him to inspect its
contents. 'I've never known a case like it. He's capable of
wickedness and vice; but he's also capable of the most
courteous, gentlemanly, and generous behaviour. He's well
enough educated, over-given to luxury and tantrums; and a
more obstinate man when it comes to admitting he's in the
wrong would be hard to find.'

'That handsome old dog', intervened Polonia, 'is as mad as
a hatter. They says he spent years among the Moors and
Jews, and when he got back he so took to studying things of
religion and *divination* he went off his rocker.'

'That's the impression I got. Our good Don Pedro's not
right in the head. What a shame! May God grant him the
sense he's lacking!'

'He's quarrelled with all the Belmontes down to the last
nephew and cousin, they hates his guts and that's why he
never leaves this place. He's a real pagan and heathen when
it comes to the good life, and there's not a bit of skirt escapes
his notice. But he's not bad-hearted for all that. They says
when people talks to him about things of religion, Catholic
or pagan, or heathen practices for that matter, that's when
he goes off the rails, because of that there *inquisiting* and
messing around with the Holy Scriptures what's turned his
head.'

'Poor man! Can you believe, my good women, that he sat
me down at his table, a magnificent table, with china fit for a
cardinal? And you can't imagine how many different courses
there were, how delicious it all tasted . . . ! And after that he
insisted I take an afternoon nap in a bed with a damask
quilt . . . Just fancy, me of all people . . . !'

'And there we were thinking he'd break every bone in your
body!'

'Well, wait till you hear this . . . He kept on going on about
me being a bishop; no, more than that, a patriarch; and
having been born in Algeciras . . . Mesopotamia that is,* and

my name being Esdras...And he also came out with the idea that the two of you are canonesses...And it was no good my denying it and insisting on the truth. He didn't hear a word I said.'

'Well, you can tell the old devil lives the good life,' exclaimed Ándara gaily getting out the food parcels. 'Pressed tongue...more tongue...and ham...Lord Almighty, look at all these goodies! And what's this here? A whopping great pie the size of a cartwheel! Just smell that now...And some pasties: one, two, three of them; chorizo, sausages...'

'Pack it up, all of it,' Nazarín said to her.

'Too right I will, so we can try it at suppertime.'

'No, my child, we're not touching it.'

'What?'

'No, that's for the poor.'

'But you can't get poorer than us, Father.'

'We're not poor, we're sated with an inexhaustible supply of that precious gift called Christian conformity.'

'Well said,' Beatriz commented, helping stuff the parcels back in the knapsack.

'And if we've been given this today and we've got no immediate need for it because our stomachs are full,' indicated Don Nazario, 'we should give it to others who need it more than we do.'

'Well, there's poor people enough in Sevilla la Nueva,' interjected Señá Polonia, 'and you can share out your treasures there all right, it's the poorest, neediest village in the whole district.'

'Really? Then that's where we'll take these leftovers from the wealthy miser's table, since they've come into our hands. Show us the way, Señá Polonia, and point out the houses of those most in need.'

'But are you really going to Sevilla la Nueva? These two here said they wouldn't go near the place.'

'Why not?'

'Because there's an outbreak of smallpox.'

'Splendid...! Well, not exactly...What I mean is that I'm overjoyed by the prospect of encountering human suffering, so I can fight and overcome it.'

'It's not reached serious proportions. There's been four cases reported these last few days. Where there is an awful epidemic is Villamantilla, eight miles further on.'

'An awful epidemic . . . of smallpox too?'

'Terrible, yes, sir. There's no one to look after the sick and those that are healthy are fleeing in panic.'

'Ándara, Beatriz,' said Nazarín getting up, 'off we go. We'll not delay another minute.'

'To Villamantilla?'

'The Lord calls us. We're needed there. What? Not afraid, are you? Anyone who's afraid or doesn't like the idea can stay behind.'

'Let's go. Did I hear anyone say they were afraid?'

They set off post-haste, and on the way Nazarín filled them in with the entertaining details of his singular visit to Don Pedro de Belmonte, the owner of La Coreja.

PART IV

I

WITH Señá Polonia acting as guide, they left part of the provisions from La Coreja with various destitute families in Sevilla la Nueva and, stopping only long enough to complete this pious mission, resumed their journey, for Nazarín would not call it a day till they were in the thick of the plague.

'I don't see why you should find the idea repugnant, my daughters,' he addressed his companions, 'you ought to have got it into your heads by now that we're not here to live the easy life or to escape toil and danger. On the contrary: we go looking for suffering so we can offer consolation, and some of that suffering is bound to rub off on us. We're not looking for fun and games but sorrow and grief. The Lord has provided us with an epidemic, into whose pestilent bosom we shall plunge like intrepid lifesavers diving into the waves to save the shipwrecked from drowning. If we perish, God will reward us. If not, we'll succeed in getting some poor wretch to the shore. So far God has ordained we should meet only good fortune on our pilgrim's way. We've not gone hungry, we've eaten and slept like princes, and no one has lifted a hand against us or frowned on us. Everything has gone our way, as if we'd been escorted by a bevy of angels charged with showering every earthly good on us. You must realize it can't go on. The world being what it is, sooner or later we're bound to meet terrible ills, obstacles, calamities and deprivations, and persecution at the hands of Satan's followers.'

This exhortation managed to win over the two women, especially Beatriz who, when it came to self-sacrifice, was the more easily inflamed by the apprentice penitent's ardour. As they'd kept up a lively pace, at sunset exhaustion forced them to rest on a hilltop from where they could see two villages, one to the east and the other to the west, and between the two a stretch of ploughed fields dotted with green woodland. The view was breathtaking, particularly at that time of day when dusk casts its melancholy spell over all the earth. From the humble rooftops smoke rose from the hearths where supper was being cooked; you could hear the bells of sheep being herded into the fold, and in both villages the church bells were ringing, summoning the villagers to prayer. The smoke, the green valley, the sunset, the tinkling and tolling of bells were all voices in a mysterious language that spoke to the soul without the latter knowing exactly what it was saying. The three wanderers gazed silently for a while at that vision of beauty spread before them, and Beatriz, who was lying at Nazarín's feet, sat up to ask him:

'Tell me, Father: that sound of church bells at this hour that's neither day nor night . . . tell me now . . . is it a happy sound or a sad sound?'

'To be honest, I don't really know. I feel the same as you: I don't know whether to call it happy or sad. I guess it makes us feel happy and sad at the same time, mixing the two emotions so you can't tell the difference.'

'I think it's sad,' Beatriz declared.

'And I think it's happy,' said Ándara, 'because you feel happy when you rest and at this hour the day gets into bed with night.'

'And I still think it's sad and happy,' repeated Nazarín, 'because those sounds and that calm are mirrors of the soul, which is sad to see the end of another day, for another day gone by takes us one step closer to death; but happy because it goes home glad to have completed the day's tasks and to find waiting for it other souls that are dear to it; sad, because the night brings with it a gentle gloom, the disappointments of the day just past; happy, because every night holds out the hope and certainty of another day, of another morrow waiting to dawn on the eastern horizon.'

The two women sighed and fell silent.

'In this,' continued the Arab from La Mancha, 'you should see an image of the sunset that is our death. It heralds the dawn of life everlasting. Death is happy and sad too: happy, because it frees us from the chains of the daily grind; sad, because we cling to our body like a faithful companion and it pains us to leave it behind.'

They carried on walking and a bit further on sat down to rest again, now well into night, under a calm, crystal-clear sky studded with countless stars.

'You know,' said Beatriz after a long, rapturous silence, 'it's so wonderful to look at the sky and find it's full of all that light, I don't think I can ever have seen it before or perhaps it's the first time I've looked at it properly.'

'Yes,' said Nazarín, 'it's so beautiful it always looks brand new, as if it were fresh from the Creator's hands.'

'It goes on and on and on,' observed Ándara. 'I never looked at it like now neither . . . And tell me, Father, will we see all that close up when we die and go to Heaven?'

'Are you so sure you'll go to Heaven? That's pushing it a bit . . . In Heaven there's no such thing as near or far . . .'

'It's all infinite,' Beatriz affirmed roundly. 'Infinite means it doesn't end anywhere.'

'All that about us being infinite,' Ándara replied, 'I don't get it.'

'Be good and you'll understand. There are two things on this mortal earth that give us a taste of infinity: love and death. Love God and your fellow men, cherish the idea of passing to a life beyond, and you'll start to grasp the idea of infinity. But philosophical concepts like this are difficult for your untrained minds, let's take a concrete example. Look at God's handiwork, and tell me if it isn't right and proper for us to bow down before the Creator of such wonders and dedicate all our deeds and thoughts to him. After gazing up at the heavens, how unworthy this wretched earth of ours seems of our desire to dwell on it! Just think that, before you were born, everything you see up there had existed for thousands of centuries and will go on existing for thousands of centuries after you've died. We live for just a moment. Isn't it natural we should hold that moment in low esteem and want to ascend to the world everlasting?'

They heaved another sigh and reflected on everything the priest had said. Then the conversation turned to more earthy matters as Ándara, while accepting that the knapsack's contents should go to others in need, protested at the idea they should not even get to taste them.

'To be good, to attain what we commonly call perfection but which in practice is relative,' Nazarín declared, 'we have to start with the things that come easiest. Before taking on the major vices, we have to tackle the minor ones. I say that because I think your love of food is the kind of habit that ought to be relatively easy to curb, with a bit of effort.'

'Yes, I like a tasty morsel all right: I know my soft spots. And the truth is I'm dying to know what these heavenly smelling goodies taste like.'

'Well, try them and you can tell us, Beatriz and I can do without.'

The wench from Móstoles submitted freely to any kind of abstinence or edification, for her spirit was starting to burn with a mystical fire* sparked by the priest's saintly ardour. She would have liked to reach the ludicrous extreme of stopping eating altogether; but since that was not a viable option, she agreed to compromise with the base needs of the flesh.

They sought hospitality at an inn and when they said they were bound for Villamantilla everyone thought they were mad, for apart from the sick hardly anyone was left in the village; the aid requested from Madrid had not yet arrived, and despair, starvation, and death reigned supreme. They improvised a bedroom in the yard among the sheep and hens, which stirred at the sound of their prayers; and dined in pastoral fashion off some fried breadcrumbs* they were given by way of alms. Ándara dipped into Belmonte's provisions without over-indulging and spent the whole night licking her chops even after falling asleep. Beatriz however did not sleep a wink: she could feel her usual symptoms coming on but in a new way she had never felt before. The difference was that the tension and agitation preceding the fit were positive, meaning that the tension was in a way pleasurable and the agitation uplifting. She felt ... almost happy to feel ill and sensed that something very special was about to happen to her. She had a slight feeling of constriction in the chest; but this discomfort was overriden by the discharges that made her tingle all over in an erratic sequence of vibrations culminating in the brain, where they turned into lovely images of things dreamt rather than seen. 'It's the usual attack,' she told herself, 'except that this time it's not the pounding of devils' hooves but the flutter of angels' wings. Who cares about being cured if being ill always makes me feel this well!'* In the early hours of morning she felt shivery and, wrapping her shawl tightly round her, stretched out on the ground to rest rather than sleep and, conscious that she was awake, she *saw things*! But if the visions she used to have were horrific, now they were glorious, though she could not explain what it was she saw or even be sure she was seeing it. She had never experienced anything so strange. And she had to repress a blind urge to fling herself at the object of her visions. Was it God, the heavenly angels, the soul of some saint, or an incorporeal spirit trying vainly to take on material form?

She refrained from saying anything about her experiences to Don Nazario when he awoke, for the day before she had heard him say, in the course of one of his sermons, that he mistrusted visions and you had to be very careful before taking seriously things (the word he had used was *phenomena*) that are simply the product of the imagination and nervous system of people whose health is unstable. After washing her face and hands she felt recovered from that comforting swoon, and the three of them downed a breakfast of bread with a few nuts and off they set again eagerly for the plague-ridden village. It was not yet 9.00 when they got there, meeting with a desperate silence and grim mistrust as they walked up the one winding street that comprised the village, with its open sewers, filthy puddles, and sharp, uneven cobbles. The two or three people they encountered on the way to the square eyed them suspiciously and outside the church, at the entrance to a building with cracks in the walls that seemed to be the Town Hall, they saw an emaciated old man who intercepted their advance with the following hostile welcome:

'Hey there, my good folk, if you've come to hawk or beg,

go back to where you've come from, all we can offer you here is desolation, death, and despair, even God's mercy has abandoned us. I'm the mayor and I should know. There's no one left but me and the priest, and a doctor we were sent when the local one died and some twenty villagers in all, not counting the sick and today's dead whom we haven't yet had a chance to bury. You'd best get packing, this is no place for beggars.'

Nazarín replied that they hadn't come to seek charity but to bring it, and would the mayor be so kind as to point them in the direction of the most desperate cases, so they could tend to their needs with all the dedication and forbearance the Lord commands.

'What's most urgent right now,' said the mayor, 'is to bury the seven dead we've got here, of both sexes.'

'Add two more to your list,' said the priest, coming out of a nearby house. 'Old Casiana's just breathed her last, and one of the sheepshearer's daughters is about to join her. I'm just rushing off to grab a bite to eat, I'll be right back.'

It didn't take much to persuade the mayor to grant Nazarín's Christian request, and the three of them quickly got down to work. But the two poor women, confronted with that spectacle of horror, putrefaction, and squalor, more repulsive than anything their naïve penitents' ardour had imagined, baulked at the prospect like children dragged to a raging battle and faced with the sight of blood for the first time in their lives. The virtue of charity, newly instilled in their hearts, was not sufficient to keep them going and they had to appeal by default to pride. The first few hours were marked by indecision, panic, and wholesale revolt by stomachs and nerves. Nazarín had to urge them on with the eloquent wrath of the desperate fighter who sees the battle in danger of being lost. Slowly but surely, praise be to God, they edged their way forward into the thick of the fray and the afternoon found them transformed, faith triumphant over disgust and charity over fear.

II

While Nazarín seemed to be in his element in the fetid atmosphere of darkened rooms, with the horrible visages of the sick and filth and suffering all around, Ándara and Beatriz, try as they might, could not—alas—get used to an occupation that elevated them overnight from the vulgar to the heroic. They had seen only the glamorous, attractive side of the Christian ideal; now they could see its true face, suffused with suffering. As Beatriz put it in her simple language: 'It's all very well to talk about going to Heaven; but how you get there and what you have to go through on the way is another matter.' Ándara ended up immersing herself in a kind of mindless activity. She conducted herself like an automaton, carrying out those repulsive tasks in a state of semi-consciousness. Her hands and feet moved *on their own*. If in earlier times she had been sentenced to such a life and faced with the choice between it or death, she would rather have had her neck wrung any day. She let herself be hypnotized by the blessed Nazarín, moving like a loose-jointed puppet. Her senses were numbed. She thought she would never be able to eat again.

Beatriz was fully conscious of what she was doing, and suppressed her natural revulsion by resorting to intellectual arguments constructed out of ideas and phrases she had picked up from her teacher. She was by nature the more delicate of the two women, with a softer complexion and a more refined physical and moral constitution, and relatively select tastes. But this handicap was offset by spiritual reserves on which she could draw to overcome her frailty, forcing herself to persevere with that odious task. Mindful of her new-born faith, she cultivated it as one fans the flames of a newly lit fire to get it firmly established; she was capable of psychological subtleties inaccessible to the other woman, and was able to derive an inner satisfaction from doing what she knew to be right, whereas the other had to appeal to her pride, whose rewards were insufficient to compensate for such enormous sacrifice. For this reason when it got to night-fall the one from Polvoranca, while showing no signs of flagging, threw in the towel with a half-hearted shrug, whereas the one from Móstoles declared herself defeated joyously, like a wounded soldier who knows that glory is the only cure.

The one who refused to admit defeat was the Arab from La Mancha. Tireless to the point of the sublime, after spending the whole day heaving the sick this way and that, washing them, giving them medicine, watching some of them die in his arms, hearing the delirious ramblings of others, when night came he desired no better relief than that of burying the twelve bodies that were still without a grave. He did so under instructions from the mayor, who insisted he could manage with the help of two men, and if only one were available, then he'd have to make do with him and the two women. The people's representative gave him the authority to act as he saw fit, impressed by his diligence and piety, and put the cemetery *at his disposal*, as if offering a guest the freedom of the billiard-table or music-room.

With the aid of a morose, seemingly half-witted old man, who it later transpired was a swine-herd, and of Beatriz, who wanted to drain the cup of sacrifice to the last and master such a terrible if edifying art, Nazarín set about collecting the dead from their homes. Not having a barrow to transport them he hoisted them on his shoulders, setting them down on the ground till they were laid out in a row. The female penitent and the swine-herd did the digging, while the mayor rushed around dealing with any problems that cropped up, insisting they weren't to do a shoddy job like the council workmen but should see to it everything was done properly, with the bodies well underground and the earth nicely shovelled back on top. Ándara had gone off to snatch three hours' sleep, after which she'd come back so her friend could take her turn at sleeping. All this was decreed by their commander, so as not to exhaust the energies of his seasoned troops.

And when all the dead were duly buried the heroic Nazarín, with no more sustenance than a bit of bread and water offered him by the mayor, returned to the germ-ridden houses of the sick, to care for them, offer them words of consolation if they were in a state to hear, wash them, and give them water to drink. At midnight Ándara went to assist three little sisters whose mother had died of the same illness; while Don Nazario took under his wing a burly woman who was ranting deliriously, and a young man they kept saying was a handsome lad, though you would not have guessed it from the horrible mask concealing his face.

A new day dawned, illumining the scene of desolation, and making the two women feel more in control and able to cope. Both of them had the impression they had been enlisted in that worthy campaign for months; for the days expand according to the amount and range of activity we pack into them. They no longer felt so sickened by the monstrously deformed faces, nor so scared of the possibility of contagion, and their nerves and stomach protested less violently at the festering pus. The doctor paid tribute to the three penitents' pious zeal, insisting to the mayor that the arrival of that Moorish-looking man and his two female companions had been for the village of Villamantilla like a visitation from the heavenly angels. Shortly before noon the church bells started ringing in public thanksgiving, and they heard that the aid sent from Madrid by the Department of Health and Welfare was about to arrive. Not before time! But better late than never. The government delegation consisted of a doctor, two nurses, a *man from the ministry*, and a host of medicines to disinfect people and things. The good news of the medical team's arrival coincided with the information that the epidemic had taken an equal hold on Villamanta, where no government relief was known to be on the way. Taking an instant tactical decision, like the brilliant strategist who in a flash rushes his troops to where they are needed, Nazarín marshalled his diminutive army; the right and left flank got in line, and the general gave them their orders:

'Quick march.'

'Where to?'

'Villamanta. We're not needed here any more. The other village has no one to help.'

'Quick march it is. Off we go.'

And by two o'clock they were blazing a trail across country, following a route suggested by the swine-herd. Nothing was left of the provisions from La Coreja, and Ándara refused the offer of further supplies from Villamantilla. The two women washed in a brook, and Don Nazario did the same further upstream. Their bodies cleansed and their hearts content, they continued on their way, which was free of incident apart from an encounter with a band of urchins whose families, fleeing Villamantilla, had set up home in some half-ruined cottages on a hilltop. The little dears had taken to whiling away the tedium of their days in exile by stoning the passers-by, and that afternoon Nazarín and his troops fell victim to their innocent *sport*. They scored a hit on the general's head and on the right flank's arm. The left flank wanted to take retaliatory action by hurling back a volley of stones. But her master restrained her, saying: 'Hold your fire. We mustn't maim or kill, not even in self-defence. Let's speed up and get out of the little devils' range, God bless them.'

So they did, but still they did not manage to reach Villamanta before nightfall. Since they had no food nor money to buy any, Ándara went on some thirty yards ahead asking everyone they met for alms. But such was the poverty and devastation in the area, nothing was forthcoming. They were starving and in genuine need of bodily sustenance. The one from Polvoranca kept complaining, the one from Móstoles tried not to let her hunger show, and the one from Miguelturra spurred them on, assuring them they'd find something to eat somewhere before the day was out. Eventually, passing a field where some men and women were busy turning the topsoil with a plough, they found succour in the form of some crusts of bread, a few handfuls of chickpeas and of vetch and carob pods, plus a couple of farthings which seemed to them a fortune. They camped out in the open air, because Beatriz said she needed a good airing before going into another plague-ridden village. Gathering some dry oak twigs, they got a fire going and boiled the vegetables, throwing in some thistles, chicory, and purslane that Ándara managed to gather in the fields; their supper was as merry as it was meagre, they said their prayers, their master gave them a brief run through the life and death of St Francis of Assisi and his foundation of the Seraphic Order, and then it was bed. Daybreak saw them enter Villamanta.

How can one describe those six days of titanic labours, in the course of which Beatriz acquired a second nature based on indifference to risk of any kind and an unshakeable, quiet courage, and Ándara an energy and diligence that did away with her slothful habits? The former threw herself into the fight against disease confident in her superior strength but without complacency, thanks to a disinterested faith that had become a habit and a degree of conviction that kept her soul's soaring temperature at fever pitch; the latter was kept going by her habitual pride and proven expertise, congratulating herself and flattering her ego like a soldier entering the fray in the hope of promotion. And what can we say about Nazarín, except that in the course of those six days he was a Christian hero, and his physical resistance miraculously rivalled his incredible spiritual energies? They left Villamanta for the same reason they had left Villamantilla, namely because of the arrival of government aid. Pleased with their efforts, their consciences glowing with the reassuring certainty they had done what was right, they conducted a verbal review of their twofold campaign, yielding to the innocent temptation to tot up the number of sick each of them had tended or saved and the bodies they had buried, not to mention a thousand pathetic episodes that would make history if anyone cared to write them up. But no one will, that's for sure, and those memorable deeds are recorded only in the archives of Heaven. And as for their need to show off by doing the arithmetic and going over it again and again, no doubt God will forgive that ingenuous display of vanity, for it is right and proper that every hero should have his story, even if it be his private version.

They set off in the direction of a village which may have been Méntrida or may have been Aldea del Fresno,* for the *Nazarine* sources are none too clear about its precise location. All we know is that it was a pleasant place, relatively prosperous, surrounded by lush farmland. On a nearby hilltop they spotted the ruins of a castle; on closer inspection, they decided it was the perfect retreat in which to install themselves for the next few days to lead a life of rest and contemplation, for Nazarín was the first to stress the importance of repose. No, the Lord did not want them to be on the go all the time, they needed to build up their physical reserves for still fiercer campaigns to come. So the director of operations gave orders for them to set up camp in the ruins of that feudal fortress, and there they would see to the necessary repair of their exhausted souls. The spot was truly magnificent, overlooking a vast stretch of the fertile valley through which the River Perales winds, with its trim orchards and lush vineyards. To get to the top, you had to climb a steep slope; but once you got there, how clear the air was, what peace and quiet! They felt more at one with Nature and totally free, like eagles dominating the heights without anyone dominating them. Having decided in which part of the ruins they would set up home, they went down to the village to beg, and that first day everything went their way: Beatriz picked up a few coppers; Nazarín some lettuces, cabbage, and potatoes; and Ándara procured a couple of pans and a pitcher for fetching water.

'This is more like it,' she kept saying. 'Why can't we stay here for good, Father?'

'We're not looking for rest and comfort,' replied their leader, 'but for constant movement and hardship. Now we can relax for a bit; but then it'll be back into the fray.'

'And who knows if they'd let us stay here anyway?' Beatriz pointed out. 'The poor man has no fixed address but carries his home with him like a snail.'

'Well, if they'd let me I'd not mind farming a bit of this slope here,' said Ándara, 'and I'd plant it with potatoes, onions, and cabbage, to feed the *household*.'

'People like us', Nazarín declared, 'have no need of land or crops or domestic animals, our vocation is to own nothing; and out of that total negation comes the affirmation that anything and everything can become ours through the practice of charity.'

On the third day the wench from Polvoranca went down to the river to wash some clothes, and when she got back to the castle Beatriz went down to fetch some water, a minor detail which cannot be passed over in this faithful account for on it hang other events of evident weight and import.

III

Nightfall saw the young woman climbing the craggy slope with a pounding heart and legs so limp she had to take the pitcher off her head and sit down on the ground to get her breath back. What had happened to her at the village fountain, down by the river in the middle of a thick clump of poplar trees? Why, something unexpected, of absolutely no significance in the general course of human existence, but for Beatriz of the utmost gravity, one of those events that in the life of an individual amount to a cataclysm, a flood, an earthquake, a thunderbolt from heaven. So what had happened . . . ? She had seen Pinto, no more, no less!

Pinto was the bane and love of her life, the seducer who had been her downfall, the object of her desires, the man who had initiated her to dreams of bliss and paroxysms of rage. And just when she had managed, if not to forget him, at least to put him to the back of her mind, just when, with that life of abstinence and that salutary mission of charity, she had managed to cure her soul of its deadly malady, the wretch had to reappear and confound her piety and cast her back into the abyss. A curse on Pinto, why did he have to turn up now, why had she ever thought of going down to the fountain for water?

Such were the thoughts spinning round her head as she sat there resting halfway up the hill. She had him still before her eyes, as he had suddenly appeared to her just a yard away from the fountain, when she was already turning away with the pitcher full of water on her head. He called out her name, and she had to clutch at the pitcher to stop it falling. It was such a shock she was rooted to the ground like a living corpse, unable to move or speak.

'I knew you were in these parts, you bitch,' he had said to her, standing with his hands in the pockets of his jacket or shirt, in a bullish posture and surly tone that betrayed a disconcerting mixture of anger and scorn. 'I saw you yesterday, I saw you come down to the village with a fellow in rags like a Moor up a date palm and a woman uglier than sin . . . So what crazy kind of life is this you're leading? What the hell do you think you're doing going round with a band of gypsies? I told you you'd end up on the streets like a tramp or a whore . . . and that's just what you've gone and done. I know all about it, you filthy slut, how you ran off from Móstoles with this apostle feller as they call him, what casts the devils out of your body by making the sign of the cross with his prayer-book, and then goes and puts them back in again.'

'Pinto, Pinto, for the love of God!' she had replied when words finally came to her lips, 'Leave me alone! I've finished with you and the world. I don't want to speak to you, let me go.'

'Wait a bit . . . for politeness' sake if nothing else, woman. Do we or don't we have any manners? Look: I still love you. Barefoot like a soul out of purgatory and all, I love you, Beatriz. My heart ain't changed. Listen to me. I can't take the thought of you going round with that hobgoblin . . . How about coming back to Móstoles with me?'

'No, never.'

'Think it over, Beatriz; think about what's in your best interest, woman. You might just make me sorry, see. I love you like I said; but you know what kind of a temper I got. That's how I am. I'm here with Gregorio Portela and the two Ortiz brothers buying cattle for the slaughterhouse in Madrid, and by tomorrow night we've got to be back where we've come from. Tomorrow I'll wait for you all day over at old Lucas's inn, you know where that is, don't you?, so we can be together just the two of us and talk about our *pretensions* . . . Be there, Beatriz.'

'I won't go; don't expect me.'

'Be there, I said. You know when I mean what I say, I mean it . . . meaning I mean business.'

'Don't expect me, Manuel.'

'Just be there . . . For the sake of somebody here as cares

for you, Beatriz; don't be stubborn, and think about your reputation that's being dragged through the mud like an old boot. Come and we can have a chat. And what if you don't? In that case me and my mates'll be up at the castle tomorrow, I know that's where you hang out, and we'll cut the throat of that apostle feller and his *lady apostle* and the whole damned host of infernal angels . . . Goodbye then. You can go now.'

That and no more was the substance of their conversation. Terrified stiff, the poor girl set off for her home in the wilds and to make matters worse she kept thinking she heard Pinto's footsteps behind her. No, it wasn't him; but in the gathering night she imagined she could see his menacing figure, handsome indeed, cruel and despotic, subjugating her through terror as before he had subjugated her though pleasure. Her brief rest halfway up the hill calmed her down a bit; but she couldn't get out of her mind the man's savage injunction nor his unforgettable figure, with his erect body and tight-fitting clothes like those of a bullfighter, his dark, fine-featured, well-shaven face, his eyes like daggers, and next to his lips a mole with a tuft of frizzy hairs growing out of it like a tassel.

When she got to the top, Beatriz's first thought was to tell the blessed Nazarín what had happened. But an obscure, inexplicable impulse that sprang from she knew not where made her keep silent. Realizing that in keeping quiet about it she was committing a fault, she rationalized things by calling it a postponement, saying to herself: 'I'll tell him over supper.' But suppertime came and just when she was about to open her mouth to speak, she felt her tongue clamped in a vice. The inhibition or restraint came from her innermost depths, and the poor woman's desire to tell all was not strong enough to combat it.

And as chance would have it, she could not have talked to Father Nazarín had she wanted to. The reason was as follows. One corner of the castle's main tower was still intact, having over the centuries defied the fury of the elements and the inclemency of time. From a distance it looked like a bone, the jaw of a huge animal. It was made of big blocks of smooth stone, tightly interlocking, and on one side they formed what from afar looked like a set of teeth, jutting out like steps up which it was not difficult to clamber to reach the top. At the highest point there was a recess big enough to hold a human figure, and a better watchtower from which to survey heaven and earth could not be found. It was to that point that Nazarín had climbed, seating himself in the recess, his head leaning back against the stone and his legs dangling. In the light of the moon, which was full, his lean figure, head, hands, and feet looked like an earthenware figurine silhouetted against the sky. Never had his Arab features been more pronounced than in that posture at that moment. He could have been taken for a holy prophet who, seeking the lonely heights undisturbed by the world's bustle and follies, does not think himself secure till he has made the stork's nest and the weather-cock's vane his own. The two women looked up and saw him at that topmost point, crowned by the stars, perhaps at prayer or sending his thoughts out to scour the sky's expanse in search of truth.*

Beatriz, even while gazing at the heavens, with her mind's eye was looking earthwards; and as her master immersed himself in contemplation of the firmament, letting his ideas race across it, encompassing a space no less than that of the heavenly bodies, her soul was engaged in a terrible struggle. If she had been forced to nurse all the lepers in the world, those suffering from the most repulsive diseases, she would have preferred it to the turmoil of that inner battle and its likely consequences. From the village, temptation was calling with a powerful magnetic pull;* and part of her innermost self commanded her to obey Pinto's summons. The sensible, proper, Christian thing to do was to tell Don Nazario; but if she told him, then she couldn't go, and if she didn't tell him and kept the appointment, it was goodbye to divine grace and the spiritual rewards earned in that life of penance! And worse still: if she didn't go, Pinto would carry out his terrible threat. So the pleasure of going would be soured by the pricks of her conscience, and the latter's triumph, if she didn't go, would mean the death of the lot of them. What was better? To go or not to go? An intractable dilemma! Even virtue was no use to her, for if she stifled the wicked impulse that like a devil's tail was lashing her whole body with waves of poisoned fire, if she stayed pure and chaste, then he'd come up the hill and the knives would fly. And if she went down and sullied herself for ever, how could she face the good Nazarín again and ask his forgiveness? Oh no, she'd be so ashamed. She'd never be able to look him in the face again. And then the poor girl would be left at the mercy of that fiend's whims and moods... Oh no, oh no... That idea, the terror of a future as shameful as the past, decided it for her. Thank God! Christ and the Virgin, whose names she invoked, must have heard her and instilled the right solution in her mind: she must tell her master all about it and face the consequences of Pinto's revenge.

The Arab came down from his watchtower, Beatriz marched up to him determined to reveal her inner conflict and once again the vice clamped her mouth shut. She said nothing. Throughout supper, making an effort to hide the fact that she was off her food and to appear calm, she considered herself the most wicked, depraved woman in the world. And as they said their prayers, she found it hard to pronounce the most moving words of the Lord's Prayer. Her old illness started to prick at different parts of her body, and to stir up the sediment left by the devils in flight... She felt a sudden urge to destroy something, and then an unspeakable panic. She had to summon all her energies, or those still at her service, to pull herself together so as not to jump up and rush off howling like a beast, or hurl herself headlong from those heights into the depths of the valley. Mercifully it did not come to that; she managed to quell her nerves and curb the mutinous malady, invoking the aid of the Virgin Mary and all the saints whose names she could remember. When she lay down to sleep, she felt calmer and like crying.

Since that ample refuge had a superabundance of bedrooms, meaning it had plenty of private, sheltered corners, the two women bedded down in one *chamber*, and in another, separated from the first by thick walls, the blessed Nazarín settled himself, soon falling into a peaceful slumber.

The young woman from Móstoles, however, could not get to sleep, and so violently did she twist and turn in bed, and so pathetic were her whimpers, sighs, and moans, as if talking to herself, that Ándara was kept awake too and asked her what was up. They started to chat and, as the words began to flow and the curiosity of the one wore down the reticence of the other, finally Beatriz told her companion all about it, including her awful doubts and temptations.

'Forget it, what you do is come clean and tell Don Nazarín the whole story,' said Ándara. 'Just think of that brute Pinto coming up here and killing the lot of us! It's not beyond him neither. And who'd defend us, when we're just a bunch of poor folks as counts for nothing? Our saint here will tell us what to do ... There's no need to worry with him around. You'll see how he'll come up with some *theorem* to save our bacon, without you getting up to no mischief.'

They talked on into the early hours of morning when, exhausted, they fell asleep. By the time they awoke, Nazarín had already for the last hour been lodged in his perch, watching the sun come up.

Ándara instructed her companion: 'Call him now; and when he comes down, you tell him.'

And then Beatriz, flooded with an inexpressible sense of relief, discovered her mouth had freed itself from the clamp that had stopped her telling her master about her dilemma; she felt the words, previously constrained by a wicked thought, ready to come flooding out and, not wanting to wait for Nazarín to come down of his own accord, she shouted out to him: 'Father, Father, come down, I need to talk to you.'

'I'm coming,' replied the priest, jumping from one stone down on to the next; 'but there's no need to rush, woman, there's plenty of time. I know what you've got to say.'

'How do you know if I haven't told you yet?'

'Never mind. See, here I am. You said you wanted ... Thank God you've decided to talk about it, my child. Something happened to you yesterday.'

'But Father, how do you know?' Beatriz asked in amazement.

'I have my ways.'

'Did you guess? Do you know things without seeing them or being told?'

'Yes, sometimes ... Depending who the person is to whom something's happened without my seeing.'

'You mean to say you have the gift of prophecy ... ?'

'That's not prophecy ... It's ... knowing.'

IV

'Did you overhear Ándara and me talking from your bedroom last night?'

'No, my child. You can't hear a thing from my *apartments*. Besides, I slept like a log. It's just that ... Last night, when we were saying our prayers, I noticed you kept getting things wrong and you weren't concentrating, when you never normally get things muddled or lose your concentration. Then I observed a scared look in your eyes ... I realized that when you went down to the village for water, you must have had an unpleasant encounter. Your face spoke almost as clearly as your lips would have done. And then ... I can see the signs on your face right now ... there was a violent storm raging in your soul, with claps of thunder and flashes of lightning. There's no way you can hide an emotional tempest or battle like that: the havoc it wreaks is too obvious, like a trail of uprooted trees left by a hurricane. You've been through some kind of struggle ... Satan touched your heart with his infernal finger, blackened with soot, running it all over your poor human frame. The angels did their best to defend you. You wouldn't give them the space they needed. You held back for a long, long time before deciding to which of them you would cede the terrain, and finally ...'

Beatriz burst into violent sobs.

'Cry now, cry till you melt, that's the sign the angels have won the fight. This time victory is yours. Prepare your soul so next time the going is easier. Temptation will try to ensnare you again. Gird yourself so you don't fall into its net.'

There was not much else the poor woman needed to say to fill Nazarín in with the details of her encounter with Pinto, and the ensuing conflict in her soul. Sobbing and sighing she blurted the whole story out, adding that now her conscience made her feel sure she wouldn't sin again even in thought; the terrible doubts wouldn't torment her again, and the Devil wouldn't lay a hand or finger on her. Ándara could not refrain from sticking her oar in, as always, and interjected: 'Well, now she's escaped those terrible temptations of hers, it's high time we set about escaping that brute and his knife or else, as sure as my name's Ana, that Pinto'll be here tonight with his butcherboys and they'll massacre the lot of us.'

'Yes, yes,' added Beatriz. 'We'll be safe if we run away. We can sneak down the other side of the hill here, it's covered in oak trees and no one'll see us. Then we can disappear over that hilltop, and by nightfall we'll be ten miles away or more and that wretch can come looking for us all he likes.'

'He will too. He's a nasty piece of work, and his mates are no better! Come on, Father.'

'Father, let's be off.'

'Run away . . . run away! How can you be so silly, have you taken leave of your senses?' said Nazarín with a stern smile, having let them give vent to their fear. 'Run away, you and I! From someone like that! Criminals run away, not people who've done nothing wrong. Thieves run away, not people who've no possessions to their name and who give what they get to whoever needs it. And run away for what reason? Because an insolent, spiteful man has said he'll come and kill us! Let him come. I'm well aware human justice won't bend over backwards to protect poor people like us. But what about God's eternal justice, which manifests itself in things high and low, in the tapestry of private life as much as in that of history, will that leave us defenceless? You can't have much faith in the workings of Divine Justice, in the guiding hand of God Almighty, if you quake like that at a villain's threats. Don't you realize the weak are the strong, just as the poorest are the richest? No, my daughters, it wouldn't be right for us to turn tail and surrender the citadel of our conscience, which can never be stormed; and that means we shouldn't be afraid of persecution, humiliation, martyrdom, or even death. So let the petty tyrant come and try to slit our throats. Has he got nothing better to do than slaughter poor defenceless people who are doing no one any harm? Truly I say to you,* my daughters, that if, instead of that wretch prompted by Satan to come and attack us, Satan himself were to appear with the combined forces of his fiercest, most vicious demons, I wouldn't be afraid and I'd not move from this spot. Stop shaking, and tonight we'll sit up waiting for these murderous gentleman sent by Herod to re-enact in our times the massacre of the innocents.'

'But it wouldn't do no harm', Ándara announced, her pride and bellicose instincts fired by her master's words, 'to be armed and at the ready. Pilgrims, to the barricades! As for me, even if it's only with the potato peeler, I'll do my bit to let those scoundrels know we don't put our heads on the block that easy.'

'All I've got is a pair of scissors that are too blunt to cut or hurt anyone,' said Beatriz.

And Nazarín, smiling, added: 'We've no need of scissors and knives, nor deadly rifles and mighty cannons; we've got better weapons than that, weapons that are more effective against whatever enemies Hell unleashes and sends against us. So keep calm and carry on as normal all day. If we run out of water, Ándara can go down to fetch some; and you, Beatriz, are to stay here. Behave as if nothing were going on and there were nothing to be afraid of; and may your hearts be as easy as your consciences are clear.'

With these words they both calmed down, and Beatriz was freed from the mental convulsions that had gripped her since the previous evening. After breakfast they busied themselves with various chores, one of them darning, the other making the stew for lunch and collecting firewood on the nearby hillside. In the afternoon Ándara went down to the village, spent a while in the church and toured the village asking for alms, getting quite a good response. In one house they gave her a bag of stale bread, in another an egg, and in several places coins and vegetables. Then she went to fill her pitcher at the fountain and arrived back at the castle as night was beginning to fall. She had no unpleasant encounters, and only one of the people she met said anything that gave cause for alarm. Who was that? Now you shall know.

On the two occasions she and Beatriz had been in the church with Nazarín, they had seen there the most grotesque, ridiculous, and ugly dwarf you could possibly imagine. He was a beggar too, and they kept coming across him in the street as they plied their trade. The said dwarf had the free run of every house, rich and poor, in all of them being subjected to practical jokes and taunts. People would shower him with breadcrumbs to watch them bounce off his monstrous head; they would give him the most ridiculous cast-offs and make him dress up in them on the spot; they would force him to eat the vilest things in return for money or cigarettes, and he provided the local lads with an excuse to live in a permanent state of carnival. The poor creature would retreat into the church to recover from such taxing attentions, and could be seen there during mass or the reciting of the rosary, huddled against a pew or under the holy-water stoup. At first sight, you would have thought he was a head scuttling around on its own accord, on two tiny feet set under his chin. Out of the sides of his green vest, a bit like the cover of a partridge-cage, there stuck out two unbelievably tiny, spindly arms. By contrast his head was abnormally large and utterly hideous, with a snout for a nose, a pair of brogues for ears, clumps of straggly hair for a moustache and beard, and beady mouse-like eyes that looked at each other, for he had a terrible squint. His voice was high-pitched like a child's, his speech crude and malicious. People called him *Ujo*, though it was not clear whether this was his Christian name or surname or functioned as both.

Those who went into the church not informed of the existence of that pitiful aberration of Nature would get a dreadful fright, seeing a gigantic head scurrying around some two feet above ground level, and would think it was some devil that had escaped from the painting over the altar depicting the souls in purgatory. That was Beatriz's reaction when she first set eyes on him, and her screams made the half dozen women praying in the church jump. Ándara burst out laughing, and teasingly engaged him in amorous repartee. From that moment on they became the best of friends, and whenever they saw one another they would exchange greetings: 'How's life treating you today? . . .', 'Not so bad but not as good as you're looking . . . How's the family?'

Contrary to appearances, poor Ujo was a kind man or perhaps one should say a kind dwarf or kind monster. One afternoon, for example, he gave Beatriz two oranges, a fruit hard to find in those parts, and the next day three strawberries and a handful of peas, from the generous pickings he always got by allowing himself to be the butt of everyone's humour. And he told them that, if they were still there in the grape season, he'd give them as many bunches as they could eat. Needless to say, Ujo knew everyone who lived in the village and everyone who came in on market-day, for he was an integral part of the community, like the weather-vane on the churchtower, the coat of arms on the Town Hall, or the face that formed the spout of the village fountain. Every carnival has its dragon,* and every village has its Ujo. That afternoon, after saying hello to Ándara in the church, he struck up the following conversation with her:

'Where's your friend then?'

'She's not come down today.'

'She's a bit of all right, Christ Almighty . . . ! To think they says she's sweet on . . . Now look 'ere, you lot up at the castle, Christ Almighty, you just watch it; the best thing you can do is be *begone*, some ugly customers in the village, Christ Almighty, they knows you, and they says yourself, the ugly one they says, back there you was a regular 'arlot, and 'er, the pretty one, 'ad something going with Manolito, the nephew of the Vinagre woman what lives 'ere, Pinto they calls 'im. And they's saying yourself and 'er, and *tother* one like a Moorish tramp, the three of you's going around together thieving . . . A pack of lies, I knows it is, but that's what folks be saying, and from what they says it looks like trouble, Christ Almighty . . . If I was you I'd stay put 'ere and let them others be *begone* . . . Go on, Ándara; I fancies you . . . Now there ain't no one 'ere to 'ear us, I can say I fancies you, Ándara...*Tother* day, when I *gived* you that egg, remember, I was *agoing* to say, "Ándara, I fancies you"; but I didn't dare, Christ Almighty. Want another egg? A bit of crackling?...'

The wench cut him short and ran out into the street. Just imagine coming out with things like that in church! The cheeky little *midge*! But if she was disturbed and alarmed by the news that Pinto was spreading rumours about them and the villagers were saying they were robbers, she could not help laughing at Ujo's declaration of love in that holy place, right in front of Our Saviour and the blessed saints. Who'd have thought it, that little tiddler, making improper suggestions like that, trying to be a man when he wasn't even a proper human being! Anyone'd think she was a freak like him! So he fancied her, did he! What a giggle...! Well I never, that ugly little *chimp*!

On her way up the hill to the castle, she forgot about the grotesque proposal, so concerned was she about the danger they were in; but when she reached the top the cool, clear air and the sight of her companions banished fear from her mind and, remembering the expression on Ujo's face as he came out with his declaration, she couldn't stop laughing. She announced she'd found herself a suitor in God's house and, when she told them it was the *midge*, Don Nazario and Beatriz had a good laugh too, and so they whiled away the hours till it was time for prayers and supper, which was lively because no one would eat the egg and, it having done the rounds and found no takers, they decided to draw lots for it. So they did and it fell to Beatriz, who refused to be singled out by fate, so finally their master resolved the stalemate by dividing it into three portions of equal size.

Evening gave way to night and the skies above were bathed in brilliant moonlight. The Moor climbed up to his watchtower, from where he surveyed not so much the firmament as the earth, as did the two women from the remains of a turret window, tense and on the alert. From the top of that stark, jaw-like pinnacle, Nazarín tried to steady their nerves with words of encouragement, even with the odd joke. Like a mystical bird, he soared high into the realms of the spirit without forgetting reality below and the need to care for his family of fledglings. The surrounding hillside was thick with silence, occasionally broken by the moans of the wind caressing the ruined walls, or by the scuttling of the nocturnal creatures that had their home in the undergrowth or in the rocks on which the castle was built.

Although the leader of the penitent community was his usual calm self, he decided the three of them should stay up all night to save the butchers the trouble of having to wake them up. The time passed uneventfully till twelve o'clock, when they heard sounds of movement at the bottom of the hill, dogs barking . . . Yes, someone was coming up. But they were still a long way off, whoever they were. Then the noise stopped as if they'd turned back, and half an hour later it started again, this time louder and clearly identifiable as the voices of three or four people beginning to make their way up the slope.

Don Nazario climbed down from his tower to take a closer look, and the three of them had not been long at their posts when they observed that the valley was no longer clearly visible. A mist was closing in, growing ever thicker, and as the moonlight met the fog it produced a dense, milky haze, obscuring everything below. The sound of voices was coming nearer.

In less than a quarter of an hour the fog spread and thickened, rising till it had wrapped in its flimsy veil roughly the bottom third of the hill. The voices started to move away. Half an hour later, the cloud was halfway up the hillside. The peak rose clear above it, and those who stood on it felt as though they were in a gigantic ship floating in a sea of cotton wool.* The sound of voices ceased.

V

Ordering them to bed, Nazarín stayed up and prayed till dawn, whose beauty he could not appreciate because of the mist. At 8.00 the valley was still shrouded in its hazy mantle, and when Ándara and Beatriz emerged from their dens they gave thanks to the Lord for sending them that blessed, timely relief, for the evil assassins had clearly tried to come up the hill and that wall of white had blocked their path. Nazarín exhorted them never to use expressions of hatred, not even against their worst enemies; he started by teaching them to forgive evil and love those who do us harm, and to rid our hearts of all trace of anger. Pinto and his associates might or might not be evil-doers. Who could tell? They'd have to make their reckoning with the Supreme Judge. The three of them should not pass judgement or speak unkindly of them, even if they had their knives at their throats. 'And to conclude, my beloved daughters, I think it's time to end this little holiday we've awarded ourselves after our previous ordeal. Tomorrow we'll continue on our pilgrim's way and today, the last we'll spend in this feudal mansion, we'll take a walk along the left bank of the river, as far as those villages you can see over there.'

He had just stopped speaking when they heard a voice coming uphill, singing a merry song. Look as they might they could see no one; but the two women recognized the voice even if they couldn't put a face to it. Finally, sticking out of the undergrowth, they spotted a carnival giant's head* working its way up the slope. 'Why it's Ujo, my sweetheart!' exclaimed Ándara, laughing. 'Here comes my one and only little boy . . . Ujo my love, my little *midge*, what have you done with that little body of yours, Christ Almighty? We can only see your head.'

By the time he got to the top, the poor monster was completely out of breath. Crossing his legs, he settled his almost invisible body on top of them, and on top of that propped his enormous head. As he had no neck, his chin almost touched his nipples. He was wearing a soldier's hat and the green partridge-cage cover. Sitting on the ground, he was hardly any shorter than when standing.

'Like something to eat, my sweet little Ujo?' the wench asked him. 'What brings you here?'

'Nothing if it ain't the pleasure of saying I fancies you, Christ Almighty.'

'And I fancy you too, my little baby face, my one and only little snail. Tired yourself out then? Like some bread?'

'No; I got some 'ere. And this bit's for you, white flour and egg it's got, see? There you go... Morning, Señá Beatriz; Mister Zarín, God be with you ... Well, I'm come to tell you, you'd best be *begone* ... Last night Pinto and 'is crowd was all set to come up 'ere; but what with the fogginess and that, they 'ad to pack it in. They couldn't see no further than the ends of their noses, Christ Almighty! Today they's gone off with the cattle ... Christ Almighty, the cattle they got! At the first clang of bells for early morning Mass, they was up and away already. But you ain't to think you can breathe free yet, Christ Almighty. Rumour 'as it there be robbers around ... A pack of lies they's telling! I fancies you, Ándara ... But steer clear of the Civil Guard;* they says they's saying if they gets their 'ands on you, they'll cart you off in a chain-gang, like a load of *terrorizers* and criminals, Christ Almighty.'

Nazarín replied that they weren't terrorists and if the Civil Guard took them to be such they'd soon be disappointed, and for that reason they weren't going to run away or leave a place where they were bothering no one. The *midge*, paying scant attention to this rebuff, tugged at Ándara's skirt to draw her to one side, saying to her: 'Let the Moor be *begone* with his Mooress, and you stay 'ere with me, ugly face. No one ain't going to lay their 'ands on you; why, you's too ugly and I fancies you ... Know I fancies you, Ándara? What's that you says? Me uglier than you? Christ Almighty, if that ain't why! You's ugly, you's a whore, and I fancies you ...! I never fancied no one before ... and I took a fancy to you when I first *seed* you, Christ Almighty!'

The wench's shrieks of mirth brought the others over and poor Ujo, abashed, could only repeat: '*Begone, begone,* or else you'll see ... Robbers ...! Chain-gang ...!'

'The little *midge* fancies me. Let him say it again ... He's my sweetheart, ain't that right? Why, of course I'll stay with my little baby face, my little tortoise. Say you fancy me again. I like to hear you say it ...'

'I fancies you, I does,' Ujo repeated through clenched teeth, detecting a mocking look in Beatriz's eye. 'Folks can think what they likes, I fancies you, Christ Almighty.'

And he scuttled off. Ándara shouted farewell to him as, sulking and slapping his head, he went or seemingly rolled downhill, not turning to look at the castle's three inhabitants. An hour later, the latter were descending the opposite slope from the one leading to the village, and walking along the left bank of the River Perales, following it downstream. They passed the spot where it flows into the River Alberche, and a bit further on they saw some labourers working in the vineyards. Nazarín offered to help, for a coin or two, and if nothing was forthcoming they'd lend a helping hand anyway, if they'd no objection. The labourers, who looked well fed and well disposed towards them, handed a spade to Nazarín, another to Beatriz, and gave the wench from Polvoranca a hoe to break up the earth. One of them picked his shotgun up off the ground and, firing a few shots into a nearby clump of bushes, got three rabbits, one of which he gave to the penitents.

'Sir,' Nazarín said to him, 'you'll be richly rewarded for this harvest.'

One of the women struck up conversation with Beatriz as they rested for a minute, and asked if Nazarín was her husband; when she replied that he wasn't, and that neither of the two women was married, she frantically crossed her face and chest. Then she wanted to know if they were gypsies, or the sort that go round villages mending pots and pans ... Were they the ones who were there last year with a bear on a chain with a ring through its nose, and a monkey that fired a pistol? They weren't; so who the deuce were they? Were they good Catholic folk or did they belong to some *protesting* sect? Beatriz replied that they were as Catholic as the next man, and what more need she say. Another woman with a dour look about her was afraid those foreign vagabonds would cast the evil eye on a skinny little girl dozing in her arms. They all gathered round and started muttering, and eventually the man with the gun summoned Nazarín to tell him: 'Here my good man, take this farthing and the rabbit and clear off, Ufrasia's got it into her head you've bewitched the little girl.'

Without complaining at this rude dismissal, they withdrew quietly and meekly. 'We must bear humiliation in silence, my daughters; our easy conscience is our consolation.' Further on they came across some more men cleaning out a ditch or pond that functioned as a watering-hole, and that in the recent storms had got clogged up with mud, roots, and other substances washed down from the nearby sewers. Nazarín offered his services and the deal was accepted. They ordered him to wade into the black slime up to his knees and Ándara did the same, hitching her petticoats up. With a series of buckets passed from one to the other and thence to a third party, they gradually drained that stinking sludge mixed with putrescent matter, and the others helped with spades. Beatriz jumped in the air with a squeal, feeling a yard-long snake coil itself round her ankle. Fortunately it was not poisonous. There was laughter and mirth, the reptile was caught, and after an hour and a half the watering-hole was clean and the penitents received three farthings for their costly labours.

They went down to the river to wash the slime off their legs, and as they were climbing up the bank, clean and ready to carry on their way, they were surprised by two sinister-looking men, with emaciated, bilious faces, their clothes in tatters, who leapt out of a thick clump of bushes and, shouting wildly, ordered them to halt.

Without further explanation one of them, waving a huge knife, intimated that they were to drop everything they had, be it money, jewels, or food. The other one, who must have had a droll sense of humour, said they were Civil Guards in disguise, and were under government orders to arrest all the thieves they found and strip them of the stolen goods on their persons. Ándara bravely wanted to resist; but Nazarín instructed them to hand over bread, farthings, rabbit, and all, and not content with that, the blackguards subjected them to a scrupulous search, which left Beatriz without her scissors and Ándara without her comb. And the joke was not yet over. As they backed away, under the bandits' strict instructions, the latter indulged in the senseless diversion of stoning them, grazing Nazarín's skull which started to bleed profusely. They had to go back down to the river, where the two women washed his head and then bandaged it with two cloths, first a white one, and on top the big check scarf Beatriz usually wore round her head. That turban added the final touch to the fervent hermit's Arabian image. Beatriz put his cap on her head, and they set off back to the castle.

'I've got a feeling in my bones,' said Ándara, 'that bad times are on the way. So far our luck's held out. Folks have given us food, been kind to us and treated us well; we worked our little miracle in Móstoles, and in Villamanta we were regular saints. Everybody happy and waiting on us hand and foot. But now things are starting to go against us; it's like the lottery, the way things change from one day to the next.'

'That's enough silly prattle,' Nazarín chided her, tired from the long walk and the heat of the sun, and flopping down in the shade of some holm-oaks. 'Don't equate divine providence with the lottery, that's just a matter of chance. If the Lord visits adversities on us, He must have His reasons. We mustn't utter the slightest complaint or for a single moment doubt the justice of Our Father in heaven.'

Beatriz sat down beside him; and the wench from Polvoranca started rummaging around on the ground for acorns. The three of them fell into a sombre, gloomy silence. Not a sound was heard but for the buzzing of the bluebottles beneath the trees. Ándara kept wandering off and coming back. The girl from Móstoles broke the silence, saying to her master:

'Father, there's an idea going round my head, an idea...'

'A presentiment?'

'That's it...I can't help feeling our luck is going to change, we're going to suffer.'

'I think so too.'

'If God wishes, that is.'

'We shall suffer, yes; me more than the two of you.'

'Why not the two of us? That's not fair. No, we'll suffer as much as you and if need be more.'

'No, let me be the one who suffers most.'

'And is that really what you think is going to happen? Is it a prophecy?'

'No, it's not a prophecy. The Lord tells me in my heart of hearts. I know his voice. It's as certain we shall endure great suffering, Beatriz, as that this is the light of day.'

A new silence. Ándara moved further off, stooping to gather acorns in her skirt.

VI

Seeing the good Nazarín look glum and pensive, when it was usually he who urged them on with his serene example and even with cheery words, Beatriz felt her soul suddenly blaze with love for the saint who led and guided them. She had felt the same fire before but never as intensely as then. Later, analysing her feelings in depth, she decided that state of mind ought not to be compared to a consuming holocaust that burns and destroys, but to a rush of water miraculously spouting from a rock and pouring out in a torrent. A river was running through her soul and, welling up from her throat, it gushed forth in these words:

'Father, I'd like you to know that, when that great suffering comes, I want to be able to love you with all the love in my soul, a love as pure as the love one has for an angel. And if, by taking your suffering on myself, I could take it off your shoulders, I'd do it no matter how terrible the pain.'

'My child, you love me as a teacher who knows a little more than you, and who helps you learn. I love you, I love both of you, as a shepherd loves his sheep, and if you go astray I'll come looking for you.'

'Promise me, Father,' Beatriz added carried away by her ardour, 'that you'll always love us as much, and swear that whatever happens we'll not be parted.'

'I never swear, and even if I were to, how could I promise you what you ask? If I have any say in the matter, we'll stay together; but what if men force us to part?'

'And what have men got to do with us?'

'Why, they're the ones who wield power, the ones who rule this kingdom so inferior to the kingdom of the soul. Just now two villains sprang on us and robbed us. Others may separate us by force.'

'Anything but that. Ándara and I won't let it happen.'

'You're not making allowances for being frail and faint-hearted.'

'The two of us faint-hearted? Don't say such things, Father.'

'Besides it's your duty to obey and respect others, and to conform to God's designs.'

Ándara came up to show them the acorns she'd found and wandered off again. A short while later, Beatriz was suddenly seized by a desperate weariness. It was like a dose of sedatives after that spasm of devotion. She couldn't keep her eyes open.

'Father,' she said to Nazarín, 'we didn't go to bed last night and I'm so sleepy.'

'Well, sleep now while you can, you may well not sleep tonight either.'

With a truly angelic simplicity and innocence, Beatriz leant her head on Nazarín's shoulder,* and fell straight asleep like a babe at its mother's breast. The errant hermit stayed gazing at the ground. Deciding eventually it was time to go back to the castle, he looked around for the other woman and saw her sitting some thirty yards away, her back turned to him and her head hanging. 'Ándara, what's the matter?'

The wench did not answer.

'But what's the matter with you, my child? Come here. What's this? Are you crying?'

Ándara got up and came over to him, dragging her feet and wiping her eyes with the hem of the skirt in which she was carrying the acorns she'd picked off the ground.

'Come here . . . What's the matter now?'

'Nothing, Father.'

'No; something's wrong. Have you had some evil thought? Or is it that your heart senses misfortune ahead? Tell me.'

'It's not that . . .' the wench finally replied, unable to find the right words to express her feelings. 'It's that . . . We all got our self-respect . . . I mean . . . our bit of pride . . . and we don't like it if . . . All right, I'll say it straight: if you love Beatriz more than me.'

'Heavens . . . ! Is that what . . . ?'

'Well, it ain't fair, because the two of us love you just the same.'

'And I love the two of you equally too. But what made you think I . . . ?'

'You always says the prettiest things to Beatriz and not to me. I know I'm thick and she's smart . . . real quick on the uptake . . . That's why she gets treated nice; and all I get is, "What do you know about that, Ándara? Stop blaspheming . . ." Never mind, I know no one cares about me except Ujo . . .'

'Well, what you've just said isn't blasphemous, it's ridiculous. Me love one of you more than the other! I may treat you differently, because your temperaments are different,* but there's no difference in the way I feel towards you. Come here, silly, and if you're feeling tired because you didn't get to bed last night either, come and lean your head on this other shoulder here, and have a little sleep.'

'No, it's getting late,' said Ándara, her tantrum over. 'If we're not careful, it'll be dark before we get back.'

'There's no way we'll get back before dark. We'll be lucky if we make it before 9.00 . . . And tonight we've got a wholesome meal of plain acorns to look forward to.'

'Those scoundrels cleaned us out all right. Ah, if I could get my hands on them . . . !'

'No insults and threats . . . Come on, this one's waking up. Ready? Off we go.'

Before it struck 9.00 they were climbing wearily up to the castle, and when they got there they camped out in the open. Supper wasn't going to take a lot of getting ready because all they had was the acorns* which, dressed with necessity more than appetite, were served and devoured forthwith. And just as they were starting to say grace and thank God for the frugal repast he had provided, they heard the sound of voices at the bottom of the hill, coming from the direction of the village. What could it be? And it wasn't just two or three people talking, but lots and lots of them. Ándara peered through the turret window and holy Mary!... not only did she hear the noise getting louder, but she saw a glow like a bonfire coming uphill, coming towards them with the voices.

'There's people coming,' she said to her companions, panic-stricken. 'And they've got beacons with them, or firebrands... You can hear their voices...'

'They're coming to arrest us,' stammered Beatriz, infected by the other woman's terror.

'To arrest us? What for? Well, we'll soon find out,' said Don Nazario. 'Carry on praying, it won't be long before we know the worst.'

He continued his prayers, for his resolute will curbed any emotion; but they, tense, scared, and jittery, ran around in circles, unable to decide whether to try to escape or shout for help... But who could they shout to? It didn't look as though this time the heavens were going to send a veil of fog to hide them.

And the noise was getting nearer, together with the ominous flicker of the torches. Now you could make out the clearest voices, and the sound of laughter and merriment; now you could catch the odd word. The procession was made up of men, women, and children, the latter lighting the way with bundles of gorse, passing the torches from hand to hand with gleeful cries as if celebrating Midsummer's Eve.*

'But what on earth...?' murmured Nazarín, remaining on his knees. 'Three harmless individuals and the authorities are sending an army against us?'

When the noisy retinue reached the summit, the two women spotted the Civil Guards. Their fate was clear.

'They're coming for us.'

'Well, here we are.'

'Excuse me, sirs,' said Ándara, 'is it us you're looking for?'

'You and Ali Baba there,' came the taunt from what seemed to be the mayor, as if the freedom or arrest of such humble folk were a laughing matter.

'And where's that blackamoor? I want to see him,' bellowed a fat brute of a fellow from the front ranks.

'If it's me you're looking for,' said Nazarín still on his knees, 'here I am.'

'Hey you,' said another skinny man, 'this castle's no home for a Moorish prince like yourself. Come and try prison instead.'

And as he spoke, he gave him a hearty kick.

'Coward!' shouted Ándara, inflamed with sudden indignation and leaping on him like a tiger. 'You swine! Can't you see he's not resisting?'

And with the potato peeler she lunged at him so savagely that, if the weapon had had a blade and point, the cretin would have had a bad time of it. As it was, she ripped his shirt sleeve and took a strip of skin off his arm. The crowd hurled itself furiously on the spirited wench, who had to be protected by the Civil Guards. But so wildly and desperately did she struggle, they had to tie her wrists. At that point she felt someone tugging at her skirt, and saw Ujo's walking head scuttling between the guards' legs.

'Serve's you right for not doing what I says, Christ Almighty! But I still fancies you, I'll prove I fancies you.'

'Out of my way, bloody little *chimp*,' was Ándara's reply, and she spat in his face.

Nazarín had got up and said quite calmly: 'Why all this hue and cry just to arrest three defenceless people? Do what you like with us. Ándara, that was wrong of you! If you want God's forgiveness, say sorry to that gentleman you've just injured.'*

'Will I say sorry, Christ Almighty!'

Blind with rage, her blood boiling, she didn't know what she was doing.

Off they all set. First went Ándara, kicking and screaming, and trying to bite through the rope round her wrists; behind walked the saint and Beatriz, their hands unbound, flanked by a curious, insolent, callous mob. The Civil Guards had to fight the crowd off. The fat man, who was walking at Nazarín's side, had the cheek to say: 'So we're a Moorish prince, are we ... a Moorish prince in exile ... ? And the crafty blighter's brought his harem with him!'

The mayor, who was flanking Nazarín on the other side,

came out with a loud guffaw and corrected his friend's statement: 'If he's a Moor, I'll eat my hat. As for this Sultana here, I know her from Móstoles.'

Beatriz and Don Nazario said nothing, they did not even raise their eyes. The merry-making and festivities wound their way downhill. It was more like a carnival celebration than a criminal arrest. As the flares had gone out, women and children kept bumping into one another, tripping and scrambling back to their feet, and at one point in the twisting path Ujo's head went rolling down the slope. What with the laughter, singing, and ribald quips, it was to all intents and purposes a public holiday for that village where the opportunities for fun were few and far between. Some people treated the whole occasion as a huge joke, and would have liked there to be wayward Moors to arrest or taunt every day of the year. The high point of the show was the entry into the village because all the locals appeared on their doorsteps to take a look at the miscreants wanted by the courts in Madrid. The children relit the gorse or furze, and the smoke made it hard to breathe. Ándara, worn out by her exertions, finally gave up her futile attempts at resistance. The other two prisoners submitted to their misfortune without a murmur.

What they called the prison was a room with bars over the door, forming part of the ground floor of the Town Hall. To get to it, you had to go through a courtyard. The Civil Guards cleared a path through to the entrance and the prisoners were taken inside, where Ándara was untied. The mayor, who despite his excessive and importunate love of wisecracks was not without humanitarian sentiments, told them they'd be given supper, and taking Nazarín off to a nearby room, no less shabby and dingy than that used as a cell, held the following conversation with him, which we reproduce verbatim.

VII

'Take a seat; I have some questions to ask you.'
'Thank you. Go ahead.'

'Well, I didn't want to embarrass you in front of all those people. They think you're a Moor. An idea that's got into their uneducated, country heads! And the fact is, you look the part, with those African features, that pointed beard, and then that turban of yours. But I know you're not an Arab but a Christian, in name at least. And I know something else, though I'd never have guessed if it weren't stated in the warrant for your arrest: you're a priest.'

'Yes, sir, and my name's Nazario Zaharín, at your service and that of God.'

'So you declare you're the same Don Nazario Zaharín for whose arrest the magistrate at La Inclusa has issued a warrant, do you? And that ugly one's a woman called Ándara?'

'The one who had her wrists tied. The other one's called Beatriz, and she's from Móstoles.'

'No need to tell me that! I know her all right. Pinto's a cousin of mine.'

'And what else do you know about me?'

'What else do I need to know? Come on now, let's have a nice friendly chat,' said the mayor, taking off his broad-brimmed hat and putting it on the table, where a lantern cast its glow on the two men's faces: one of them ruddy and beaming, the other sombre and austere. 'Do you think it right and proper for a gentleman of the cloth to take to the roads like this... barefoot, in the company of two whores... well, not Beatriz... but that other one... In God's holy name, my dear Father! When you get to Madrid, I expect your lawyer will try to get you off on grounds of insanity, because if you're in your right mind, there's no soul in Christendom would defend you and no law that wouldn't declare you guilty.'

'I believe myself to be entirely sane,' replied Nazarín calmly.

'We'll see about that. I'd say you're not. If you're off your head, you'd be the last person to know! But for heaven's sake, Father Zaharín, choosing to live like a tramp, and keeping company with a couple of tarts...! And I'm not saying that on religious grounds; all of us claim to be believers, some of us more than others, because it's the thing to do, because we respect the status quo. I'm saying it for your sake, and out of consideration for society in these enlightened times. A priest going around like that...! And you should see the accusations against you! That you hid that jezebel in your house when she knifed another whore like herself; that then, between the two of you, you set fire to a building or a freehold property... And to cap it all, the two of you take to the roads, you as an apostle and she as your *lady apostle*, and prey on people's gullibility, curing the sick by offering them drinking water, raising fake corpses from the grave, and delivering sermons against those of us who've got a little something to fall back on... My, my, Father, and you say you're not mad! Tell me: how many miracles have you worked in this municipality? I heard you tamed the lion of lions, the owner of La Coreja... You can be honest with me, I won't take it out on you or betray your secrets. Tell me now, and forget I'm the mayor and you're just a prisoner under arrest. In this room there are only two good sporting fellows: an open-handed sort of mayor who doesn't stand on ceremony, and a little priest with itchy feet who's going to tell us all about his apostolic and *mussulmanic* adventures... all about them, mind you...! Wait a second: I'll send for some glasses.'

'No, please don't bother,' said Nazarín, interrupting the mayor's gesture. 'Listen to what I've got to say, which will be brief. First, sir, I don't drink.'

'Goodness gracious! Not even some lemonade? No wonder they take you for a Moor.'

'Second, I'm innocent of the crimes ascribed to me. I shall say that to the magistrate, and if he doesn't believe me, God knows my innocence and that's enough for me. Third: I'm not an apostle and I preach to no one; all I do is teach Christian doctrine, in its simplest, most basic form, to anyone who cares to listen. I teach it through my words and my example. Everything I say I put into practice, and I see no particular merit in doing so. If that's made them take me for a criminal, it's of no importance to me. My conscience accuses me of no crime. I've raised no one from the dead, nor have I healed the sick: I'm not a doctor and I can't work miracles, because God, my Lord and Master, has not given me the power to do so. That's all I have to say, sir, and that being so, you're free to do what you like with me, and whatever trials and humiliations fall on my head I accept them submissively and serenely, without fear or complacency either, for no one will find in me the sinner's pride or the bigot's conceit.'

The good mayor was left not a little disconcerted and non-plussed by these arguments, no doubt because he was expecting the priest to come out with some cynical confession, in other words to dance to his tune. But dance he wouldn't. So there were two possibilities: either Don Nazario was the most ingenious, crafty rogue God had ever let loose in the world as an example of his creative talents, or else he was . . . but who the deuce could tell what he was, or whether those grave words, spoken with such simplicity and dignity, were true or false?

'Well, sir, let's see now,' said the mayor, realizing wise-cracks would get him nowhere with a man like this. 'The thing is, if you take things so seriously and literally, you'll have a bad time of things. Be sensible and listen to me, I'm a practical man and, though I shouldn't say so myself, I've had my smaltering of education; a bit weak on the Latin but strong on common sense. This person you see before you had a go at studying for the priesthood; but the Church wasn't my cup of tea, I was more interested in what you can see with your eyes and touch with your hands, I mean the concrete world or factual knowledge, they're my forte. And how, in these practical times, these essentially practical times of ours, when there's so much factual knowledge around, am I to believe that a sensible man can take seriously the idea of teaching by his example everything that's written in the Gospels? It can't be done, my good man, it can't be done, and anyone who tries it is either mad or will end up falling victim to . . . yes sir, falling victim to . . .'

He couldn't find a way of finishing the sentence. Nazarín didn't want to get into an argument, and answered him crisply but politely:

'I believe the opposite. It not only can be done, it is being done.'

'But come on now,' continued the mayor, realizing or sensing his opponent's powers of refutation, and wanting to rise to the occasion by appealing to the arguments he remembered from his trite, superficial reading. 'How are you going to convince me it can be done...? Me, a man of the nineteenth century, the age of the steam engine, the electric telephone and the printing press, that vehicle... of public and private freedom, this age of progress, that flood-tide... this age when knowledge has freed us from all that old-fangled fanaticism! Why, that's the word for what you're saying and doing, fanaticism! I wouldn't criticize religion as such, or object to us accepting the Holy Trinity, even though the best mathematicians can't make head or tail of it; I respect the beliefs of our elders, the Catholic Mass, religious processions, christenings, funerals with all the trappings, etcetera... What's more, I wouldn't deny that there *be*... I mean, are souls in Purgatory, and that bishops and cardinals are a good thing, and parish priests too of course... and if pushed I'll even accept things like papal bulls... right... and I'll also concede there's got to be a *big beyond*, and it all needs to be said in Latin... But that's my lot, adherence to tradition and all that. I respect religion, I've a lot of respect for the Virgin and even pray to her when the children fall sick... But give me a bit of leeway; don't ask me to believe things that are fine for women but not the sort of things we men should believe in... No, that's not for me. Don't give me that line. I don't believe you can put into practice all the sayings and teachings of that great social reformer, that genius... I wouldn't belittle him, not at all, that exceptional being...! And my arguments for maintaining it can't be done are as follows: man's goal is to live. You can't live without eating. You can't eat without working. And in this age of progress, what must man look to? Industry, agriculture, bureaucracy, trade. Now there's the rub! Boosting our wine exports, balancing the books in the public and private sector... building loads of factories... transport systems... workers' clubs... workers' housing...

education, schools, public and private welfare...Not to
mention sanitation, urbanization, and other major advances...Well, your mysticism won't bring us any of that;
what it'll bring is starvation, public and private ruin...
Just like the monasteries and convents before!* The nineteenth century has said: we don't want religious orders
and seminaries but trade treaties. We don't want hermits
but great economists. We don't want sermons but narrow-
gauge railways. We don't want Church fathers but chemical
fertilizers. Oh, my good sir, the day we have a university in
every modern town, an agricultural credit bank in every
street, and an electric machine for cooking in the kitchen of
every home; oh, when that day comes there'll be no more
room for mysticism! And I like to think...this is all my own
idea...that if Our Lord Jesus Christ were alive today, he'd
think the same as me, and would be the first to give his
blessing to our advances and would say: "This is my age, not
the one I lived in...My age is this and not my own."'

He came to an end, and mopped his perspiring brow with
his handkerchief; it had been no mean task for him to
deliver, birth pangs into the bargain, that lengthy erudite
speech with which he expected to knock the unhappy hermit
for six. The latter gave him a pitying look; but since
politeness and his customary humility would not let him
reply with the contempt he felt he deserved, he simply said:
'My dear sir, you speak a language I don't understand. The
language I speak is also incomprehensible to you, at least for
the time being. Let's say no more.'

The mayor was not of this discreet opinion, being not a
little put out that his well-chosen and well-turned arguments
had made no impact on that fanatic or cynic or whatever he
was, and he decided a different approach was needed to
make him lose his cool. A tortoise like this would stick his
neck out only if you put a firebrand to his shell. So fire was
what he would get, meaning sarcasm, ridicule, and scorn.

'Don't be like that, Father; if you're going to take it all so
seriously, forget everything I've said. I'm an ignorant man
who's only read things of our century, theology's not my
strong point. So let's say you're a saint. Well, I'll be the first

to take my hat off to you, and I'll even carry you through the streets on my shoulders if it comes to that. You'll see how the people will bow and worship; and you can do your bit by giving us a couple of miracles, real big ones, mind you, like multiplying our wine vats, and bringing us the new bridge that's planned for the future, and the Great Western Railway, which is our prime *desideratum* . . . And on top of that you'll find plenty of hunchbacks to straighten, blind men whose sight needs restoring, cripples dying for you to tell them to get up and walk, not to mention the dead in the cemetery who, as soon as you summon them, will come rushing out to parade round the village and see the improvements they owe to me . . . So there's the new Jesus Christ for you . . . all mankind's problems solved! The whole world will be ablaze when word gets round we're preaching the coming of the new millennium! "Public and private salvations undertaken. For a modest fee." The truth of the matter is that right now we're sending you to jail. The time for suffering has come, comrade. But you won't be crucified: you'll escape that fate. No need to steel yourself, Father, that kind of martyrdom is out of fashion nowadays, it's a thing of the benighted past; you won't enter Madrid on the back of a donkey but escorted by the Civil Guard; you won't be received with palms unless it's a slap in the face. And what's this barbarous religion you're bringing us anyway? My bet is it's the Mohammedan creed . . . and that's why you've brought your Moorish harem with you . . . to preach by your example, of course . . .'*

As Nazarín took no notice and remained unruffled, showing no signs of being the slightest bit affected by his jibes, the worthy mayor was thrown off balance once again, and changing tack and adopting a bantering, familiar tone, he slapped him on the back and said:

'Cheer up, good man, don't let it get you down. These things are sent to try us. This going round preaching like an apostle, my dear friend, has its ups and downs, especially when it falls on deaf ears. But not to worry; the law will be satisfied with shutting you up in a madhouse, and you won't even get a flogging, that's a thing of the past . . . "Penance without pain, I mean without the whip... Death and martyrdom, with tea and toast..." Ho ho...! Anyway, as long as you're in this civilized borough you'll be well looked after because the law is one thing but enlightened thinking is another. And if what I've said has needled you, treat it as a joke, that's my style... As you can see, I'm a sporting sort of fellow... which doesn't mean I don't commiserate with your misfortune. I'll put my staff of office to one side, and we're not mayor and prisoner any more, but two good chums who like a bit of a laugh, a couple of old dogs who know a few tricks, agreed...? And by the way, you could have found yourself a better class of dame for your harem. Beatriz's not so bad. But that other one...! Where on earth did you pick up that sight for sore eyes...? Anyway you must want something to eat.'

Nazarín responded only to this last sentence:

'I'm not hungry, sir. But I imagine those poor women could do with some food.'

VIII

Meanwhile in the prison proper, the two women, the two Civil Guards, and a few individuals who had wangled their way in, among them that important personage Ujo, were busy chatting away. Beatriz, as soon as they got inside, went up to one of the guards, a tall, good-looking lad with an attractive military mien, and tapping him on the sleeve said:

'Hey, are you Corporal Mondéjar?'

'At your service, Beatriz.'

'So you recognized me?'

'Why, of course!'

'I wasn't quite sure, I was thinking: I could swear that's Corporal Cirilo Mondéjar, who used to be stationed in Móstoles.'*

'I recognized you; but I didn't like to say anything. It upset me to see you with that crowd. And you might as well know there's no charge against you, if you're in jail it's of your own choosing. The warrant of arrest is for him and that other woman. The only reason we've brought you here is because you were with them. Anyway, the mayor will tell you whether you can go or whether you're to stay.'

'The mayor can say what he likes, I'm staying with my friends.'

'Even if they march you off in a chain-gang?'

'Whatever happens, and if they lock them up in jail, I'll go too. And if they have to appear before the High Court, I'll be there with them. And if it's the gallows, they can hang the three of us.'

'Beatriz, you're out of your mind. We'll leave you in Móstoles with your sister.'

'I said I'm going wherever Don Nazario goes, and nothing will make me abandon him to his fate. Do you know what I'd do if I could? Why, I'd take on my shoulders all the trials and tribulations that lie in store for him, all the insults they're going to hurl at him, all the maltreatment and punishment he's going to endure . . . But how silly of me, Cirilo! I nearly forgot to ask: How's Demetria, your wife?'

'She's fine.'

'I'm very fond of Demetria. And tell me, how many children have you got now?'

'One . . . and another one on the way . . .'

'God grant them good health . . . And you're happy, aren't you?'

'Not complaining.'

'Well, watch out, don't offend God or he may punish you.'

'Me? What for?'

'For persecuting the good, and I don't mean myself.'

'You mean the male prisoner? It's nothing to do with us guards. That's the judge's problem.'

'Judge, mayor, Civil Guards, it's all the same thing. They don't stop to think, they've no sense of what's right and wrong . . . And I don't mean you, Cirilo, you're a good soul. You won't persecute God's elect or let the wicked torture him.'

'Beatriz, are you crazy or what's got into you?'

'Cirilo, you're the one who's crazy if you let your soul be damned for siding with the wicked against the good. Think

of your wife, your children, and remember if you want God
to protect them, you must defend His cause.'

'How?'

Beatriz lowered her voice, for although everyone else there
was gathered round Ándara, chatting and laughing at the
other end of the cell, she didn't want to be overheard.

'Why, that's easy. When you take us off as prisoners, you
just turn a blind eye and we'll escape.'

'Sure, and I'll take a pot shot at you too.* Beatriz, don't
talk such nonsense. Don't you know how the Civil Guard
operates? Don't you know what our orders are? And you can
come out with a hare-brained idea like that! I'll not disobey
orders for anything in the world, and rather than shame my
uniform, I'd prefer to lose wife, children, and all. It's a point
of honour, and it's not my personal honour that's at stake,
Beatriz, it's the honour of the Force . . . Of course it'd be nice
to be moved by pity . . . But in the whole of the Force you'll
not find a single officer who is, moved by pity I mean, not
when on duty. The Civil Guard doesn't know what pity is,
and when the Law, that's our reason for existence after all,
orders us to make an arrest, we make an arrest, and if it
orders us to shoot, we shoot.'

The good sergeant said this with such upright conviction
and honesty, and his eyes, his posture, his tone of voice so
clearly demonstrated his fervent devotion to the Order of
Chivalry of which he was a professed member, that the girl
hung her head and sighed, saying:

'You're quite right, I don't know what I'm saying. Don't
take any notice of me, Cirilo. Everyone has his own creed.'

The hangers-on who had come to find out what was going
on abandoned the corner where Ándara was, and came over
to Beatriz and the sergeant. The other wench was left with
only Ujo for company who, standing, came up to just above
the waist of his sweetheart, who was sitting down.

'I got something I want to say to you,' he said to her
as soon as he found himself alone with her, 'You treated
me bad, Christ Almighty . . . I thought you was better
mannered . . . But even if manners ain't your strong point,
and you gone and spat in my face, I still says I fancies you,

Christ Almighty ... I says it even if you goes and spits on me again.'

'Me spit on you?' Ándara replied gaily, recovered from her earlier bout of anger. 'I must have done it without meaning to, my little baby face, my funny little *midge*, everybody's little darling. That's just my style: when I want to say I fancy someone, I spit on him.'

'Want to know something else? When you went for Lucas, 'im at the inn, with that knife of yours ... all of a sudden you was real beautiful ... Christ Almighty, there I was seeing you and I never knowed it was you! 'Cos you's ugly, Ándara; and it's 'cos you's ugly and a fright I fancies you, and I'd take on the 'eavenly 'ost in person to get you out of trouble, Christ Almighty what art in 'eaven!'

'Bravo, my little shrimp, my little big-headed snail! Did you say that fellow I knifed is the innkeeper?'

'Old Lucas.'

'The other day you said you lived at the inn.'

'But I moved out yesterday after I got kicked by a mule. Now I lives with old Juan the blacksmith.'

'Oh, just think of my little snail all snug and cosy at the blacksmith's! Well, just you listen to me, Christ Almighty: you say you fancy me, do you?'

'Cross my 'eart.'

'Well, if you want me to believe you, what you've got to do is go and fetch me from where you're living, from the blacksmith's that is ... all the things I'm going to ask you for.'

'And what's that?'

'Some scrap iron. Get me some scrap iron. How you get it's up to you. He must have all sorts of junk lying around the place. And bring me some nails ... No, not nails ... Yes, yes, a couple of long nails; and then a knife, a good sharp one, mind you. And a file ... one that really eats into things ... Bring the whole lot nicely tucked away under that vest of yours, and ...'

They cut short the conversation when Nazarín came in together with the mayor, and the latter, making a show of his generosity and humanitarianism, qualities which were not incompatible with his being above all a jolly good fellow, said to them: 'Now, *mesdames*, how about a bite to eat? The supper's on me, I hope you realize; there's nothing in the kitty to cover expenses. As for you, Reverend Father, since you're not hungry, why don't you give those bones of yours a little rest . . . ? You guards there, the prisoner gives us his word he won't try to escape. Isn't that what our prophet here just said? And you, my lady disciples, had better watch your step. Luckily we've got a prison better than you could hope for in a village like ours, with iron bars the envy of the Model Prison in Madrid.* So, short of a miracle, you'll not be getting out of here. Right then . . . those who've come to nose around are in the way. Clear the cell. Ujo, out!'

Clear it they did, and the only people left, apart from the hapless penitents, were the mayor and the local magistrate who discussed the prisoners' transfer, which would have to wait for a day to allow them to join up with various other delinquents and vagabonds who had been picked up in Villa del Prado and Cadalso. Then the bailiff brought in the supper, which Ándara and Beatriz barely touched; the mayor said good night to them, the Civil Guards and bailiff locked up with much jangling of keys and grating of bolts, and the three unhappy prisoners spent the first half of the night in prayer, and the remaining half sleeping on the tiled floor. The following day brought some consolation as several of the villagers, concerned at their sorry plight, came to offer them food and clothing, which was not accepted. Ujo managed to climb up the door to the courtyard like a spider and, hanging on the bars, conversed with the two women. At night the other prisoners arrived who were also being sent to Madrid: namely, an old beggar, accompanied by a little girl whose provenance was being investigated by the courts, and two evil-looking fellows in whom Nazarín instantly recognized the bandits who had robbed them in the early evening of the day of their arrest. The two of them had broken out of prison in Madrid, where they were up before the High Court for parricide in one case, in the other for stealing from churches. All four were herded into the small room, which made everyone eager to be let out into the fresh air and for the chain-gang to be on its way. No matter how tough the going was, it could never be as bad as that pile of unwashed bodies packed into a dark, cramped, insanitary cell.

Next morning, at crack of dawn, once the necessary documents had been signed and sealed, they were given their marching orders. The mayor turned out to see Nazarín off, saying to him in his usual bantering fashion: 'Just to show you there's no hard feelings, my prophet friend; I'd like you to think of me as a pal, a good-humoured sort of fellow who's been much entertained by you and your gang, and the *sporting* way you've turned vagrancy into such a convenient, easy-going religion ... Ho ho! And I don't mean offence, I can't help admiring your genius, that grey matter you've got there ... Because there's no flies on this gentleman here, none at all, and I'm only sorry you didn't want to come clean with me ... I repeat that I don't mean offence. Actually I've taken quite a shine to you ... I wouldn't like you to go without us shaking hands. Here's some food I've brought for you to put in your knapsack.'

'Much indebted to you, sir.'

'And tell me: wouldn't you like some clothes, some old breeches of mine, some shoes or sandals ... ?'

'Many thanks. I've no need of clothes or shoes.'

'That pride of yours! Well, the gesture's genuine. It's your loss.'

'I'm extremely grateful for your kind attention.'

'Goodbye then. You know where we are. I'd be glad to see you get off, so you can carry on your mission. Believe you me, you'll attract plenty of disciples, especially if the government keeps on putting up the taxes ... Farewell ... Have a good trip ... Enjoy yourselves, girls.'

They left and, it being so early, not many people came out to give them a send off. First and foremost among the few curious stragglers was Ujo's swaying head, which continued to escort the object of his fancies till his tiny legs gave out. After being forced to fall behind, he could be seen leaning against a tree, his hand held to his eyes.

The Civil Guards made Nazarín and the old beggar take

the lead. Behind them came the little girl belonging to the latter, holding Beatriz's hand; then Ándara; next the two convicts, tied together by the elbows; and bringing up the rear, the Civil Guards, rifles slung over their shoulders. The sorry convoy made its way along the dusty road.* They walked in silence, reflecting on their several case-histories, which for their sins could not have been more different... They each carried their own world in their head, and the travellers or peasants who saw them pass by bracketed all those lives together under a common label: 'Vagrants, delinquents, scum'.

PART V

I

AFTER half an hour's walking, the old beggar, tired of Don Nazario's reluctance to talk, tried sounding him out:

'You must be used to these treks, eh comrade?'

'No, sir: it's the first time...'

'Well, in my case... I make this my fourteenth trip. If only the miles I've got under my belt were shilling pieces...! And I'll tell you something in all confidence: do you know who's to blame if I keep finding myself in this position? Why, Cánovas* himself... I'm not exaggerating.'

'Don't tell me!'

'You heard right. Because if Don Antonio Cánovas hadn't resigned the day he did, right now you'd see me reinstated in the job they threw me out of in 1842, all because of the Moderates* and their intrigues, yes sir, my nice little job as an *articulated* clerk on sixty pounds. My *province* was Customs and *Excision*. Well, Don Antonio messed me up by not hanging on for just one more day: the official order was all ready for His Majesty to sign... But there's so much scheming goes on...! They went so far as to bring the government down just to stop me getting my job back.'

'The lengths people will go to!'

'This person you see before you has got two daughters, one of them married in Seville to an individual with more money than he knows what to do with; the other married my son-in-law, naturally enough, a rotter and the reason all my *estate* is bound up in lawsuits... Because the fortune I inherited from my brother Juan who died in America, which is in the region of a quarter of a million, I'm not exaggerating, well, I can't claim it till next year, if I'm lucky... Because, between them, the lawyers, the consul out there, and my son-in-law conspired to put a spanner in the works, just to mess me up... He's a right one is my son-in-law. With the first bar I set him up in alone, he frittered away a good three hundred of mine, and if anything that's an underestimate. And it was him who turned it into a gambling joint, which got me six months in jail till I was proved innocent, and... Just my luck: the very day I was due to come out of prison, I had a dispute with an associate who tried to cheat me of some eighty pounds, and they kept me in for another six months, I'm not exaggerating.'

Seeing that Nazarín was not interested in his life story, he tried another tack.

'I heard you're a priest ... Is that right now?'

'Yes, sir.'

'Well I never ... On my various trips I've seen all sorts. But I've never seen a gentleman of the cloth in a chain-gang before.'

'Well, now you have. You've got a new titbit to add to your collection.'

'And what brought this about, Father? If I might ask ... A little slip, I suppose. I saw you were in female company and that looks like trouble to me. Any man who gets mixed up with the weaker sex is done for, mark my words. I ought to know, I was once involved with a respectable lady, from the cream of the aristocracy she was. And the trouble she got me into! What with her and a friend of hers who was a marchioness, they robbed me of three thousand or more, I'm not exaggerating. And they had me up in the courts to boot. Women! Don't talk to me about women unless you want to make me lose my cool. It's all because of a female cousin of my son-in-law, who's got a refreshment stall and is the mistress of a lieutenant-general, that I'm in this tight spot now, because they gave me this little girl here to take to an aunt and uncle of hers in Navalcarnero, and they refused to have her if I couldn't guarantee they'd be paid six years' upkeep, I'm not exaggerating ... Women, *alias* the fair sex, are to blame for everything, for which reason, my friend, I'd advise you to give them up and ask your bishop's pardon, and don't get mixed up in protestant, heathen sects again ... What do you say to that?'

'Nothing, my good man. You can go on talking as much

as you like, but leave me out of it; I've nothing to say to you, it's clear you wouldn't understand me.'

Meanwhile Beatriz tried asking the little girl what her name was and who her parents were. But the poor child seemed to be completely traumatized and couldn't get an answer out. Ándara, with the Civil Guards' permission, moved up to the front to talk to Nazarín and take his mind off things, and the old beggar fell in with Beatriz. During their first halt for rest, the convicts who were tied together plagued the two women with obscene, ribald remarks. They all sat down on the ground to eat, and Nazarín shared what the mayor had put in his knapsack with his fellow prisoners. The Civil Guards, surprised at the unhappy priest's continued docility and submissiveness, invited him to a drink; but he refused, begging them not to take offence. It has to be said that, if the two guards' initial opinion of the strange prisoner they were escorting was not exactly favourable and they took him to be an out-and-out hypocrite, in the course of the journey they came to revise their moral assessment of him, for the meekness of his replies, the uncomplaining forbearance with which he endured every hardship, his kindness, his gentleness gradually won them over, and they ended up concluding that, if Don Nazario wasn't a saint, he was the nearest you could get to it.

The first day was hard going since, to avoid spending the night in Villamanta, still infested with the plague, they marched them straight on to Navalcarnero. The two convicts were in a filthy mood, and it got to the point where they lay down in the middle of the road and refused to go on, the Civil Guards being obliged to resort to threats. The old man could scarcely keep going, and strings of curses issued from his toothless mouth. Nazarín and his two companions did their best not to show their exhaustion and carried on stalwartly, notwithstanding the fact that the two women took turns to carry the little girl. They finally got there dropping with fatigue, well after dark. The superior lay-out of the jail at Navalcarnero allowed the Civil Guards to rest in the officers' quarters, while the prisoners, after being given something to eat, were locked up, men and women in separate cells, for the accommodation was sufficient to permit such generally convenient segregation. It was the first time the pilgrim and his two companions, whom the chain-gang were already jokingly referring to as *lady disciples*, and also as *lady nazarenes*, had been separated; and if they were upset at not having him at their side and being able to listen to his words and talk to him about their common adversities, he was just as distressed at having to say his prayers on his own. But what else could he do but accept things as they were!

The night was an abominable one for Nazarín, locked up in the dark with a bunch of hardened criminals: for, in addition to the two convicts from the chain-gang, the cell had three other inmates who insisted on chanting and bawling obscenities, as if carried away by a rising tide of lewdness. The previous inmates found out from the two newcomers (whom, for lack of any other designation, we shall call the *Parricide* and the *Sacrilegious Thief*) that Nazarín was a priest, and between them they set about constructing their own version of his story as religious impostor or charlatan. They made scurrilous remarks out loud about the iniquitous ideas which, according to them, formed the basis of his teachings; and as for the women he was with, one of them claimed they were nuns who had absconded from a convent, another that they were pick-pockets who specialized in lifting the purses of women in church. The improprieties they said to our good Nazarín's face are not fit to be repeated. One convict called him the Gypsy Pope, another asked if it were true he carried a phial of poison round with him to tip into village fountains and cause smallpox. Half-jokingly, half in earnest, they accused him of stealing children to crucify them in accordance with the rites of his idolatrous creed; and all of them, to cut a long story short, subjected him to a flood of indecent, brutal abuse. But the culminating lunacy of that stupid, repugnant charade came when they asked him to celebrate a kind of black mass for their benefit, threatening to beat him up if he didn't immediately start reciting the satanic liturgy, coming out with expressions of endearment and snatches of

Latin that echoed but were a travesty of the true Catholic Mass; and while one of them went down on his knees in a grotesque parody of prayer, another took to slapping his lower parts aping the way genuine Christians beat their breast in contrition, and all of them chanted *mea culpa, mea culpa* in a riotous pandemonium.

Faced with such brazen irreverence, not against his person but against the Holy Church, Nazarín lost his saintly composure and, fired with a righteous anger, rose to his feet and upbraided the vile rabble in this brave and dignified fashion:

'How can you be so shameless, so degenerate, so blind! Insult me as much as you like; but pay respect to God's Majesty, for He created you and gave you this life, so you could use it not to curse and mock him, but to engage in acts of piety, acts of love towards your fellow men. The depravity of your souls, defiled by every vice and evil that tarnishes the human race, pours forth from your lips with all that foul-mouthed talk of yours and pollutes the air around you. But you still have time to mend your ways; even for hardened offenders like yourselves, the path of repentance is always open, the well of forgiveness never dry. Heed the warning while you can; your souls are sorely and gravely damaged. Turn to the way of truth, of good, of innocence. Love God your Father, and your brothers; do not kill, do not blaspheme, do not bear false witness, do not sin in word or deed. Just as you would not abuse a stronger man, do not abuse those who are weaker. Be kind and compassionate, eschew injustice, and by avoiding evil words you will avoid evil deeds, and by freeing yourselves from evil deeds, you will free yourselves from crime. Remember that he who died on the cross endured insults and suffering, and gave his blood and life to redeem you from evil . . . And it was you, in your blindness, who dragged him before Pontius Pilate and set him on the road to Calvary; you who crowned his divine head with thorns; you who scourged him and spit on him; you who nailed him to the cross as a criminal!* And if you do not recognize that it was you who killed him, and who go on killing him, scourging him and spitting on him every day of your lives; if you do not admit your guilt, and shed bitter tears for your heinous crimes; if you do not seek God's mercy quickly, this very minute, remember there is no remission for you; remember you are damned and the flames of Hell are waiting to claim you for all eternity.'

The blessed Nazarín was inspiring and awesome in his brief oration, uttered with all the wrath and grave solemnity of the Scriptures. There was no light in the prison except for that of the moon which shone through the high barred window, playing on his head and bust, whose fine features were thrown into relief by the gentle glow. The initial impression produced in the convicts by that terrible indictment, and by the orator's ringing tones and mystical figure, was one of shock. They were left unable to move or speak. But for all its intensity, the impression quickly wore off and, evil being so deeply lodged in their tarnished souls, they soon rallied and reverted to their usual perversity. The lewd insults started flying again and one of the scoundrels, the one we have agreed to call the *Parricide*, who was the most insolent braggart of them all, stood up arrogantly, as if wanting to outdo the other bandits in barbarity, came up to Nazarín who was still on his feet, and said to him: 'I'm His Satanic Majesty's bishop, and I'm going to confirm you. Take that.'

As he said 'Take that', he gave him such a punch in the jaw that Nazarín's frail body was sent hurtling to the ground. From the poor man's lips as he lay there humiliated came a groan, guttural sounds that might have been a barely articulated clamour for revenge. He was a man, and the man had at some point to reassert itself; for charity and patience, though deeply rooted in him, had not drained all the vital sap of human emotion. The struggle in his will between the man and the angel must have been as terrible as it was short. Another groan was heard, a sigh that seemed to rend his soul. The rabble were laughing. What did they expect Nazarín to do? Turn on them in anger and lash out at them, if not with blows being so outnumbered, at least with insults and sneers to match their own? For one moment, something of the kind might have seemed about to happen, as the penitent made an effort to get up, prising himself on to his knees, his head down, his chest flat on the ground, like a cat crouching for the kill. Finally he raised his chest off the floor, and there was another sigh that made his lungs heave as if about to burst.

His reply to the indignity he had suffered was, as it had to be, midway between the divine and the human.

'Brutes, when you hear me say I forgive you, you'll think me as much of a coward as you are yourselves . . . and I have to say it! Oh bitter cup!* For the first time in my life I find it hard to tell my enemies I forgive them: but I tell you I do, even if my heart is not in my words, because it's my Christian duty to do so . . . So I tell you I forgive you, cowards; I also tell you I despise you, and I feel ashamed I can't keep the two emotions separate in my soul.'

II

'Well, take that for your forgiveness,' said the *Parricide*, landing him another punch, though not so hard this time.

'And that for your scorn.'

And all of them but one fell on him and, laughing cruelly, laid into him, punching him in the jaw, the back of the head, the chest, the ribs. In fact, that mass assault was less an expression of brutality and vindictiveness than a crude and callous practical joke by men used to rough behaviour, for they did not hit him hard, but hard enough to cover the poor priest's body with bruises. The latter, grappling with his emotions more resolutely than before, desperately imploring God's aid, appealing to his deepest convictions and fanning the faith that burned in his soul, offered no resistance and uttered not a single protest or cry. The others got bored with their heartless joke, and left him lying on the ground unable to move. He said not a word: all you could hear was his wheezing as he tried to get his breath back. The convicts also lapsed into silence, as if after that bout of brazen, savage taunts their souls needed a spell of gravity. The sinister mixture of mockery and anger that characterizes the brutal and often bloody jests of hardened criminals tends to give way to black depression. In the ensuing lull, the only sounds were Nazarín's desperate gasps for breath and the mighty snores of the old beggar, fast asleep, blissfully unaware of the rumpus. Perhaps he was dreaming he had finally come into the quarter of a million from his brother in America.

The first to break the silence by speaking was Nazarín, who heaved his aching bones up off the ground and said: 'Now at last ... with your new round of brutalities, the Lord has allowed me to recover my normal self, and here you have me in all my Christian humility, free from anger, from the urge to hatred and revenge. You've behaved towards me in a cowardly fashion; but there must have been other occasions when you've behaved bravely if not heroically, for even crime has its heroes. It's not easy to be a lion; but it's even harder to be a lamb, and that's what I am. I can tell you I forgive you with all my heart because the Lord Above commands me to do so; I can also tell you I don't despise you because the Lord commands me not to despise you but to love you. I regard you as my beloved brothers, and your wickedness and the risk you run of damning your souls for ever fill me with sorrow, and that sorrow is so great and my soul so burns with sorrow and love, that if right now I could at the cost of my life secure your repentance, I'd gladly endure the most terrible martyrdom, ignominy, and death.'

A fresh silence ensued, heavier than the last because the old man's snoring had stopped. After a short while that mood of sombre expectancy, in which their brooding consciences, stirred and churned, seemed to go through a fermentation process, was broken by a voice. It came from the convict we have chosen to call the *Sacrilegious Thief*, the only one who throughout the attacks on the poor errant priest stayed still and silent. He spoke as follows, from the corner where he was lying:

'Well, if you ask me, taunting and laying into a defenceless man like that ain't a proper way for gentlemen to behave, not on your life it ain't, and what's more, if you ask me, it ain't a proper way for decent folks to behave, and if pushed I'd go so far as to say it's the sort of thing ruffians and bullies do. And if that's too close to the bone for comfort, too bad, I always was one for calling a spade a spade. Fair's fair, and what's clear as daylight needs saying. So there . . . now you know; and you'd also better know I'm prepared to stick by what I've said, right here or anywhere else you care to name.'

'Shut your mouth, spoilsport,' said one of the mutinous crew, 'we know the likes of you. Fancy simple Saint Simon here coming out with a speech like that!'

'It came out because I felt like it, and I ain't apologizing neither,' declared the other convict with a menacing coolness, clambering to his feet. 'Because I may be bad, but I always defended the weak and never hit no one when he was down; and there's times I gone without, rather than see someone go hungry. Necessity makes a man what we is; but just because we helps ourselves to what ain't ours, that don't mean we can't feel compassion.'

'Shut up, you stooge, you got no gumption except when it comes to ratting on your friends,' the *Parricide* said to him. 'You always was a sanctimonious sort. Not for nothing you only steal from churches, where you don't risk your skin because the images won't blab when they sees you take their silver, and the Holy Wafer and the Monstrance lets themselves be stolen without so much as an *upon my soul*! You ungrateful bastard, you'd be nothing without the likes of us! And look at you acting and talking big . . . ! Why don't you shut up before . . .'

'Go on, threaten me again, now we ain't got no weapons. That's you all over. Wouldn't I like to see you outside, in the open air, no holds barred, and then I'd tell you insulting and hurting a poor defenceless man, what's naturally good and gentle and don't bother no one, that's something only cowards do, like yourself, for example. You ain't fit to be no one's son or brother, you ain't even born of man and woman!'

They flew at each other in a fury, and the others rushed to pull them apart.

'Leave him to me,' the *Parricide* was shouting, 'I'll tear his heart out with my teeth!'.

To which the other replied: 'You're only squawking because they're holding you down . . . I'm ready whenever you are to string your guts up, even the crows wouldn't touch them.'

And planting himself squarely in the middle of the cell, with a defiant, provocative glare, he went on:

'All right, you gentlemen just shut up and listen to what I got to say. I tell you straight, I'm prepared to defend this good man here as if he was my father; so now you know, out of all the thieves, ruffians, and cut-throats in this place, there's one decent thief* here has a good Christian soul, and takes the side of this man what lets you taunt him without opening his mouth, and lets you beat him without fighting back, and forgives you instead of insulting you. And I'm telling you now, if you don't like it you can lump it, this is a good man and I'll even go so far as to say he's a saint, and I'm willing to take on any man as doubts it. So let's see now, you scum, anyone here deny what I just said? If anyone disagrees, you can step forward; and if you all step forward, I'm ready for you.'

So earnestly and dramatically did the *Sacrilegious Thief* speak out that the others were left dumbstruck and stared aghast at his face, barely visible in the moonlight. Some of them, the least violent, tried to defuse the tension by cracking jokes. The *Parricide*, biting his lip, was mumbling obscenities and threats. Flopping on the ground like a lazy dog, he simply said: 'Go on then, sissy, make a song and dance of it to bring the guards running; and as usual they'll pin it on me, and it'll be the innocent what pays for the guilty.'

'You're the one making a song and dance of it, bully-boy,' retorted the *Sacrilegious Thief*, striding across the cell, now fully in control of the terrain. 'You're making a rumpus because you knows the guards always blames me whenever there's a fight...I stand by my words: this good man's a saint, and I don't mind saying so to all the cut-throats in Christendom, a saint, listen to me and get that into your blockheads, a saint, and anyone who touches a hair on his head will have to answer to me for it, here or wherever.'

The Civil Guards finally heard the commotion and opened up the door from the adjoining room, telling them to be quiet.

'We was just fooling about, sirs,' said the *Parricide*. 'It's that blooming priest's fault, he kept going on at us with his sermons and wouldn't let us sleep.'

'That's not true,' the *Sacrilegious Thief* declared boldly. 'The priest's not to blame, and he wasn't doing nothing of the sort. It was me what was giving a sermon.'

A few curses, and the threat of a sermon from their rifle butts, were enough to shut the whole lot up, and a respectful silence reigned throughout the jail. Some time later, after the *Parricide* and his crew had sunk into comatose oblivion, as if sleeping off their barbarism, Nazarín went to lie down in the corner where the *Sacrilegious Thief* had previously been. The latter came to lie down beside him, without saying a word, as if his tongue were tied by a superstitious reverence. The priest sensed his awkwardness and said to him:

'God knows how grateful I am to you for defending me. But I wouldn't like to see you get into trouble because of me.'

'Sir, I did it because I felt like it,' replied the robber of churches. 'No need to thank me, it was nothing to write home about.'

'You took pity on me, and you were incensed by their callous behaviour towards me. That means your soul isn't entirely rotten; if you want to, you can still be saved.'

'Sir,' the other man declared with genuine remorse. 'I'm a wicked man, and I don't even deserve to be here speaking to you.'

'That wicked? How wicked?'

'Really wicked, wicked as you can get.'

'Let's see now: how many thefts have you committed? How about . . . four hundred thousand, say?'

'Not that many . . . In churches, only three, and one of them's hardly worth mentioning . . . St Joseph's rod, that's all.'

'And how many people have you killed? Eighty thousand?'

'Only two: once to get my own back on someone what insulted me; the other time because I was starving. There were three of us who . . .'

'Keeping bad company never did anyone any good. So when you look back and think about your crimes, do you feel pleased with yourself for committing them?'

'No, sir.'

'Do you feel indifferent towards them?'

'No, sir, not that neither.'

'Do you feel sorry?'

'Yes, sir ... Sometimes only a bit sorry ... I get together with the others and, with all of us thinking bad thoughts, the feeling sorry goes away ... But other times I feel more sorry ... like tonight, really sorry.'

'Fine. Have you got a mother?'

'Not that you'd notice. My mother's a wicked woman. She's been in Alcalá jail these last ten years, for stealing a child and killing it.'

'Lord have mercy on us! Have you any relatives?'

'None.'

'And would you like to lead a different kind of life ... like not to be a criminal, not to have anything on your conscience?'

'I'd like to ... but it ain't that easy ... You get sucked into things ... And necessity makes you ...'

'Forget about necessity, ignore it. If you want to be good, it's enough for you to say just that: I want to be good. If you repudiate your sins, however evil, God will forgive them.'

'Are you quite sure about that, sir?'

'Absolutely sure.'

'You really mean it? So what do I have to do?'

'Nothing.'

'And nothing's enough to get you saved?'

'Nothing except repent and not sin again in future.'

'It can't be that easy, it just can't. What about doing penance ... ? I'll be expected to pay for it in a big way.'

'All you have to do is endure suffering, and if human justice condemns you, resign yourself and accept your punishment.'

'But they'll send me to jail, and in jail you learn things worse than what you knew before. They can let me go free and then I'll be good.'

'Free or in jail, you can be whatever you choose. Just think about it for a minute: as a free man you've been bad. So why are you afraid of being made bad by prison? Suffering is the way to regeneration. Learn to suffer and it'll all come easily.'

'Will you teach me how?'

'I don't know what they're going to do with me. If we stay together, I'll teach you.'

'I want to be with you, sir.'

'That's easy. Think about what I've said and you'll be with me.'*

'Just by thinking about it?'

'That's all. See how easy it is?'

'I will then.'

As they were conversing thus, the light of dawn was creeping through the high barred window.

III

And while the violent scene just described was taking place in the men's cell, in the women's quarters all was peace and quiet. Ándara and Beatriz were alone with the little girl, and spent the first few hours talking about the nasty turn their mendicant mission had taken, but both of them were resigned to misfortune and nothing in the world would make them abandon that holy man who had agreed to let them share his life of virtue. They made a thousand guesses as to what the future might hold in store. What most upset Beatriz was having to go through Móstoles, and the embarrassment of having people there see her in a chain-gang escorted by the Civil Guard. Vanity was something she frowned on; but the test the Lord had sent to try her was a stiff one, and she'd have to muster all her Christian valour and faith to come through victorious. Having got this off her chest, she burst into a flood of tears; and the other woman tried to console her, without success.

'You're not under arrest. You can tell the Civil Guards you're not going to Móstoles and then join up with us later.'

'No, that'd be a cowardly thing to do, and it'd go against what he's told us so many times. Run away from hardship, never! The thought of going through my village makes me feel bad enough; it'd be even worse to have Don Nazario say: "Beatriz, how soon you've tired of carrying your cross",* and that's just what he would say. I'd rather go through with the whole awful business of passing through Móstoles, no matter what happens, than hear him say that. I'm prepared to face the shame; I just hope God will set it against my sins.'

'Your sins!' said Ándara. 'Come on, don't *execrate*. Mine are much, much worse. If I started crying about them like you are, there'd be so many tears I could take a swim in them. There's plenty of time left for crying. I've been bad, but so bad! Apart from the lies I've told and the trouble I've caused, I've borne false witness, I've insulted people, I've hit and bitten people . . . and I've filched scarves and farthings and things worth more than that . . . and then there's the sin of having loved all those men and leading a life of vice.'

'No, Ándara,' replied Beatriz, making no effort to hold back her tears, 'you can try and console me as much as you like but you won't succeed. My sins are worse than yours. I've been so wicked.'

'Not as wicked as me. Look here, I'll not have you making yourself out to be worse than me, Beatriz. A wickeder hussy would be hard to find, I'd even say impossible.'

'No, no, I've sinned more than you.'

'Come on! Don't be so hard on yourself . . . Tell me now, did you ever set fire to a building?'

'No; but that's nothing.'

'So what have you done then? Bah. Loved Pinto . . . That's chickenfeed!'

'And worse, much worse . . . If only one could be born again . . . !'

'You'd do exactly the same as before.'

'Oh no, I wouldn't; not me.'

'I'd be a bit more careful, Christ Almighty; but I'd not make no promises . . . To tell the truth, I'm sorry now about all the mischief and cheating I got up to; but seeing as rainy days are on the way, or so he's told us, seeing as we've no choice but to put up with the troubles ahead, you won't find me crying; there'll be plenty of time for that later on.'

'But I want to cry, I want to,' said Beatriz, refusing to be cheered up. 'I want to cry for the things I've done wrong, why, there's loads of things I've done to offend God and hurt my neighbour! And I can't see how I'll ever be able to shed enough tears for all that guilt to be wiped clean.'

'Why, how can God not forgive you, when you've turned over a new leaf and now you're as good as gold...? But getting God to forgive me is going to be like drawing blood from stone. You see, Beatriz, I'm rotten to the core: when we was up at the castle, I felt envious of you because I thought he loved you more than me. Envy's a terrible crime now, isn't it? But then when they arrested us, and I saw how you came with us despite not needing to, and how you wanted to be as much of a prisoner and criminal as us, the wicked feeling went away; believe me, Beatriz, it's gone altogether now, and I love you with all my heart, and I'd take your sufferings on my head.'

'And I would yours.'

'But I don't want you to cry so much; because the awful things we done, me more than you, we're purging them with these hard times and this disgrace. I'll not cry... because my temperament's different from yours. You're soft, I'm hard; you're one big loving heart; and I say it's fine and dandy to feel sorry and suffer, like he says we got to, but I think you also got to defend yourself against all the wickedness in the world.'

'Don't say that... God's our defender. Let God take care of us.'

'Sure he can take care of us. But God's given us hands, he's given us lips. And what's the use of lips, if not to tell a few home truths to them as denies our Nazarín's a saint? What have we got hands for, if not to save him from them as tries to harm him? Oh Beatriz, I'm a natural fighter; my temperament *was born* like that. Take it from me: folks only learns the hard way; and if we wants everybody to see his goodness and declare him a blessed saint, a bit of stick won't do no harm. Never mind the hardship and suffering; that's fine by me. But seeing injustice done, and hearing them say things what ain't true, that makes me see red. And it's not that, when it comes to it, I ain't capable of being a *lady martyr* like the best of them; but don't it make you weep to see him among murderers in a chain-gang, when his only *delinquence* has been to comfort the poor, heal the sick, and generally be one of God's angels and one of the Virgin's seraphim? Well, if he'd give me half a chance, I swear I'd let all hell loose; and even if I didn't get much in the way of help, I'd set him free and wipe the floor with Civil Guards, judges, and jailers; and I'd parade him through the streets, proclaiming to all and sundry: "Here you have someone who knows the truth of this life and the next, who never committed a single sin, and whose body and soul are clean as a communion plate; our saint and the saint of the whole world, Christian or not."'

'Oh I agree we should worship him, but what you say about resorting to violence, Ándara, that's no good. What can the two of us do? Even if we could ... You know what the commandment says: "Thou shalt not kill." And we mustn't kill even our enemies, or hurt any of God's creatures, not even the most criminal ones.'

'I wouldn't go on the warpath in my own defence, to save my own skin. They can stone me to death and quarter me alive: I'll not turn a hair. But when it comes to a good man like that ... ! Believe you me: people won't see the light if there ain't someone to give a kick in the pants to those that's slow on the uptake.'

'But not kill people.'

'Then they can stop killing people first ...'

'Ándara, don't say things like that.'

'Beatriz, *let you be* as much of a saint as you like; let me do things my way, there's got to be more than one road to salvation. Tell me now: is there such a thing as devils ... ? I mean wicked people, what persecutes the good, and is responsible for all the dreadful, unjust things you come across in this crooked world? Well, let's declare war on the devils. There's some folks fights them with benedictions ... Casting out devils is fine for them as knows how; but to wipe out evil and rid the world of it, benedictions ain't enough, fire and sword are needed too. Mark my words: if there weren't no fighters about, real fighters, mind, the devils would rule the roost. Tell me: isn't St Michael an angel?

Well, he's got a sword all right. And St Paul, isn't he a saint? Well, in all the statues they *paints* him with a sword. And St Ferdinand and other folks you see on altar-pieces? They got soldiers' uniforms . . . So let me do things my way; I got my reasons.'

'You frighten me, Ándara.'

'Beatriz, you're a sinner, I'm a sinner. Each of us'll purge our sins as best we may or can, depending on our natures . . . you with tears, me with . . . God only knows!'

As they were speaking, the first light of day stole through the high barred window.

IV

As soon as men and women were reunited, after daybreak, to continue on their sorry journey, Beatriz and her companion ran to see Nazarín to find out what sort of a night he had had. There is no need to describe their acute distress at the sight of the bruises on his venerable face, the terrible weals on his arms and legs, and his whole body near to collapse. The face of the one from Móstoles went as white as a sheet, and in her agitation she didn't have the presence of mind to ask him who was responsible for that monstrous act of savagery. The arms of the one from Polvoranca twitched as if they were tied and she were trying to break free; she clenched her fists and gnashed her teeth. The convoy set off in the same order as the day before, except that Nazarín was holding the little girl by the hand, with Beatriz at his side, while Ándara took the lead with the old man. The latter filled her in about what had happened in the men's cell the night before. 'I never found out how it all started, because I was fast asleep. I was woken by the ruffians shouting, and saw them laying into that poor devil of a priest, punching him from head to toe . . . I'm not exaggerating. The whole crowd joined in, apart from one of them who later came to Nazarín's rescue, and made the others toe the line. Of those two convicts bringing up the rear there, tied by the elbow, it was the one on the right, the one up for parricide, who was responsible for hitting and abusing that master of yours; the one on the left, the one up for stealing candlesticks and cruets from churches, he took the victim's side against the bullies. Then he got together with the priest, who had a long religious talk with him about repenting.' Hearing this, Ándara looked round and eyed the two of them up and down; both were evil-looking individuals, but she could instantly tell which was which: the bad one had a bilious face, bristly beard, brawny muscles, unhealthy rolls of fat, and walked with a slouch; the good one was lean, with a sad-looking face, tight-knit brows, and a straggly beard, and walked with a firm gait, his eyes trained on the ground.

As they trudged on, Nazarín told Beatriz about the incident, attaching little importance to the whole affair. The only thing that pained him was that the first blow had almost made him turn on his aggressors in anger; but he'd made such a huge effort at self-control that he'd quickly brought the beast of wrath to heel and succeeded in asserting his Christian meekness. But among the events of that night none was so edifying and gratifying as the brave stand one of the malefactors had taken in his defence. 'Instead of acting big by egging his associates on, the sinner let his heart be touched by God. And later on we talked, and I was overjoyed to see a glimmer of repentance in his soul, as he started to open up to me. I thank God for making me the object of such blows and insults, if they've brought a lost sheep into the fold!'

After that, they talked about Beatriz's embarrassment at having to go through Móstoles, and her resigned acceptance of the shame, in atonement for her sins. Nazarín urged her not to care what people thought of her, if she wanted to progress in that new life; anyway, worrying about whether the future would be black or rosy was a waste of time, for no amount of reasoning can tell us what lies ahead; we go through life like blind men groping in the dark, and only God knows what the morrow will bring. Which means that more often than not, when we're expecting something awful to happen, we end up being pleasantly surprised, and vice versa. So onwards march, and may the Supreme Architect's will be done tomorrow as today.

Beatriz felt comforted by his words, and less apprehensive

about going into her home village. Ándara fell back to join them, and after chatting for a while about how hard the going was, moved off to share her time between those at the front and those in the rear. She noticed that the two convicts tied together were not talking to one another, as they had the day before, nor relieving the tedium of the march by cracking jokes and singing songs. Walking beside the one on the left for a bit, she tried to strike up conversation with him, for the guards had no objection to the convicts talking to the prisoners who were allowed to go loose, a charitable gesture not incompatible with carrying out orders.

'How's it going?' she said to him, 'Tired? If I could get the guards to tie me up in your place, I'd be only too glad to see you walk free. That's the least you deserve for having the guts to wipe the floor with that fiend next to you. God will give you your reward. Just repent heart and soul, and in the Lord's eyes it'll be as if you'd returned all the silver you stole from him, with a coating of gold into the bargain.'

She got no reply from the thief, who was plunged in gloom, as if weighed down by some invisible burden. Then the mischievous woman went round to the other side to walk beside the convict accused of parricide, and quietly, so no one could hear, kept hissing in his ear words to this effect: 'I'd like to be a snake, a real big snake with huge fangs, so I could wind myself round you and choke you and send you to hell, you brute, you coward.'

'Guards!' the bandit shouted weakly, almost plaintively. 'This here lady's bothering me.'

'I ain't no lady.'

'This here whore then... I ain't bothering no one... and she keeps saying she's a snake what wants to give me a hug and a kiss... I ain't in the mood for party games and hugging and kissing, woman. Get off my back and stop pestering a man what can't stand the sight of women, not even the word in print.'

The guards ordered her to the front, and soon after the convoy stopped off at an inn for a rest. Back on the march again, it was not yet evening when the towers and spires of the great town of Móstoles came into view, and as they got nearer they were greeted by the odd villager and a posse of urchins, for word had got round that the Moorish miracle-worker from La Mancha was in the chain-gang along with Beatriz. They were some 200 yards from the first houses when three men appeared who spoke to the guards, asking them to stop for a minute so they could have a few words with the prisoners. As soon as she saw them coming, Beatriz recognized them: one of them was Pinto, another his brother Blas, and the third an uncle of hers. The poor woman had to marshal all her spiritual energies to avoid dying of shame on the spot. Their object was precisely to find out if she were under arrest, and when they heard she was detained *at her pleasure*, they were flabbergasted, and insisted she leave the convoy and go with them, so she'd be spared the embarrassment of going through the village in a chain-gang of murderers, thieves, and *apostles*. And their amazement knew no bounds when they heard Beatriz boldly declare nothing in the world would make her abandon her companions in misfortune, and she'd stay with them to the last, even if it meant facing hardship, prison, or the scaffold. Words cannot describe the fury of the three men of Móstoles, and in all likelihood they would have taken it out on her physically had the guards' presence not restrained them.

'You shameless, brazen hussy!' Pinto spat at her, livid with rage. 'I always knew you'd end up as a whore, taking to the roads with a band of robbers. But I never thought you'd sink so low … Get out of my sight, you filthy slattern! I don't know how I can bear to look at you. I can't believe my eyes … ! To think you've turned into a harlot, running after that scarecrow, that fraud and charlatan, what goes round villages cheating people with his lies and witchcraft, and his bag of *mussulmanic* tricks!'

'Pinto,' Beatriz replied gravely, bracing herself to meet the challenge, her headscarf pushed forward to shade her face, her fingers toying with one of the ends in front of her mouth. 'Pinto, go away and let me see this through, I'm not bothering you and I don't want anything to do with you … If I've got to suffer shame, so be it: it's no business of yours. Why come looking for me like this, when for me you're something from the past, you might as well be dead and buried. Go away, and never speak to me again.'

'You whore . . . !'

The guards cut him short, ordering the convoy to resume its march. But Pinto, beside himself with anger, went on letting the insults fly: 'You whore, you can thank your lucky stars these gentlemen here are escorting that sluttish body of yours; if not, I'd lynch you on the spot and cut that scoundrel's ears off!'

The three men were left ranting and raving, and the chain-gang paraded through the main street of Móstoles, mobbed by the curious crowds eager to snatch a look at them, especially at Beatriz. The latter, firm to the last, without arrogance, without flinching, as if draining a bitter cup in whose bitterness lay the remedy for her ills, endured her agony, and when they entered the prison gates she felt she was entering the gates of Paradise.

V

The wretched prisoners' quarters in Móstoles (or wherever, for here again the *Nazarite* chronicles are none too clear about the precise location) were appalling, for what was called the prison deserved the name only on account of the shocking conditions it had in common with all institutions devoted to the correction of criminals. It was a ground-floor extension of the Town Hall, built in an earlier century to evade a tax on bedrooms, its front door giving on to the street and at the back a yard full of rubble, disused timber, and stinging nettles. If the sanitary conditions and decorum required by the law were non-existent, security was *purely mythical*, to quote the prison governors' official report requesting state funds to build a new purpose-built jail. The old one, which may or may not still be in existence, was notorious for the frequency with which breakouts took place, its inmates not needing to go to such risky lengths as scaling high walls or digging underground tunnels. The usual escape route was through the roof, which was wonderfully rickety and precarious, so that anyone could dislodge the rotten rafters and lift and replace the tiles to his heart's content.

From the moment he was locked in that festering slum, Nazarín started to shiver with cold from top to toe, as if in an icebox or some freezing Purgatory, and the shivering was accompanied by a searing pain running through his bones, as if an axe were making matchwood of them. He flopped to the ground, wrapping his cape round him tightly, and before long was burning with an unbearable fire. It was a Purgatory in which flames sprang from ice. 'What I've got is a fever,' he said to himself, 'a terrible fever. But it'll go away.' No one came over to ask if he were ill; he was brought some food on a tin plate, which he left untouched.

Beatriz was asked to leave for the simple reason she wasn't under arrest, and so naturally *had no right to a place* in that edifice dedicated exclusively to those sought by the law. The distraught woman begged and pleaded to be allowed to stay, insisting she was a voluntary criminal under self-ordained arrest, but to no avail. Apart from her distress at having to abandon her friends, she was scared at having to go out into the streets of Móstoles, where she was bound to bump into someone she knew. There was only one person she wanted to see, her sister; and she, so a neighbour had told her at the prison gate on her way in, had gone off to Madrid a couple of days before, taking the little girl with her, who was now completely better. 'The strangest things keep happening to me!' she kept saying. 'Most criminals hate being in prison and want only to be free. I hate being free, I don't want to be let loose in the streets, all I want is to be a prisoner.' In the end the town clerk, who lived next door, took pity on her and offered to put her up, which allayed at least some of the exalted penitent's anxieties.

Don Nazario was truly sorry not to have Beatriz at his side, but relieved to know she was spending the night next door and that they would go on to the end of their *via crucis* together. As the night progressed, the errant priest felt worse and worse, and so lonely and abandoned* he nearly burst into tears like a child. It was as if his energies had suddenly deserted him, and his Christian adventures were to end in an inglorious womanly swoon. He asked the Lord to help him endure the trials that lay ahead, and the miraculous energies came flooding back into his soul, at the same time as his temperature soared alarmingly. Ándara came over to give him a drink of water, which he had called out for several times, and they briefly talked, their conversation being strangely disjointed and at cross purposes. Either he couldn't make himself clear, or else she didn't have the mental agility to adjust her replies to what the poor hermit was saying.

'Go to sleep, my child, and get some rest.'

'Please stop calling out to me like that, sir. Try to stay awake. Pray out loud to keep a bit of noise *agoing*.'

'Ándara, what time is it?'

'Sir, if you're cold, keep walking round the cell. I hope our troubles are over soon. I'm glad Beatriz's not here; she's not a fighter, she thinks you can sort everything out by weeping and moaning.'

'Tell me, are they all asleep? Where are we? Have we got to Madrid?'

'We're here. I'm a real fighter. Stay awake, sir . . .'

And suddenly she went away, like a ghost vanishing or a light going out. These incoherent snatches of conversation marked the beginning of a phase during which the priest was seized by a colossal doubt: 'Was what he could see and hear around him reality, or was it a projection on to the outside world of his feverish delirium? Where was reality located? Inside or outside his head? Did the senses perceive things or create them?' He racked his brains trying to find an answer to these big questions, appealing first to common-sense argument and then to observation. But what use was observation in that murky half-light that blurred the edges of people and things, making everything look unreal? The jail took on the form of a huge cavern,* with a roof so low a man of average height could not stand up in it without stooping. The roof had two or three skylights in it, or perhaps there were twenty or thirty of them, letting in a feeble light which might have been that of a cloudy day

or that of a cloudless night. Following on from the first
chamber he could see a smaller one, intermittently illumined
by the reddish flicker of a lantern or candle. On the ground
were the prisoners, lying wrapped in rugs or blankets, like
bales of cloth or sacks of coal. At the far end of this second
chamber he saw Ándara, whose head kept lighting up with
a strange luminosity, as if her loose, unkempt hair were
radiating ghoulish shafts of electric light. She was deep in
conversation with the *Sacrilegious Thief*, both of them
gesticulating so wildly and extravagantly that his arms
betrayed her intentions, and her arms his. The robber of
churches grew taller and taller till the upper half of his body
disappeared through the roof; he kept reappearing upside
down like an acrobat.

As for the passing of time, Nazarín's mind and senses grew
increasingly confused and bewildered; after what felt like
hours and hours of seeing nothing, he seemed in the space of
just a few minutes to see Ándara come over to where he was,
lift him up and put him down again, saying so many things
to him that, if written down, they would have filled the
pages of an average-length book. 'This can't really be happening,' he kept saying, 'it can't be! But I can see it, I can feel
it and hear it; my senses can't be wrong!' Finally Ándara
grabbed him by the wrist and dragged him forcibly into the
second chamber. That there was no doubting because his
hand hurt, so impatiently did the valiant wench from Polvoranca tug at it. And now the *Sacrilegious Thief* was
picking him up in his arms, ready to push him out through a
hole opened up in the roof, like a cache of contraband
stowed away by hardy brigands.

No, that couldn't be Ándara's voice telling him: 'Father,
we've got to climb out, since we can't walk out.' Nor could
the voice of the *Sacrilegious Thief* be saying: 'You first,
sir ... When you get out on the roof, jump down into the
yard.'

But if the good leader of the *Nazarites* was no longer sure
of anything, there was and could be no doubt about the
following utterance which he distinctly heard himself saying:
'I'm not escaping; I'm not the kind of man who runs away.

If you're feeling faint-hearted, you can escape and leave me behind.' Nor could he doubt that he struggled against superior forces to stop himself from being tossed out on to the roof like a ball. The robber of churches deposited him on the ground, where he was left lying like a corpse, unconscious except that he could still see what was going on, through a blur of incredulity, indignation, and horror at the thought of going free. He didn't want freedom, for himself or for his followers. Out of the first chamber, reeling like a drunk, came one of the sacks of coal which suddenly took on human form, looking to all intents and purposes like the *Parricide*. With cat-like alacrity, changing with the greatest of ease from sack of coal to light-footed beast, he leapt out of the hole in the roof and vanished.*

At that point Nazarín, making a supreme effort, managed to get a few words out and, pushing away Ándara's shoulder which was weighing down on him like a slab of granite, murmured: 'Anyone who wants to go may do so ... Anyone who runs away parts company with me.'

The wench, her face pressed to the ground, rubbing her nose and mouth against the filthy floor-tiles, sat up and interrupted her sobs to say: 'I'll stay then.'

The *Sacrilegious Thief*, who had climbed up on to the roof as if in pursuit of his fellow convict, reappeared with a scowl and clenched fists. 'No ... no escaping,' Ándara cried out to him in a strangled moan. 'He says no ... no escaping.'

Nazarín clearly heard the *Sacrilegious Thief*'s voice repeat: 'No escaping. I'll stay.'

The two of them must have picked him up off the ground because the good pilgrim was aware of being transported effortlessly through the air; and the ensuing delirium, which robbed him of sense and speech, left him conscious only of how ill he felt, an awareness that registered itself as follows: 'I've got galloping typhus.'*

VI

He woke up even more dazed and disturbed, not knowing whether what he saw was real or imagined. He was being taken out of prison, dragged by a rope round his neck. The road was rough and overgrown, full of sharp stones. The pilgrim's feet were bleeding, and he kept stumbling and falling, hauling himself up through a combination of his own laborious efforts and merciless tugs on the rope from whoever was holding it. Ahead he could see Beatriz, transfigured. Her common beauty was transformed into a celestial radiance, beyond all earthly beauty, and her face was ringed by a translucent glow. Her hands were white as snow, as were her feet, which glided over the stones as if they were clouds, and her robes shimmered with the light of dawn.

He could not see the other individuals travelling with him. He could hear their voices, whether pitying or harsh and mocking; but their bodies were hidden in a dense, suffocating, chalky fog, made of sighs of anguish and beads of sweat... All of a sudden a brilliant sun broke through the fog, and Nazarín saw coming towards him a band of malefactors on foot and horseback, waving swords and toting guns. The first band was followed by another, and by yet another, forming a vast and terrible army. The dust kicked up by boots and hooves gradually blocked out the sun. Those escorting the prisoner went over to the enemy camp, for those massed forces were hostile and advancing on him, the saint, the penitent, the humble beggar, with bloodthirsty cries, bent on defeating and destroying him. They set upon him furiously and ferociously, and the strange thing was that, though they kept on pounding and knifing and stabbing his feeble body, they did not kill him. And though he made no effort to defend himself, not even by scratching them like a child, the fury of those serried ranks of seasoned warriors could not prevail against him. Thousands of war-horses and chariot wheels passed over his body, and yet that huge army, sufficient to wipe out and raze to the ground an entire city of errant or sedentary penitents and hermits, did not touch a hair on the blessed Nazarín's body or draw one drop of his blood. They kept on slashing at him wildly, coming thick and fast, for hordes and hordes of ravaging barbarians were pouring over the turbulent horizon.

And the battle raged on, for the greater his resistance and miraculous immunity to their mighty blows, the greater the clamour of that never-ending enemy. Would they finally succeed in crushing the humble, innocent saint? No, that was unthinkable. Just when Nazarín was starting to be afraid that vast enemy army might, if not kill him, at least capture him, who should he see coming from the East but Ándara, transfigured into the bravest, most handsome female warrior imaginable. Clad in shining armour, with a helmet like that of St Michael, on its crest not plumes but rays of sun, riding a white steed whose hooves pounded like rolling thunder, whose mane streamed in the wind like driving rain, and which sent everyone flying as it sped on like a hurricane, the terrible Amazon plunged into the thick of the fray, and with her sword of fire lunged and hacked at the ranks of men. The manly wench was a glorious sight as she fought on single-handed, aided only by the *Sacrilegious Thief* who, also transfigured into a warrior angel, rode behind her wielding his club, with each blow crushing a thousand men. In no time at all they had routed the *anti-Nazarite* forces, and the celestial Amazon, inspired with martial valour, shouted: 'Get back, vile rabble, forces of evil, envy, and pride. I'll wipe you out and exterminate you if you don't ackowledge my lord for the saint he is, the only way, the only truth, the only life. Get back, I say, I'm stronger than the lot of you, I'll turn you all to dust and a bleeding pulp, and what's left of you will fertilize the new kingdom on this earth . . . And that kingdom shall be ruled by its rightful ruler, Christ Almighty!'

As she spoke, her sword and her fellow warrior's club rid the world of that plague of vermin, and Nazarín walked on through pools of blood and mounds of mangled flesh and bones, covering the earth for miles around. The angelic Beatriz was looking on from a celestial tower at that scene of death and reckoning,* in dulcet tones imploring God's forgiveness for the wicked.

VII

The vision came to an end, and everything returned to the grey, nebulous bounds of the real. The rough road reverted to what it had been before, and those accompanying Nazarín on his martyr's way were restored to their normal form and clothing, the guards were guards, and Ándara and Beatriz two ordinary women, one a warmonger, the other a peacemaker, their headscarves knotted under their chins. The point came when, even if he summoned up all his energies, the holy pilgrim could go no further. A feverish sweat was pouring from his brow; his head was throbbing as if cleft by an axe, and an unsufferable weight pressed down on his right shoulder. His legs would not sustain him; the skin on his feet was so raw it kept peeling off on the stones underfoot. Ándara and Beatriz lifted him up in their arms. What a relief to rest, to float in the air like a feather in the wind! But the two women soon tired of carrying him and the *Sacrilegious Thief*, who was tough and wiry, picked him up like a child, saying he would carry him, not just to Madrid, but to the end of the world if need be.* The guards took pity on him and tried to console him, saying: 'Don't worry, Father; when we get there, they'll let you off because you're mad. Of the wanted men that we pick up, two out of every three get off on grounds of insanity, guilty or not. And even if you're a saint, that won't be what saves you, it'll be your madness; the reason of unreason is all the rage nowadays, meaning it's madness that makes you a genius or an idiot, an exception to the rule for better or worse.'*

After a while Nazarín saw them enter a street that sloped steeply upwards, and the curious bystanders turned to watch him go past in the *Sacrilegious Thief*'s arms, flanked on either side by his two female co-penitents, and followed by the train of wretches picked up along the wayside by the Civil Guard. He began to doubt, as before, whether the people and things he saw on that painful climb were real or projections of his deranged mind. At the far end of the street, he saw a huge cross come looming into view,* and if for a split second his soul was ecstatic at the thought of being nailed to it, he quickly checked himself with the following reflection: 'I'm not worthy, Lord, I'm not worthy of the sublime honour of dying on your cross. Not for me that kind of sacrifice, with an altar for a gallows, an apotheosis for an agony. As the least of God's servants, I want to die alone and forgotten, with no crowds at my feet, no crown of glory. I want no one to witness my death, no one to talk about me, no one to watch me, no one to pity me. Far from me all pride. Far from me the vainglory of martyrdom. If die a martyr I must, let it be in the greatest secrecy and obscurity. May my executioners be neither persecuted nor reviled, may God alone assist me and receive my soul, without my death being proclaimed to the world, reported in print, sung by poets, or becoming the motive of public protest or celebration. Let them throw me on a dungheap and leave me to die, or kill me anonymously and bury me like an animal.'

Upon which the cross disappeared from view, and with it the street and the crowds; and after an unspecified lapse of time, he found himself completely on his own. Where was he? He felt as if he had just come round from a deep sleep. No matter how hard he looked around him, he could not work out what part of God's universe he was in. Was this some sphere of mortal existence, or of eternity? It occurred to him he was dead; it also occurred to him he was still alive. A burning desire to celebrate the Eucharist and commune with the Supreme Truth filled his soul, and the desire materialized instantly as he saw himself in his vestments before the altar, an altar so ethereal it seemed untouched by human hand. He said Mass with immense devotion, and as he took the Host in his hands, Christ addressed him thus:

'My son, you are still alive. You are in my blessed hospital, suffering for my sake. Your companions, the two fallen women and the thief who follow your teachings, are in jail. You cannot say Mass, I cannot be with you in body and blood, and this Host is the deluded figment of your imagination. Now take a rest, you have earned it.

You have done something for me. Be satisfied with that. I know you will go on to do greater things.'

*Santander, San Quintín.**
May 1895

THE END

EXPLANATORY NOTES

1   *Tía Chanfaina*: the nickname Chanfaina means 'stew'; it can also have the figurative meaning 'mess'. Tía is literally 'aunt' but can also be applied colloquially (usually rudely) to women in general.

Fair Town of the Bear and Strawberry Tree: a reference to the coat of arms of Madrid.

entry into Madrid of Queen Elizabeth of Valois: Elizabeth of Valois was married to King Philip II of Spain by proxy in 1559, and came to join him in Spain in January 1560, at the age of 14. As the text indicates, elaborate festivities were staged to celebrate the event.

ingenuous contemporary informant *to whom I owe these pearls of wisdom*: Peter Bly (*Pérez Galdós*: Nazarín, 11) notes that Galdós takes this quotation verbatim from Antonio Capmani y Montpalau, *Origen histórico y etimológico de las calles de Madrid* (Madrid: Quirós, 1863), 21. Galdós's narrators frequently claim (sometimes correctly, often mendaciously) to be 'chroniclers' basing their stories on historical sources. Galdós is here conflating Zola's insistence on documentation with Cervantes's pretence in *Don Quixote* that he has done archival research and that (from Part I, ch. 9 onwards) his novel is based on a translation of an Arab historian's text.

2   *Estefanía la del Peñón*: a reference to the nearby Calle del Peñón, mentioned later in the novel.

7   *Señá*: popular contraction of 'Señora'.

rich source of material for an ethnographic study: Galdós's 'ethnographic' classification of the occupants of the lodging-house shows the obvious influence of Darwin's *Origin of Species*. The second half of the nineteenth century saw the birth of anthropology as a discipline: the Spanish Anthropological Society was founded in 1865, modelled on its French counterpart; 1874 saw the creation of the *Revista de Antropología* (*Anthropological Review*), and 1875 that of the Anthropology Museum in Madrid. As in Galdós's concept of ethnography illustrated here, the emphasis was on 'physical anthropology'; that is, the classification of species: see Luis Maristany, 'Lombroso y España: Nuevas consideraciones', *Anales de Literatura Española*, 2 (1983), 366.

9 *Nazarín*: the name 'Nazarín', technically the affectionate diminutive of 'Nazario', sets up an obvious parallel with Jesus of Nazareth. The term 'Nazarene' (or 'Nazarite', found elsewhere in the novel) was used of Christ's followers and applied pejoratively to the early Christians; in particular it was used to refer to early Jewish Christians. The 'Nazaríes' or 'Nazaritas' were also the Islamic dynasty governing the Kingdom of Granada from 1231 to its fall to the Catholic Kings in 1492. In addition to the Christ parallel, Nazarín's Moorish appearance is stressed throughout, reminding the reader of Christ's Semitic origins (a point made by Renan in his influential *Life of Jesus* [1863]), and also of the important role played in Spain's history by the Moors prior to the enforced imposition of Catholicism as the sole national religion in 1492.

it ain't natural: the colloquial language in this paragraph has been translated freely, but I have tried to keep the veiled Christ parallel with this suggestion of Nazarín's unnatural origins. The Spanish speaks of Nazarín's birth being greeted as an extraordinary event, but, as with the phrase 'It ain't natural', leaves it unclear whether the new-born child is a portent because he is superhuman or subnormal.

Papal Nonce's kitchen: in Spanish the phrase 'go tell the Papal Nuncio' means 'tell me another'. I have given a literal translation (malapropism included), so as to keep the ecclesiastical reference and the implied equation of the Papal Nuncio's palace with hell (cf. 'the Devil's Inn').

10 *Miguelturra*: a village to the south-east of Ciudad Real (La Mancha). The first of many obvious Quixotic parallels (Don Quixote also being from La Mancha). Galdós's novels feature a variety of eccentric characters who originate from La Mancha. The name Miguelturra sounds comically barbaric in Spanish ('baturro', from the Aragonese village of the same name, means 'uncouth').

his full name is Don Nazario Zaharín or Zajarín: in the opening paragraph of the *Quixote*, Cervantes makes fun of his mock historical sources by noting their disagreement over the name of his hero (Quijada or Quesada), rejecting both versions for a hypothetical Quejana. (Quixote—meaning 'cuisse' or thigh armour—is the name Cervantes's hero adopts when he sets out on his chivalric adventures.)

11 *Corpus procession*: the Spanish has 'la Minerva', the name popularly given to the procession of the Eucharist on successive Sundays after Corpus Christi from the various parish churches of Madrid. The name derives from the Church of St Mary upon Minerva in Rome (built over a former temple to Minerva), the home of the Congregation of the Holy Body of Christ set up by Pope Paul III to promote the cult of the Eucharist.

13 *as the classical rules of proportion tell us*: the Spanish has 'according to the calculations of Don Hermogenes'. A Greek architect of the second century BC, Hermogenes laid down the rules of proportion on which Vitruvius would base his famous treaty *De architectura*. The phrase has become an idiom in Spanish (cf. the English 'Hobson's choice'); I have given a rough paraphrase, since the name Hermogenes would mean nothing to the average English reader.

17 *Buddhist*: the novel's exploration of spirituality shows the influence not only of the late nineteenth-century Catholic revival, but also of the contemporary interest in Eastern religions (see the character Don Pedro Belmonte, with his oriental past, in Part III). This orientalist vogue entered Spain via Paris.

Diogenes: Diogenes the Cynic, born 414 BC, is remembered as an eccentric individualist who chastised vice, despised wealth, and exalted the poor.

18 *nice little living*: the Spanish 'canongía' (modern spelling 'canonjía') has the double meaning of 'canonry' and 'sinecure'.

30 *Tiñosa*: nickname meaning 'scabby'.

Tripita: nickname meaning 'paunch'.

31 *jail*: the Spanish has 'la galera' ('the galleys'), the popular name of the women's prison in Madrid.

32 *Pelada*: nickname meaning 'bald'.

36 *Camella*: the nickname 'Camella' (a mispronunciation of 'Camelia') means 'she-camel' with reminiscences of the verb 'camelar' ('to chat up', 'to lead on').

43   *you'd have swung for it*: in Spain the common death penalty, until its abolition in 1977, took the form of garotting, not hanging. I have preferred colloquialism to accuracy.

45   *cops*: the Spanish here is 'caifases' (literally 'Caiaphases'), a slang term referring to officers of the law (Caiaphas being the High Priest before whom Christ was taken after his arrest). Galdós takes advantage of this popular usage throughout the novel to underpin the parallel drawn between Nazarín and Christ, both persecuted by the law.

     Señor Rubín, the priest at St Cayetano's: a returning character from Galdós's best-known novel *Fortunata y Jacinta* (1886–7). In the earlier novel, Nicolás Rubín is known principally for his stupidity, greed, and coarse table manners.

55   *Peludos*: 'hairy'.

58   *La Canóniga*: literally 'canonness', here implying 'canon's concubine'.

59   *setting forth in search of adventures*: an implied comparison of Nazarín to Don Quixote, who also set out from home in search of adventures. If Don Quixote's motive for doing so was his desire to emulate the romances of chivalry, Nazarín is motivated by a desire to put the Gospels into practice; the ironic implications of this parallel between the Gospels and the romances of chivalry are obvious.

62   *tertiary*: lay member of a religious order. The Franciscans, in particular, offer associate status to lay persons or secular clergy wanting to continue their role in the outside world; such persons (members of the Third Order) are buried in the Franciscan habit. In the late nineteenth century, this practice was frequently abused and functioned as a kind of spiritual insurance policy. In Spain it had come to signify a bigoted form of neo-Catholicism. It is not surprising that Nazarín rejects the suggestion.

64   *errant priest*: another implied reference to Don Quixote playing the role of knight errant. Although 'itinerant priest' would read better in English, I have kept the formula 'errant priest' (or 'errant hermit', etc.) throughout, so as to retain the chivalric connotations. The ambiguity of the word 'errant' ('itinerant'/'erring') also captures the moral ambiguity of Galdós's depiction of his latter-day Christ.

67 *Civil Guards*: the Civil Guard was set up in 1844 to deal with the problem of rural banditry inherited from the War of Independence (1808–14) and the First Carlist War (1837–40), in both of which guerrilla bands played a vital part. A branch of the military, the Civil Guard had special jurisdiction over the rural areas, with orders to arrest vagrants of all kinds.

69 *St Isidore*: the patron saint of Madrid, whose feast day on 15 May is a big popular event.

70 *Sagasta*: Práxedes Sagasta (1827–1903), leader of the Liberal Party, served as Prime Minister 1871–2, 1874, 1881–3, 1885–90, 1892–5, and 1901–2. The political stability of Restoration Spain was based on a gentleman's agreement, known as the 'peaceful rota', between Sagasta and Cánovas del Castillo (leader of the Conservatives) to rig elections so as to alternate in power. Galdós was 'made' a member of Parliament for Sagasta's Liberals in 1886, representing a district of Puerto Rico he never visited; his term of office concluded in 1890 with Sagasta's fall from power. It is not clear which of Sagasta's falls from power is alluded to here, since the novel—unlike Galdós's earlier fiction—makes no reference to specific historical events.

72 *typhus*: a dangerous fever, contracted from lice and prevalent in crowded tenements in the nineteenth century.

Only say the word, Don Nazario, and the little girl'll be healed: a reference to the Roman centurion at Capernaum, who asked Christ to heal his servant with the words, 'Lord, I am not worthy that thou shouldest come under my roof: but speak the word only and my servant shall be healed' (Matt. 8: 8; see also Mark 7: 6 and Luke 22: 42). Galdós's novel *Misericordia* (1897) also ends with a reference to this biblical episode.

75 *like Magdalenes*: the first of several references to Beatriz as a latter-day Mary Magdalene. Like the Mary Magdalene of popular iconography, Beatriz is a repentant fallen woman with a penchant for weeping.

79 *Devils*: in the New Testament, Christ is repeatedly shown curing people possessed by devils, including Mary Magdalene.

hysteria: late nineteenth-century medicine was obsessed with investigating hysteria, seen as an exclusively female complaint (see Introduction, pp. xv–xvi). This passage shows that Galdós was familiar with the medical debate, probably via his close friend Tolosa Latour, an eminent doctor who provided him with medical information for his novels.

81 *Pinto*: the Spanish phrase 'estar entre Pinto y Valdemoro' ('to be between Pinto and Valdemoro', two villages to the east of Móstoles) means to be unable to decide between two alternatives. Beatriz will hesitate between her attraction to Pinto and her allegiance to Nazarín, whose Moorish appearance incidentally echoes the name Valdemoro ('Valley of the Moor').

84 *wayfarer*: Ándara is referred to here, as on subsequent occasions, as 'la andariega' ('wayfarer'): the contraction of her name Ana de Ara to Ándara foreshadows her later role as Nazarín's follower.

as if she'd been raised from the dead: a reference to Christ's raising from the dead of Jairus's daughter. Like Nazarín, Christ insists that he has not performed a miracle: 'the damsel is not dead, but sleepeth', and commands his disciples not to broadcast the incident (Mark 5: 39, 43).

85 *that intimate form of address*: Nazarín here addresses Beatriz by the familiar 'tú' for the first time, indicating her role from this point on as his favourite (her name evokes the 'Blessed Disciple' referred to in the Gospel of St John). There is a hint that Nazarín is not immune to Beatriz's physical attractions, emphasized by the narrator on their first acquaintance.

93 *Orient*: I have translated 'Oriente' here as 'Orient', rather than 'Middle East', to keep the orientalist connotations. Belmonte's association of Nazarín with the Orient testifies to the *fin-de-siècle* fascination with Eastern religions; Belmonte's orientalist fantasy is, however, shown to be utter lunacy. The heroine of the sequel novel *Halma* (1895), who comes under Nazarín's spiritual influence, has also travelled in the Orient.

94 *remarkable shape of his skull*: a reference to the theories of the Italian criminologist Cesare Lombroso, who, building on the earlier nineteenth-century pseudo-science of phrenology, proposed that the various forms of mental abnormality were congenital and manifested themselves in physical ('zoological') factors such as the shape of the skull. See Introduction, pp. xiii–xv; and Luis Maristany, 'Lombroso y España: Nuevas consideraciones', *Anales de Literatura Española*, 2 (1983), 361–81.

97 *Salome dancing; Salome with John the Baptist's head*: the subject-matter of these paintings is typical of *fin-de-siècle* taste (cf. Wilde's and Richard Strauss's *Salome*, and the paintings of Gustave Moreau). Their combination of oriental religiosity and sado-masochistic sensuality is also reflected in Galdós's novel (though the sexual dimension of Nazarín's masochism is veiled). Nazarín's position in this scene is clearly mirrored by that of St John the Baptist in the paintings; like Nazarín, St John the Baptist is an iconic representation of male masochism.

Pius IX: Pope from 1846 to 1878, he convened the 1870 Vatican Council which proclaimed the doctrine of papal infallibility. Belmonte, similarly, is incapable of admitting he has got things wrong.

98 *indicated one of the chairs to Nazarín*: an implied parallel with the *Quixote*, where the Duke and Duchess feast Don Quixote at their table (Part II, chs. 31–2). The whole of the Belmonte episode parallels that of the Duke and Duchess in the *Quixote* (Part II, chs. 30–57). The aristocrats' acting out of Don Quixote's chivalric delusions leaves the reader wondering if they are not more mad than their guest; in the same way, Belmonte's fantasies will escalate to the point that Nazarín's ideals begin to sound entirely rational by comparison.

99 *Leo XIII*: Pope from 1878 to 1903, succeeding Pius IX. Known as the 'founder of Catholic sociology', Leo XIII was known for his social concerns. His encyclical *Rerum novarum* of 1891 (four years before the writing of *Nazarín*) had set out a charter of workers' rights and employers' obligations, in an attempt to provide a Catholic alternative to the growing threat of socialism (see Introduction, p. x).

Man is beginning to show signs of weariness ... and of a welcome return to the spiritual: an explicit reference to the Catholic revival, and interest in esoteric and Eastern religions, which triumphed in France in particular in the late 1880s and 1890s. This religious revival was picked up eagerly by Spanish intellectuals, who even at their most Liberal were reluctant to adopt an entirely materialist position (Galdós is a classic case of this ambivalence).

100 *With all the advances in technology ... the distribution of wealth is increasingly unjust*: Nazarín's attribution of social injustice to progress in general rather than to a particular

political system is echoed by Galdós's journalistic articles of
the 1890s (see Introduction, p. xii).

100 *announcing that we're nearly out of the desert and that the
Promised Land is near, with its pleasant valleys and fertile
hills*: in his 1897 speech on reception to the Spanish Royal
Academy—reprinted in English in Labanyi (ed.), *Galdós*
(1993)—Galdós used a similar messianic metaphor to
describe this *malaise*, about which he was more pessimistic
than Nazarín: 'It could be said that society has reached a
point at which it finds itself surrounded by high cliffs that
block the way forward. Cracks are appearing in these harsh
and fearful crags, opening up paths or escape routes which
may lead us to open ground. But we tireless travellers were
counting on some supernatural voice to tell us from on high:
this is the way, this and no other. This supernatural voice has
not yet made itself heard . . .'

*politics has burnt itself out . . . political problems . . . have
been resolved without mankind finding a new heaven on this
earth*: as in his journalistic articles, where he talks of political
problems having been resolved because the formerly
disenfranchised middle classes now have access to power,
Galdós seems here to be using politics in the narrow sense of
the right to vote. The 'peaceful rota' which led to the stability
of the Restoration produced mass cynicism about the value of
parliamentary democracy. A curious feature of Nazarín's
creed is that, like Tolstoy's religious utopianism, it poses a
highly political challenge to established values while claiming
to be apolitical.

101 *mediocrities promoted to celebrities, and celebrities promoted
to the status of national hero*: in a journalistic article of
1893—'Confusions and Paradoxes', quoted in Peter B.
Goldman, 'Galdós and the Nineteenth-Century Spanish
Novel: The Need for an Interdisciplinary Approach', *Anales
Galdosianos*, 10 (1975), 8; reprinted in Labanyi (ed.),
Galdós—Galdós similarly bemoaned the triumph of the
'average' and the loss of outstanding individuals he felt had
come with democracy. Here Galdós anticipates the national
critique of the 1898 Generation and of Ortega y Gasset, who
attributed Spain's decadence to a lack of 'great men': a view
dangerously attractive to a later generation of Spanish right-
wing intellectuals who would support Franco's Nationalist
uprising against the Second Republic.

> *we'll see the appearance of one of those towering giants of the Christian faith ... who'll lead mankind to the end of its travails before despair hurls it into the abyss*: this apocalyptic messianism chararacterizes much European *fin-de-siècle* thought, notably that of Nietzsche who would exert a profound influence on the younger Spanish writers of the 1898 Generation.

> *The society of men is diseased. It's looking for a cure*: this medical metaphor is again characteristic of the 1898 Generation's analysis of Spain's 'decadence'.

102 *That's what I believe: What I Believe* is the English title of Tolstoy's profession of religious utopianism, which Galdós owned (and annotated) in the French translation *Ma religion*. This speech by Nazarín, with its denunciation of property and its doctrine of non-resistance to evil, directly echoes Tolstoy's ideals.

105 *Aldjezira*: this appears to be either Belmonte's or Galdós's attempt to render Azerbaijan; or possibly a reference to the Iranian city of Ajab Shir, in Azerbaijan. Either way, the misrepresentation permits the nice joke on p. 110, in which Nazarín thinks Belmonte is talking about the Spanish port of Algeciras.

110 *in Algeciras ... Mesopotamia that is*: see above note.

116 *The wench from Móstoles submitted freely to any kind of abstinence ... for her spirit was starting to burn with a mystical fire*: the link here between mysticism and lack of eating reminds the reader of the connection between Beatriz's earlier hysteria and anorexia, reinforcing the suggestion that mysticism and hysteria are positive and negative sides of the same disorder.

> *dined in pastoral fashion off some fried breadcrumbs*: the Spanish 'migas', a sort of couscous made by frying breadcrumbs, is a traditional shepherds' dish.

117 *Who cares about being cured if being ill always makes me feel this well*: the use of oxymoron in this statement is typical of mystical discourse, cf. St Teresa's famous 'I live because I die and die because I live'.

123 *a village which may have been Méntrida or may have been Aldea del Fresno*: the reference on p. 140 to the nearby confluence of the Rivers Perales and Alberche identifies the

village as Aldea del Fresno (see Map 2). Galdós is here, like Cervantes in the *Quixote*, making fun of his text's pretensions to historicity, by pointing to the unreliability of his alleged documentary sources.

128 *The two women ... saw him at that topmost point, crowned by the stars ... in search of truth*: this scene, with Nazarín's figure bathed in moonlight, is a reworking of the Transfiguration of Christ, observed by the disciples as he prays on a mountain top (Matt. 17; Mark 9).

with a powerful magnetic pull: in the late nineteenth century magnetism and hysteria were closely associated through the use of hypnotism (called 'magnetism' in Spanish) to treat the disorder.

133 *Truly I say to you*: a reminiscence of Christ's repeated phrase in the New Testament, 'verily I say unto you'.

135 *Every carnival has its dragon*: Spanish carnival celebrations traditionally include a dragon, carried on two men's backs like a pantomime horse, which emits fireworks from its mouth and behind.

137 *The peak rose clear above it ... in a sea of cotton wool*: this scene seems to be a second allusion to the Transfiguration; cf. the note to p. 128.

138 *carnival giant's head*: alongside dragons (see note to p. 135), 'cabezudos' (grotesque giant papier-mâché heads) are stock elements of the Spanish carnival tradition. The persistent association of the dwarf Ujo with carnival reinforces the motif of 'the world upside down' that runs throughout the novel, implying that Nazarín, in his desire to turn the established order upside down, is also a 'monstrous' aberration of nature.

139 *Civil Guard*: see note to p. 67.

144 *Beatriz leant her head on Nazarín's shoulder*: a reminiscence of the Blessed Disciple (cf. Beatriz's name) who leans his head on Christ's shoulder at the Last Supper (John 13: 23); see also Leonardo da Vinci's famous painting *The Last Supper*.

145 *I may treat you differently, because your temperaments are different*: here the dreamer Beatriz and the practical Ándara occupy the roles of the sisters Mary and Martha respectively (Luke 10: 38–42). Christ chided Martha for complaining that he let Mary sit listening to him while she worked in the kitchen; in the same way, Nazarín chides Ándara for

complaining that he lets Beatriz sit talking to him while she gathers food for supper.

acorns: as Don Quixote reminds us in a famous speech, acorns were the traditional food of the Golden Age, when there was no 'yours and mine' and 'everything was common to everyone' (*Don Quixote*, Part I, ch. 11). Don Quixote's vision of the Golden Age is virtually identical to Nazarín's utopian vision of a primitive Christian communal existence. Acorns are thus appropriate food for this re-enactment of the Last Supper.

146 *Midsummer's Eve*: the Noche de San Juan (Midsummer's Eve) is traditionally celebrated in Spain with bonfires and paganistic rituals.

147 *say sorry to that gentleman you've just injured*: an allusion to the Arrest in the Garden, in which Christ rebukes Peter for cutting off the ear of one of the high priest's servants, in an attempt to resist arrest (Matt. 26: 51–2; John 18: 10–11; Luke 22: 50–1).

153 *Just like the monasteries and convents before*: the disentailment of Church land was a central plank of Spanish Liberal reform, from the late eighteenth century through to the mid-nineteenth century. The Liberal politician Mendizábal's celebrated law of 1841 nationalized all Church property, in order to put it up for sale to private bidders; a further law of 1855 consolidated this process. In practice, the reform aggravated social injustice since the land formerly owned by the Church was bought up by a new entrepreneurial middle class, who refused the peasants the communal grazing rights they had previously enjoyed. As Galdós noted in a newspaper article of 1890, 'now we [the middle class] are the tyrants': see Goldman, 'Galdós and the Nineteenth-Century Novel', 7; reprinted in Labanyi (ed.), *Galdós*. It is logical that the mayor, with his stock Liberal belief in private ownership, should regard disentailment as a sacred principle in direct conflict with Nazarín's insistence on communal ownership.

154 *My bet is it's the Mohammedan creed... to preach by your example, of course*: here the mayor takes on the role of Pontius Pilate presiding over the mocking of Christ. Like Christ, Nazarín replies with silence. Like Pontius Pilate, the mayor plays a double game, condemning Nazarín while claiming to be motivated by humanitarian principles.

155 *Corporal Cirilo Mondéjar, who used to be stationed in Móstoles*: a fundamental rule of the Civil Guard is that they be stationed in areas other than that of their origin, to avoid conflict between local loyalties and obedience to orders. A source of popular grievance, this rule led to justifiable accusations that the Civil Guard behaved towards local citizens like an occupying army. Galdós's Civil Guards are shown to be ordinary, decent folk.

157 *I'll take a pot shot at you too*: a reference to the notorious 'ley de fugas' ('law of escape'), which gave the Civil Guard the right to shoot any prisoner attempting escape. A major complaint against the Civil Guard was their abuse of this law to execute prisoners summarily.

159 *Model Prison in Madrid*: Galdós refers to this by its popular name 'el Abanico' ('the Fan'), which it acquired on account of its radial layout.

161 *The sorry convoy made its way along the dusty road*: Nazarín's forced march back to Madrid in a chain-gang echoes the end of Part I of *Don Quixote*, where the protagonist is brought home captive in a cage.

162 *Cánovas*: Antonio Cánovas del Castillo (1828–97), leader of the Conservative Party, is credited with being the architect of Restoration Spain, under which (until 1892 at least) Spain enjoyed an unprecedented period of political stability and economic boom. Prime Minister 1874–81, 1883–5, 1890–2, and 1895–7, he was assassinated by an Italian anarchist in 1897.

Moderates: after 1820, Spanish Liberalism split into two tendencies: the Extremists ('los exaltados') and the Moderates ('los moderados'). The Moderates held power, under the authoritarian General Narváez and others, from 1843 till the 1854 Revolution led by General O'Donnell. The Moderates ceased to exist as a political entity after the consolidation of the Liberal Party under Sagasta in the 1870s; see note to p. 69.

166 *Remember that he who died on the cross ... nailed him to the cross as a criminal*: throughout this passage, contrary to convention elsewhere in the novel, there is no capitalization for 'he', 'his', and 'him' referring to Christ. The implication is that Nazarín is putting himself in the position of Christ, which technically is blasphemous.

168 *Oh bitter cup!*: a reference to the Agony in the Garden, when Christ exclaims, 'O my Father, if it be possible, let this cup pass from me: nevertheless not as I will, but as thou wilt' (Matt. 26: 39; see also Mark 14: 36).

171 *one decent thief*: from this point on, the *Sacrilegious Thief* occupies the role of the Good Thief crucified alongside Christ. The *Parricide* occupies the role of the other (unrepentant) thief.

174 *'I want to be with you, sir'*... *'Think about what I've said, and you'll be with me'*: cf. Luke 23: 42–3: 'And he [the Good Thief] said unto Jesus, Lord, remember me when thou comest into thy kingdom. And Jesus said unto him, verily I say unto thee, today shalt thou be with me in paradise.'

175 *'Beatriz, how soon you've tired of carrying your cross'*: the first of several explicit parallels with the Stations of the Cross.

183 *so lonely and abandoned*: cf. Christ's words on the cross: 'My God, my God, why hast thou forsaken me?' (Matt. 27: 46; see also Mark 15: 34).

184 *jail took on the form of a huge cavern*: an implied reference to Plato's cave, where reality is seen only obliquely through the shadows it casts on the inner wall of the mind.

186 *he leapt out of the hole in the roof and vanished*: in Luke 23: 39–40, the Bad Thief asks Jesus to show that he is Christ by saving them from crucifixion; whereupon the Good Thief rebukes him, recognizing that, unlike Jesus, they deserve punishment. In Galdós's novel, the *Parricide* will escape, and the *Sacrilegious Thief* will (reluctantly) reject the opportunity to evade punishment.

typhus: see note to p. 72. The connection between typhus and lack of hygiene suggests that Nazarín's contraction of the disease is the direct result of his profession of poverty: an implied ironic comment on his spiritual ideals.

188 *that scene of death and reckoning*: this vision of Armageddon is typical of the late nineteenth-century and early twentieth-century revival of millenarian thought, in which the answer to decadence is seen, by thinkers of the political right and left, to lie in universal destruction leading to the birth of a new order. Here the vision of a purifying holocaust is the product of a literally diseased mind, since Nazarín is suffering from typhus.

189   *saying he would carry him . . . to the end of the world if need
      be*: here the *Sacrilegious Thief* takes on the role of Simon of
      Cyrene, who carried Christ's cross to Calvary.

      *reason of unreason is all the rage nowadays . . . an exception
      to the rule for better or worse*: the most direct reference in
      the text to the theories of the Italian criminologist Cesare
      Lombroso (1836–1909), much discussed in Spain in the
      1890s, on the relation between madness, genius, and
      criminality. See also note to p. 94, and Introduction pp.
      xiii–xv. This passage betrays Galdós's disillusionment with
      democracy as the 'rule of mediocrity', and his nostalgia for the
      'outstanding individuals' he felt were no longer possible: see
      note to p. 101. If in his journalism he left open the question of
      whether universal equality is better than general prostration
      offset by a select minority of 'great men', his novelistic
      depiction of a latter-day saint is ironically undercut
      throughout by the Lombrosian suggestion that genius is a
      form of madness, or even of criminal deviance.

      he saw a huge cross come looming into view: Nazarín's entry
      into Madrid, in which he climbs uphill towards a cross, marks
      the final stage of his ascent to Calvary (a Calvary which, of
      course, is the product of his feverish delirium).

190   *San Quintín*: the summer residence Galdós had built for
      himself in Santander between 1891 and 1893.